Advance Praise for *Big Shadow*

"Preternatural, radiating warmth and coldness and colour
and light, *Big Shadow* brims with intelligence and wit.
While one world flickers in the background, our narrator
enters another, but by the end, we see that the flickering is,
amazingly, reality too. I never quite knew where this novel
was taking me, which is exactly where I wanted to be going."
—AMINA CAIN, AUTHOR OF *INDELICACY*

"*Big Shadow* is a quietly radical novel in which
a strange woman in an absurd world disorients us
so the story can remind us that actually, it's this
life that is absurd, it is we who are strange.
Marta Balcewicz's unflagging focus on the beauty of
the world's lost and forgotten things beseeches us
to stay still, just for a second, and pay attention.
Funny, moving, and a pure delight."
—THEA LIM, SCOTIABANK GILLER PRIZE–SHORTLISTED
AUTHOR OF *AN OCEAN OF MINUTES*

"Marta Balcewicz's *Big Shadow* is a deft portrait of artistic ambition and the troubled pursuit of truth. This story of everyday grifters—the small town proselytizers and desperate musicians—captures how difficult it is to untangle oneself from the narratives that are imposed. Smart, ironic, and tender, with prose as sharp as a scam, *Big Shadow* is the first of many excellent Balcewicz novels to come."

—ISLE MCELROY, AUTHOR OF
PEOPLE COLLIDE AND *THE ATMOSPHERIANS*

MARTA BALCEWICZ

BIG
SHADOW

a novel

Book*hug Press
TORONTO 2023

Library and Archives Canada Cataloguing in Publication

Title: Big shadow / Marta Balcewicz.
Names: Balcewicz, Marta, author.
Identifiers: Canadiana (print) 20220458316 | Canadiana (ebook) 20220458367
ISBN 9781771668316 (softcover)
ISBN 9781771668323 (EPUB)
ISBN 9781771668330 (PDF)
Classification: LCC PS8603.A485 B54 2023 | DDC C813/.6—dc23

The production of this book was made possible through the generous assistance of the Canada Council for the Arts and the Ontario Arts Council. Book*hug Press also acknowledges the support of the Government of Canada through the Canada Book Fund and the Government of Ontario through the Ontario Book Publishing Tax Credit and the Ontario Book Fund.

Book*hug Press acknowledges that the land on which we operate is the traditional territory of many nations, including the Mississaugas of the Credit, the Anishnabeg, the Chippewa, the Haudenosaunee, and the Wendat peoples. We recognize the enduring presence of many diverse First Nations, Inuit, and Métis peoples and are grateful for the opportunity to meet and work on this territory.

1
—

For a while I had a job where I'd watch the passing clouds. In a notebook that I always carried with me, I'd write, "That one went on its way," "There was nothing unusual in that one." I learned how the clouds set themselves apart, by becoming shapes that had nothing to do with one another: wedding veils, curdled milk, trails of horse droppings perfectly spaced out. I learned their proper names: *cirrus, stratus, nimbus.* The clouds in the opening credits of *The Simpsons* are *stratocumulus,* for example. Nephology is the study of clouds and nephrology is the study of kidneys. I could tell you so much more; I was hyperaware and educated. I walked around always tense, and looked upward a lot so that at the end of the day I'd feel an ache in my neck and shoulders.

Calling the cloud job a "job" is inaccurate. There was no hiring. I was really just spending time with the only two people I knew. I saw little of them and for the most part sat stationed outdoors. My cousin Christopher and his friend Alex felt I was uniquely qualified to be the one who observed, and outside, on a lawn, the perspective of a sky is clearer. Once the weather warmed up, I didn't think to mind. I also hadn't thought to mind during the earlier spring days when this all started. Only then, I'd bring out a blanket. The job and the cloud watching it involved had been invented entirely by Alex. And it was par for the course that if he had an idea, Christopher and I usually went along with it. Or at least we considered his idea very seriously, so that it felt like a job to finally execute it. There isn't much to do when there's nothing but lawn and more lawn around. There's not much to do when you're young and stuck together like we were.

For a time I became one with my job in the way anybody with a serious calling would, and I thought myself essential. A surgeon or a president must look at their hands a hundred-plus times every day. In their palms and their hardened fingers dwell their accomplishments, like a list displayed by a computer. I had the same compulsion. I thought my notebook notations weren't far from saving a life. I'd sit on the sun lounger with a novel in my lap and the cloud notebook underneath it. In a cup set on the grass at my side, I kept a slim fountain pen that I especially liked to use. Even at the height of it—when I felt no outward disdain—the task of monitoring the sky was idle-work, in the most painful, extreme sense of stopped, sleepy, and dead. I suppose I took it too literally at points, though sometimes not literally enough.

"Do you sense something coming," Alex would say. "That's all it's about, a *sense*." I sensed a lot of things on any given day, and the frustrating thing about sense is that it's always highly impressionable. In answering him, I pretty much always said, "I sensed nothing relevant today and sensed nothing the day before either." Having the cloud notebook, I could at least hold it up and point to the notations. "Nothing," "nothing," said my notes. Though sometimes I would elaborate: "An extra-large nimbus moved so slowly, I thought it was stopped. I was sure it was the Big Shadow. The trees were whipping, it was obviously windy, so why no movement? But then I saw that the cloud was shrinking, which *is* movement. It was shrinking very fast, actually. Imagine standing on a set of tracks, watching a train leave the station. Eventually it's a toy, soon after it's a dot, soon after that, nothing. It's all about the angle from which you (the subject) watch the object (the cloud), which is also called parapraxis."

I'd insert short-lived drama like that, written colloquially, and a little fancifully, as if it were conversation. But it was embellishment only. "Parapraxis" came from James Joyce's *Ulysses*—though I'd only read its long introduction. I was grasping at straws. The earth spins, hemispheres rotate, clouds are just vapour procured by oceans, no more. I'm sorry it's nothing bigger.

THE LAWN WHERE I sat while on the cloud-watching job was part of a property belonging to Alex. Since we were only days past the end of high school and not yet eighteen, the accurate way of stating this was that the property where I sat while on the cloud job belonged to Alex's mother, a lady with money. The money she had took her far from us—I figured spots like Italy, because of her new life partner, and his business, or a stock he'd invested in that'd done well, and maybe children of his who needed more tending to than self-sufficient Alex. These ideas were just pulled from movies showing rich-people preoccupations. She may have been staying with a friend or sister in town, only a forty-minute drive away, even working a nine-to-five job—we didn't know; we could be so myopic. Perhaps Alex's mother was an ordinary person.

When she had been around, she saw to it that the property was maintained to a certain standard. There was a better selection of food, and bottled water with gas. Since she'd left, the old landscaping company still came by, but they'd turned lazy and left the lawns uneven. Over time, the hedges grew so tall one could easily miss the house when driving down the country highway. I tried my best to be a type of substitute and made myself in charge of handing the landscapers their pay. Though just that spring, one of the younger workers had backed his motorized mower into the fencing. The machine knocked down the row of posts, a good quarter mile. He made eye contact with me; I was sitting outside with a blanket. I'd heard the *whack* and put down my book. And yet he only turned the gear shifter and continued on his way, never addressing the incident. I suppose he only saw a child. He knew there was no one in charge.

What I was, ever since my early days of being there, was something more of an honorary tenant or sometime special guest. I took shears to that hedge once, just to experience the violence of this absurd, sharp object. I found many things in the shed, which sat behind the large coach house that sat behind the main brick house. I played badminton. I completed homework, for all the grades until the end of high school. I watched a lot of films and read the many books that filled the shelves in the coach house, books with paintings and photography, and books with plots and poems. The books came from Alex's father; he'd lost interest in them years before. There were two acres of land all around, which meant the neighbours were visible but it was hard to discern what they were up to. Here was what Alex's mother called a "countrystead," a foil to the city home that Alex's father kept in their divorce. A place of upholstery and picture frames with scenes of horses, people, and other animals, none of them in conversation with one another. A home where her mother and her mother's mother had died, she would repeat, as if that were a good thing, when I knew from reading her son's many books that in some cultures that much death would make a home unsellable.

The thing that made the property truly stand out from the country homes around it, the hefty, brown-bricked rectangles— some with coach houses, others with renovated barns, some converted to appeal to berry-picking people from town—was a large, empty concrete swimming pool Alex's mother had promised to fill since we were kids. By now the cracks in its walls had grown so wide, winter after winter having clawed at them, that a whole forest sprouted from within. And so when you looked across the lawn, the pool appeared as no more than a sudden twenty-yard-long valley, perfectly convincingly natural but for the pastel-yellow diving board at its deep end, on which I often saw raccoons, and once, a pair of deer teetering.

SUMMER HAD BEGUN earlier that week and a new heat immediately set in. On one of my last days at the countrystead, in the late morning, I watched Alex and my cousin leave the property in the car they shared, a compact Honda the colour of a human bone. "Back soon," Christopher called to me from the passenger window as Alex steered them out of there. The tires ground the rocks of the driveway. I brought my knees higher on the sun lounger.

Two hours later, I heard the crunch of their return. They parked the car so that its back faced the coach house door. Christopher began unloading boxes. From what I could make out from my station on the lounger, most of the boxes held lemon-flavoured iced tea. Christopher's shirt stuck to his back and he repeatedly wiped his forehead. Alex had darted into the coach house the moment he'd finished parking. No one asked if the shade falling over the lounger was comfortable for me or if I cared for some of their lemon iced tea. After my cousin lifted the last of the boxes, he went inside and shut the door. The coach house was beautifully old and wooden, though renovated and outfitted for living in modest luxury. In addition to the book-shelves, it boasted a couch, desk, kitchenette, and a bathroom with a bathtub. It sat thirty steps behind the main house, sepa-rated by the driveway, which was oval in shape and allowed cars to come and go without having to reverse. They had the AC going, I could hear. The noise of the unit, for someone stuck outdoors as I was, was offensive. The higher they cranked its cooling set-ting, the more offensive it got.

EARLY EVENING, I left the sun lounger, the book I had been reading, and the notebook with the clouds. In the main house, I passed through the rooms, upstairs and downstairs. I checked for any-thing I might've left and felt I needed. I looked under the beds where those mothers had passed, where those mothers might've been conceived, by the mothers' mothers and fathers. The bed undersides held studded leather luggage and zippered plastic bags with furs. I saw solitary slippers and what I thought were abandoned golf balls, but turned out to be used Kleenex, hard-ened and decades old. I checked the bathrooms, and in the kitchen, I sat for a while, eating an apple brought by the woman who came by to dust and wipe down the place. I took my time with the apple and studied the cupboards, hyperconscious of their shape and colour and pre-emptively nostalgic. The still of the house, its absolute quiet, gave the scene a monastic air. At my house, the sounds of the row houses touching our row house flowed undeterred. There were the blenders and vacuums of neighbours, and then my mother, who was like a blender and vacuum combined. Maybe that had been it all along. Maybe I spent time here because I needed quiet, as a fundamental personality trait, the way I also needed oxygen, film, and art. I started on a second apple.

IT WAS CLOSE to nightfall when I awoke in one of the dead mother bedrooms. Wouldn't you know it, the light was still lingering. It must've been close to ten. I'd brought more apples upstairs. The cores had turned rusty and their stench hung over the bed. My cousin tugged on my foot; I realized that's what had woken me. He was backlit but still recognizably Christopher, a thin-framed boy, generally good-intentioned. "Come outside, there's so much happening," he said, quietly, as if afraid to wake me, which made no sense seeing that I was staring straight at him. His hand let go of my foot and he crouched on his haunches, on the small rug by the bed's end. Alex was not in the room.

"So much happening? I find that hard to believe," I said. But I was already lifting my knees and sliding my legs off the mattress.

In the backyard, sitting at the edge of the pool, Alex delivered a long-winded talk on the importance of our "present moment," by which he meant yesterday's solstice, the way the days now dragged and dragged. There was *more* day, in the simple sense of quantity, yeah. And so more opportunity for us to be attuned to it, and measure some kind of change, or witness it, articulated in something like a weird cloud shape passing overhead, maybe a shape that beckoned us. The bottom line was that I shouldn't nap in the early evening when I could be sitting on the lounger with my head pointed up. He didn't say it meanly, but I understood the gist. "There's a task to be done and you're the best at it, I think." Funny how he never thought we should wake up at the crack of dawn, that *I* should wake up at the crack of dawn, rather, like some farmer or his rooster. If I was sleeping over at Alex's on a summer day, I would get up at nine or ten, just like them. God knows a lot of clouds passed overhead without anyone registering a thing.

Still, I supposed there was truth in saying the days stood out for the way they now lasted longer, not so much began sooner. Here we were, minutes to ten, and the pool was all buttery gold accents. And Alex's and Christopher's shoulders, aglow as if dressed in orange sweaters. Their faces a boiling pink. The trees no longer green but a tropical type of red, their trunks included. The whole scene, generally, looking like fire and flames, just gushing the undeniable beauty of the sun saying goodbye.

I'd sat with Christopher and Alex in this way, at the pool's edge, with our legs lowered into its leafy basin, for so many years by that point. Those two were all right when all was told, though of course I preferred Christopher to Alex. The whole cloud obsession was new, but they were still the same two humans, one of them "blood" and "pretty much a sibling," as my mother reminded me daily, using her uncomfortable medieval language, all because her brother was his father.

"My mother's fixing the pool this summer," Alex said out of the blue. It had no connection to what he'd been saying just before, about how the days were lasting longer and the implication that I was slacking. "I don't know if we'll be around still to see it, but we might get a few weeks, or a few days, who knows." He then elaborated, saying his mother had called him that day, to announce that she'd finally set a wedding date with this new man, for early fall. The wedding would happen at the countrystead, with concrete patching up the pool cracks.

"Imagine the Big Shadow comes in the middle of the wedding?" Christopher said. "During whatever moment is the most important."

"The vows are usually the most important part, and it could happen," Alex said.

"Yeah?" My cousin started laughing. I don't know what he imagined exactly, but it gave him such delirious pleasure he was now rocking back and forth. A cloud parks itself above a renovated pool and casts a singular shadow, so that there's no doubt in our minds, so that we know this is not nothing. The bride, groom, and guests pause their dancing. The band, the balloons, the bowties, they all stop. Everyone turns toward us, but we're already gone, somehow, somehow we've been transported by the Big Shadow, to where, we don't yet know. For the guests, our absence causes no alarm, only a sense that something has happened. It's the cue blip on a film reel, too quick for pedestrian eyes.

Christopher hunched his shoulders and went on laughing. I hadn't seen him so possessed in weeks. I thought he might topple into the pool. He was that excited, actually shaking from the thought of how hilarious and equal parts fantastic that transcendental exit would be.

AROUND THREE IN the morning, I left the upstairs bedroom and padded out of the main house. The property had no hint of light. It was a moonless night, apparently. The motion sensor lights that had worked at some point were unplugged, or their wires had been chewed through by insects. The place didn't have a security system. I had overdressed by wearing jeans. I wanted to have the jeans with me because they struck me as more valuable than the shorts I'd been wearing. I left the shorts on top of the mother bed, along with my toothbrush and some hair clips that didn't fit in my jean pockets. The cloud notebook I hid in an armoire drawer, under a pile of antique bras, stiff and pointy as zeppelins.

I'd seen characters walk out of unwanted jobs in movies, and sometimes it was a forgettable comedy, but other times an intense and inspirational drama, so that your whole life could change just from watching it. This brief quitting scene would barely warrant mention in a plot summary on the back of the vhs box—because it's merely inciting action and more likely there's a romantic story at play, because what else is the human race moving toward but connection between two someones. What an inspiration, though, seeing a character carry out the screenwriter's order of "character walks out." Someone brave, without a mother in their head and no established friendships, or someone momentarily muting their mother and friends, an even more impressive skill.

The night was sultry, just as the day had been, or even worse. The heat had been consistently rising ever since the previous day's afternoon. Once I was past the hedge fence and on the country highway, I relaxed and forgot about how hot my legs felt in the jeans. It was a beautiful road, with the tall grass that grew alongside the shoulder reflecting a dapple of light from faraway properties. My sneakers generated the slightest grind, like I was on a soft beach. I saw a low, flat animal cross the road before me, a weasel or possum; there was a brook nearby that swelled to a river during rainy seasons, and I believed the animals lived there. Dandelions bloomed unimpeded around the drainage grates. The land was as vast and quiet as I'd ever experienced it. The scene had, I think, an epiphanic quality, or whatever it is that floods a person with realizations that normally stay out of reach.

I thought about my mother, tucked in bed in our apartment back in town, the soundtrack of her sleep apnea, the glass of water at her bedside, and a fan set to maximum—a tragic tableau, like most snapshots of her life. I thought of Christopher next, a twin image of my mother: curled in a lonesome sleeping shape, on the fold-out sofa, in the middle of the coach house, dreaming of clouds. They both lacked self-awareness, and both were so pathetic. I was practically a parent to them, in the sense that parenthood is a position of stewardship where one is more perceptive and attuned to norms than their hapless, bumbling ward. I was a single parent, too, with all the hardship of that. I stopped for a moment and thought of turning around to grab Christopher. But the mechanics of it were impossible. Or were they? I could tap him awake and ask him to help out with a strange sound I was hearing. Alex would remain sleeping, and a couple of minutes later, it'd be the two of us on the road, off to my mother's apartment. I turned around but saw only dark.

Or *would* Alex remain sleeping? He'd assume I'd heard the Big Shadow arrive. He and Christopher would ask me a series of questions, turning wild and gathering objects in their arms. I'd have no answer to give and would feel forced to return to bed. Come morning, a day exactly like the last would roll out. I'd have nothing to do. I'd probably watch the clouds.

Now I walked a lot faster. I saw how constricted I was, so much so that any thought, even one of escape and breaking away, involved making triangulations with the only three people I knew: Mother, Christopher, Alex. *Go from Alex's home to your mother's, perhaps bring Christopher with you, or perhaps not.* There are so few shapes you can make when you know practically nobody. I was like a bird measuring the world only in parameters of cages, plus the humans who refilled her feed and replaced the shit-stained newspaper. It's possible I summoned Maurice Blunt right then, while walking down the country highway. Because, I would say—if Maurice and I were ever to talk about it—the act of summoning comes at one's lowest point, and is subconscious, or at least the most effective type of it is.

THE RAMP FOR the highway, the real highway with six lanes, became visible. I wasn't sure that walking on its shoulder was legal, but figured there couldn't be too much traffic that early in the morning. I felt giddy as I started out on the curve of the ramp. I had never walked on a ramp. It was possible no one had ever walked on a ramp. I heard a tractor trailer zip past beneath me with all of its parts rattling. The walk home would probably take four hours. I wasn't sure how I'd calculated that, but I had the sense that I could figure out my whole life if given this block of time just for thinking. I tripped on the toe of my sneaker and lost control of my body, then steadied myself and thought of the incident as funny, that's how positive I felt. For just the slightest moment I considered that maybe this feeling, this rapturous positivity, was the result of the Big Shadow having come after all. That I was already gone, in a better place, the moment of passage erased from my memory. But the sound of gravel under my feet grounded me. I was definitely still here, on earth, all parts of me intact. Most importantly, I was without those two.

I'd walked a good three-quarters of the way down the ramp when a set of headlights lit up the road from behind me. I projected onto the asphalt as a powerful creature with legs twenty feet long. I didn't turn around; that seemed the best way to convey that what I was doing was normal. I did step sideways, toward the shoulder, trying to signal *there's room for us both, I am just like you, keep driving.* I waited to be outpaced, but I could tell from the sound of the motor that the car was slowing down. The engine shut off after coming so close the hood practically touched my elbow. My cousin tapped the horn and its ridiculous goose honk dispelled whatever serious mood our stand-off could've had. The passenger window was down, the door was unlocked, everything was just so. Christopher drove me the forty minutes to my mother's house. We didn't speak until he'd parked us in front of the triplex and I asked if he wanted to sleep over. He rolled his eyes and turned the ignition back on.

"I'll keep on the lookout for clouds from here," I said and pointed at the living-room window, though in retrospect, I should've ended it with a slam of the car door like in a film, or maybe complete silence and a controlled stepping away.

"See you soon," he said in response, as if nothing we'd just done was unusual. "Oh, and Alex said to tell you the heatwave we're experiencing, that's *something*. It wouldn't be this hot for no reason.

I mean, it pretty much feels like hell."

I said again, "I'll be on the lookout," and he said, sure, yeah, and even smiled in a way that passed for cordial. I supposed he was calling my bluff; it was something Alex had taught him. I shut the door and he drove away, neither more quickly nor slowly than he would have on any other night.

2
—

was in bed the morning after the highway incident when the phone started ringing. My mother was at work and the apartment was empty. I let the ringing run its course, but a second after the phone went quiet, it started again.

I threw off the bedsheet and took my time walking down the hall. I'd been sweating in my sleep, quite badly it looked like. My feet left prints on the floorboards. My pajamas stuck to my thighs, all around, and when I shifted their elastic waistband I saw that it'd left a welt, moist and violet, on the tender skin of my stomach.

"Mom," I said when I picked up the receiver. There was no need for hellos or who is its. She asked why I hadn't been answering. "It's too hot to be awake," I said. She then started on something, but immediately a sound like sizzling took over the line, as if someone had turned on a fryer. She yelled, "Judy! I can't hear anything." Her tone was inexplicably tragic. "I can't," she said, with such terminal sadness. She behaved as if cut off from the past, though on every other occasion she behaved as if immune to the present. We both knew that our hallway phone was broken;

the fryer sound had been with us for many years by that point. Alex had diagnosed her shrillness and alarm as something "purely pathological." He'd sometimes give her condition a more specific name, but that name would change with each mother-story I told, and we accepted that there was a certain rotation at play, a galaxy of conditions within which I was unfortunately caught.

I laid the receiver in my palm and wiggled the cable that came out of its bottom. With my foot, I nudged the long cable that ran from the phone base to the wall, and I used my index finger and thumb to squeeze the electrical tape patching a break. I brought the receiver back to my face. "Mom?" I said. The intrusion had passed. I leaned against the wall, facing the phone, its lone hook, and the pale-yellow wall around it. Our broken phone was cheap, like everything else in the apartment. It was an $11.99 unit with no caller ID screen, the most offensive shade of green plastic to have been moulded by the people of Radio Shack. We had the same exact model in the kitchen, wedged between the fridge and the microwave, with an answering machine hooked up to it. My mother knew not to leave messages. She knew how many rings to let pass before hanging up to start again.

From next door, where the kitchen of the neighbours' row house touched our hallway, I could hear a blender working through a late breakfast smoothie. My mother was undeterred. We spoke about the heat, how the patrons at the public library where she worked were already complaining. The homeless had grouped near the AC vents. The computers had been turned off, apparently to save electricity. "The grid might explode," my mother said, though she had the sense to correct herself, and added, "or whatever it's called, when too many people turn on their AC." Of course we had nothing close to air conditioning in the apartment. We spoke a little about whether the cold should be rationed, through some kind of communism, and how exactly that would work. When I say "we spoke," it was mainly my mother talking. Eventually a colleague summoned her. She told me she loved me, and to stay safe. She'd been so overcome by the heat, she'd forgotten to ask about Alex and Christopher and why I wasn't with them.

A few minutes later, I was sitting in a bathtub filled halfway with tepid water, reading a short story that reimagined the life of Yoko Ono. My mother brought me magazines from work, the more obscure, arty kinds that went out of circulation quickly. Here was a story about Ono as a ghostly puff, just some vapour, floating around the Midwestern states, which had a lot of lakes and lonely women in them. She visited single mothers and some widows, and imparted a silent wisdom, conveyed to them in their sleep. She appeared as a green mist, sometimes brown, with a mouth and long hair identifying her as Yoko Ono. Over time, her mentees came together, drawn by their unofficial membership, intuitively meeting by a lakeside at the right time and place. They became friends and confidantes, sharing stories of their losses, but also boosting themselves through communal grief and the power that their various losses had bestowed upon them.

The story had a lot of scope—Alex used this term to describe certain films, even some people—but somehow the author managed to fit it all into three pages. The story also had long spells of silent, uneventful writing, and a lot of detail left out, though somehow this only worked to give it force and an air of realism. It'd been a long time since I'd experienced that kind of excitement when reading something. I reread the story, forgetting for a moment about the infernal heat, which despite the cool puddle of water I'd poured myself, had flushed my upper body, causing sweat to pool in my collar, the spot between my nose and lips, and the insides of my ears. Of course, what struck me most about the story was the premise of this shifting vapour, which pretty much mirrored, or mirrored if the mirror were placed at some distance, at a slight angle from its subject, some of the things that Alex had been prophesizing for the past four months. His belief was more so founded on the three of us making it out of here rather than a coming together of strangers. But still, the similarities were striking. And it was odd the way the story had come to me by chance, being the first thing I picked up in the bathroom, out of a large stack of options.

My mother had taken the towels out for laundry, so I padded, dripping and nude, to the hallway, toward the phone. I was clutching the magazine and felt somewhat entranced, and a little physically anxious. My plan was to call Christopher and Alex to tell them about the story, or rather about how randomly I came upon it, making it the most overt sign I'd intercepted yet, even if it hadn't come from staring up at clouds.

I wasn't sure whether I was about to deliver big news. I figured the news was technically good even if indeterminate. Or, the news would become determinate, would take on its true good shape, once it was processed by Alex.

On the first cycle of rings, no one picked up at the coach house. I tried again, in case they were outside, and I also tried the number of the main house. Christopher finally picked up. His voice had its usual emaciated tone, or maybe it was just overheated. Either way, it didn't sound like something big had descended upon them that morning. "Who's this?" he said because I hadn't yet said anything. I was deciding what to say, whether to start with how I had just flipped to the Yoko Ono story, which would've been honest. Though, while the phone had been ringing, I'd started to lose confidence in my reading of it and the excitement that that reading called for, objectively speaking. Of course, the heat that we were suffering was also unusual, very objectively—I wanted to comment on that. The way the grid might implode, and my extreme sweating. "Judy," my cousin followed up, "is that you? Are you able to speak?"

Or I could start by bringing up what had happened earlier that morning, when the world was still dark and he'd picked me up off the highway. I could say that sometimes, as of late, I didn't really think I was meant for sitting on the lawn of Alex's mother's place, acting as a barometer and waiting for something unsubstantiated, making nothing notes, and attuning myself to absent sensations.

"Judy!" my cousin said, and this came out as a death scream, in the same deranged category that my mother's voice belonged to, whenever she believed she'd just lost me to the broken phone, or if I didn't answer straightaway when sitting behind a locked bathroom door, or from underneath my bedsheet. Their reactions were equally senseless, yet so sincere that you had to wonder whether there was something wrong with them. More than anything, I wanted to ask my cousin to come over and move into this apartment. In my simple understanding of it, the problem was one of geography. Also inaction, ennui, and depression. Once he moved here, I could discuss with Christopher the idea of him applying to a college. Or signing up for classes at the university in town, where I'd already been admitted. We'd take long, daily walks during which I'd ask what he thought of this or that attractive woman, or man, or whether he'd spoken to his father lately, or how he felt about his mother having a new husband and child, who by then were far from new. I had the sense that without Alex around, we'd each learn who the other was to such an exciting degree, neither he nor I would ever think of leaving any place again.

By now the phone sounded like wrapping paper being balled. Christopher had pressed the receiver to his shirt. He was probably running. The phone at the coach house was cordless so there was no telling the places he could run. After a while I made out voices. Christopher's was saying: "The Big Shadow's here. Judy's trying to communicate from it. I think—it's happening—" He sounded fiendish and out of breath. Next, I heard Alex's standard intonation, that sociopathic composure, obsessed with commandeering his little world, really just the product of insolence and money. "It's Judy?" he said. "Wait, how do you know she's—"

I could tell the receiver was being passed from hand to hand and I hung up, immediately unplugging the cable that ran from the phone base to the wall. I unplugged the kitchen unit as well. The apartment became a precious silent, a world without cousins, mothers, friends, or ideas. Though soon the cracks in the floor let through the sound of *The Price Is Right*. Our downstairs neighbour had cranked the volume to watch the numbered wheel spin, excited to see whose life would change for the better. The Yoko Ono story felt years in the past. Actually, it was embarrassing, the way it'd worked me up. I collected my pajamas from the bathroom floor and used them to wipe the trail of water running from the bathtub to the hallway and to the kitchen.

I AWOKE IN the mid-afternoon to my mother speaking my name. She crouched over me, spreading her knees uncouthly and patting me on the head too hard. Her work purse was still attached to the side of her body. She'd come home early; the library shut down for heat reasons. She assumed our phone had stopped working from the temperature and hadn't noticed that I'd unplugged the cords. I let her do whatever. I answered her questions, saying no, I was not collapsed, not seeing double. It was only a nap on a day when the temperature, the humidity, and the sun had colluded to play a terrible trick on us. Maybe Alex was right, and this was prophetic. I felt too worn out to care. I'd fallen asleep on the uncarpeted part of my bedroom floor in my underwear and a camisole. My scalp was soaked, as if I'd just taken a shower. My mother sat over me for a few minutes, silent and monitoring. Then she stood up and said, "Okay!" and I knew she was off to do something that she believed would make me better.

A short while later, we were on the living-room couch, the TV tuned to a sitcom starring teenagers with problems that were nothing like my own. My mother had taken her skirt off and stretched her legs across the coffee table, pointing her feet toward opposite ends of the room. I lay on my side, with the top of my head pressed into her naked thigh. She'd lain a wet towel over my forehead, scented with lavender oil, which she said had "revitalizing properties." The scent, mingling with the unmoving air of our living room, metastasized to the stench of old lady perfume. But I didn't care about that either. I wanted to gag, and to sleep, and to be at my house, but also not there at the same time. I couldn't hold it in any longer and said, "I think Christopher should just live here, no?" I thought she and I might have an unprecedented, honest conversation about the things I'd been feeling lately. But instead, her hand wandered to my scalp and picked up a piece of my hair. "I actually can't understand why you're not at Alex's right now," she said. "If I had the option to escape to the country..."

For the next while, she rattled on about breezes, shade, and the fact of Alex's mother's air conditioner. Her ideas on the countrystead had cemented ten years prior, during a brief halcyon era when Alex's mother's guilt over the divorce had translated into supervision. And that supervision translated into free babysitting that allowed my own mother to work both day shifts and through the night. Here was a place where lavender sprigs grew out of the soil and asked to be picked into a rustic bouquet, for the vase in the breakfast nook, next to the tumbler of maple syrup. Here was a swimming pool, even if unfilled, and *Nutcracker* ballet tickets at Christmastime. Pizza parties with high-quality pizza, not from a chain. Admission to the water park. Alex's mother, when we were eight, offered to take us all to Disney World, though that was too much for my mother—Florida? No, no; that state is full of rape. Alex and Christopher had gone and had a very nice time on the roller coasters. Before Alex got his driver's licence, there was a glorified cabbie specifically paid to drive him into town and back, so he could stay at the neighbourhood school despite his parents' divorce. Christopher soon started taking advantage, and spent nights at the coach house. His mother had remarried around then, after the strangest man one could ever meet—my mother's brother—left her out of the blue and moved to the woods of British Columbia. I took advantage as well. It was no secret that the countrystead was a welcome vacation. We stuffed our homework in the trunk and were chauffeured out of the school parking lot, like children of a president or a very famous actor.

WHEN THE SITCOM ended, my mother stood up to reposition the fan, tugging its head too forcefully in a direction it wasn't meant to twist. I watched a screw fly off the back and roll underneath the TV stand. She eventually opted to drag the entire fan closer to me. It was a military-green industrial-looking model, given to us by a neighbour who'd since passed away. My mother's pocked thighs flexed as she pushed and pulled at the fan. Her skin was white as paper and criss-crossed with purple railroads that came to abrupt ends, nothing going anywhere. Her underwear was an orange juniors' pair she'd bought for me years earlier. The synthetic trim had itched so badly, I took it off the moment I got to school. Was my mother putting up with that itch now? I believed she had the will to ride it out. She was like a nun in burlap or Jesus with his crown of thorns. Her heels called the most attention, with their crusted, yellowed rim exactly like on a piece of cheese. She was not an old woman; she'd had me at twenty-seven. But by syphoning all life into me, she'd degenerated unnaturally quickly.

"Here, see," she said, about the new breeze. The fan was so close now I could barely open my eyes. The commercial break ended. Another episode of the same sitcom began, with its four stock characters. My mother curled herself on the couch in a new way, tucking her feet so that my head was forced to lie on their hard parts. The smell of chicken crept in from the kitchen. She did not have the sense to not cook on a day like today. She said that as long as she used the pressure cooker it was fine—because any heat and energy, well, it would all go *into the bird*. She said chicken was a lean meat, as if that made it suitable for a day that felt like hell finally folding us in. Her hand travelled back into my hair and the hackneyed character delivered his first line, about a high school dance or football touchdown. "He's very cute," my mother said. "Which is your favourite of the guys on this show?"

I sat up, forgetting about the lavender compress on my head. It fell to the floor and for a second I thought a piece of me had broken off, like a loose brick in a windstorm. Very little would've surprised me at this point. "I need to pee," I said and left her on the sofa. After a few minutes on the toilet, I could see that nothing would come out. Practically speaking, I'd been peeing out of my scalp, my chest, my back, and my forehead all day. I flushed the toilet and walked past the living room to the hallway. I lifted the phone receiver, stared at the wall for a moment, and set it back in its cradle. "Looks like the phone is working again," I said. I plugged the phone back in, both in the hall and in the kitchen. I reentered the living room and spread my arms. "I just spoke to Christopher. You're right that it makes more sense to be out in the country today."

My mother didn't turn to me, she was so out of it from the heat. She said, "On a day like today, yes. On a day like today, yes." She was also partly distracted by the brain-numbing plotline of the episode. I said Christopher and Alex would pick me up soon, we'd get ice cream, and head back to the countrystead, with its breezes and amenities, everything money could buy. "Smart girl," she said, and then told me that she'd pack up the chicken, that Christopher, Alex, and I could eat it together before having the ice cream. She stretched her arm toward me, donating her last energy to the wiggling of her fingers. She signalled that we should touch, one final time, before I left for that glorious locale.

3

I stood on the street looking up at our living-room window to check for my mother's face in the insect screen. On a normal day, the sun would've started to signal its intention to set, and the temperature would've been waning at some welcome rate. It was the time of day when birds should've been behaving differently than a few hours prior, and new types of persons would go walking the streets, while the opposite types of persons would return home and lock their doors. But the heat and the unwavering light had flattened all sense of routine. The street was empty, in fact, and quiet but for the drone of AC units. The effort of getting dressed, combing my hair, and walking downstairs from the third floor with the chicken in a plastic bag had drained me to the point that taking a single step felt precarious. I believed this wasn't that different from descriptions I'd read of NASA astronauts returning home and stumbling like colts, the earth more alien to them now than the planets and moons they'd gone to see. I had to sit on the curb to rest, and I watched our window screen for a while longer. It was the first time I'd told my mother I would be picked up by Christopher and Alex, but upon coming downstairs, had no car waiting for me and no destination either.

Two short blocks north, the street on which my mother and I live arrives at an east-west throughway with shops and a bus route on it. I turned to the right, only because I'd been walking on the right side of the street. Or maybe because left was the way to the countrystead. Soon I passed under the marquee of the repertory cinema where Jeremy, my first boyfriend, had worked. His title, as I remember it, was "assistant junior theatre comanager."

Passing by the repertory cinema wasn't good for me these days. Jeremy and I had met in the final week of winter when I'd gone to see *Jane B. par Agnès V.*, part of a French documentary showcase, with Alex and Christopher of course. After slipping out to go to the bathroom, I returned to the theatre and was faced with a horrifying flat dark that could only be described as what you'd see if accidentally buried alive. After my eyes adjusted somewhat, I saw that each row in the theatre had a complete set of heads, everyone the same height, the same hairstyle, no one wearing a hat, no seat appearing vacant. The then-scene in the documentary was particularly low lit, too. I believe Jane Birkin might have been in a cemetery even, or it was nighttime and she was sitting alone in her apartment, in Paris. Either way, I panicked. I didn't bother attempting to figure out which row it was I'd come out of. Instead, I fled to the lobby, where I pretended to be immersed in the mechanics of the vintage popcorn machine, until Jeremy walked by, asked if everything was cool, and offered me a free pass to the next day's screening of *News from Home*, to make up for all my troubles.

I went to see *News* on my own. By the time Alex and Christopher discovered I was going, the tickets were sold out. I told them I'd found the pass on the floor, inside the women's bathroom.

After the screening, Jeremy and I talked film theory: strategies of distanciation, also will to allegory a little. He showed me the theatre manager's storage closet, from which he encouraged me to pick out a film poster to take home for free. I grabbed the closest tube. I figured anything in that closet was bound to be good. When I said this to Jeremy, he gave me a long and happy look. "That's an unusually positive approach," he said, which seemed the complete opposite of how I'd ever thought of my approaches.

Outside, by the domed ticket window protruding from the front of the theatre, Jeremy told me I was mature for my age, which was three years less than him, and that I resembled, coincidentally, Jane Birkin's daughter Charlotte. I'd never interacted with someone ostensibly interested in me. It's possible I was coming out of a plain or even ugly phase that winter, my face bones settling into "interesting" or "French" or whatever Charlotte G. was—at least to the discerning eye. But of course, discernment was all that Alex ever preached appreciation for. I assumed he and Christopher would approve of Jeremy, especially how he could hold his own in a conversation on film and theory. In the alley between the theatre and a submarine sandwich shop, Jeremy and I made out for a couple of minutes, my one hand crushing the film poster, the other at rest on his shoulder. The whole experience— fortuitous meeting, free ticket, fantastic conversation—seemed out of the movies. And so I acted like I was in a film, feeling as good as I later would when walking that highway ramp, when seeing myself projected as twenty times bigger than I actually was, freed from my cousin, Alex, and my mother.

I had never kissed anyone before and was surprised by how much space Jeremy's tongue took up in my mouth. A couple of minutes in, he moved the flaps of my winter coat apart, opened his hand, and pressed his palm into my lower ribs, over the T-shirt I wore underneath my sweater. He made his hand travel slowly up my torso, the heel of the hand applying maximum lateral pressure. The heel bulldozed over my right breast, pushing its modest bulk of fat upward, the way the glaciers moved across our earth way back when, sparing absolutely nothing. "Did that feel nice?" he asked afterward, sounding so sincere I had no choice but to say, "Yes, thank you, it did." Ten minutes later, I was at home, lying on the couch next to my mother in the same old way, the top of my head resting against her thigh. My ribs on the right side burned like I'd fallen into fire. My right breast burned the most and its nipple felt torn. But I could barely contain myself; I was smiling into the couch cushion. I understood that burning to be the cousin of the proverbial blood-stained bedsheet, a badge of my now having a boyfriend. My mother had the TV tuned to CNN, unusually loud because a woman in rural Pennsylvania had just murdered her infant. Or she was a suspect, or in custody, or was only a person of interest.

"I can tell she did it," my mother said. "Look at her eyes. That's a wolf, not a human being." She went on without waiting for confirmation, about all the things that made this mother guilty. I shrugged but all I could think about was Jeremy. My mother rubbed and raked at my scalp and I shut my eyes and pictured those fingers as his: picking up strands, laying them back down gently, over and over, like a tender, meticulous weaver.

AFTER HALF AN hour of walking, I arrived at the university. I'd walked to the campus often in my life. For two summers, I went to see my mother, who worked at one of its libraries until she was fired for what the letter she brought home called "antisocial behaviour." She'd hated the job, saying there were "politics," but trudged on, she explained, for the end goal of my free tuition. The campus looked like a pretty, neo-Gothic amusement park set in the centre of our city, with its turrets, chocolate-coloured bricks, and gardens. A clock tower announced that it was five past seven. I set the bag with the chicken at the base of the tower, for a hungry student or a racoon to find. In front of the psychology building, I saw a groundsman kneeling by a bed of tulips, all dead. The bed had been colour-blocked, to create an abstract version of the university crest. The flowers now lay collapsed across the dirt, their heads like runny rubber.

I stopped to watch the groundsman. I was curious to see what he'd do because, as I saw it, there was nothing to do but walk away and try again next spring. I was perhaps hoping for an interaction. The truth was, I wasn't sure where I was headed and felt the impending horror of the inevitable turnaround, the return to my mother's couch. The groundsman sensed me standing behind him. "If they'd only held out for a little while longer, you know?" he said, glancing over his shoulder. "Just a few more minutes." I left him and the flowers, and went to sit on the steps of the library, the very library where my mother had worked, the steps where we'd often sat when I was on summer holidays, eating the sandwiches she'd prepared for our lunch.

I had taken the groundsman's words to be gardener nonsense. Meaning, I hadn't thought to take him literally. But soon enough, minutes after I sat down, I heard the first clap of thunder, distant but unmistakable. Of course, anyone who would've thought about it would know that the heatwave was due to go out. After days of rising temperatures, the atmosphere and its mystery layers had been pushed to their limits. What followed was the stuff of time-lapse cinematography. As if flicked on by a switch, the sky went from its happy robin's egg blue to the dirty colour of a river. The air began to move. I felt a breeze and, for the first time in days, something like relief as the perspiration was wiped from my thighs, my arms, and the back of my neck. Soon the birds started to act out, emerging from their hiding places to draw frantic figure-eights. Back home, my mother had likely gotten off the couch to unplug the television, microwave, and toaster. The electric lights lining the campus paths blinked and came on, their night sensors tricked because the sky was now a mix of brown and orange. And then the air became completely still. As quickly as they'd appeared, the birds hid away. Aside from the thunder, there was nothing. Not a human, motor, or animal to be seen or heard.

The sky flashed once and shot its starting pistol. The concrete underneath me quaked. The facade of the library faced a large, oval lawn; from its opposite end, a residence building looked back at the library. It was where the first-year students lived, and now that summer was here, all of the windows had been thrown open to air out the smells they'd left behind. The last of the day's cottony denseness melted away. The breeze came back as a proper wind. My hair flew to one side. The white standard-issue curtains of the first-year residence flung themselves out of the windows. I could easily make out what was inside each room: a bunk bed pressed against a wall, beige paint, some kind of corkboard stuck to the wall opposite the window, a small rectangular mirror, rooms so drab and identical they looked like prison cells.

Two more flashes, a couple of cracks, and the rain arrived. The residence building disappeared. I was left with three feet of world, just to where my shoes reached. I heard the lawn turn to slop, its snails start to rattle, and its worms start to squirm. It was Kurosawa's *Rashomon*. The rain in that film is a character unto itself, that's how much scope it has.

The stairs were protected by a roof, but even so, a mist sprayed me on the legs, arms, and face. I winced and shielded my eyes. Christopher's mother, my aunt Tamara, had once told me, "That's how it is at Niagara. From a thousand feet away, the spray hits you so that you're pretty much drinking the famous falls." While my aunt was on the honeymoon of her second marriage, Christopher had stayed with me and my mother. We'd watched the classic film noir thriller *Niagara*, starring Marilyn Monroe, which had come on the TV by chance, causing my mother to whoop, "Stranger than fiction! Stranger than fiction!" about the coincidence. At one point, she made a joke that even then I could recognize was in poor taste. We'd just watched an attempted murder, involving a rowboat and the violent water of the Niagara River. My mother, still riding her strange high, said, "I hope this doesn't happen to your mom. After all, we don't know her new husband too well." She'd been kidding, most likely, but my cousin went hysterical. My mother's high plummeted to its converse low as she tried to calm him down for what turned out to be hours. The three of us eventually ended up on my bed, with inconsolable Christopher still sniffling, his face red and blue, and my mother repeating apologies that I could see he was refusing to hear.

I sat next to them, a hand on each of their bodies, sensing that sunrise was imminent, that soon Christopher and I would head off to our third-grade classroom with its atlas and aquarium. In that bedroom, touching them both, I was filled with the under-standing—which even then I experienced as repugnant—that I was tethered to them now, simply by having witnessed just how much was wrong with each.

THE RAIN SOFTENED for a short moment and entered a seesaw stage, intensifying and letting up in turns. During one of these intervals, when the rain thinned, I saw a man shoot out of a gate that led to the first-year residence building. The tulip man, was my first thought, the university groundsman. His shape was distorted by the rain and at one point I lost him. Then I saw him again, stopped under a tree, and thinking better of it, continuing on, sprinting across the lawn toward where I was sitting. He reached the bottom stair in time to the next thunderclap. The lightning and the sound of sky being ripped down its middle were nearly simultaneous by this point. "Shit," he said, "that nearly got me." He was breathless but seemed to find the situation funny. He might've been embarrassed about being so out of shape. By the look of his features, I guessed he was fifty or forty years old. He was a tall person, at least six feet two in his pair of cowboy boots, slightly more than my cousin's six feet, though unlike Christo-pher, this man had girth. The buttons on his shirt strained from the push of his gut. He'd been holding a leather jacket over his head and he tossed it onto the stairs. He then tilted his head back, shut his eyes, and started combing his hands through his hair, pressing it into a slick-back with slow, regular strokes.

I watched him pat himself before me and was filled with the sense that I was part of a TV commercial filmed inside a person's shower, something intimate selling me a cosmetic. I was not the subject of the commercial, but I was more than a mere audience member sitting in front of her television set. I was there, inside. I was wet just as he was. I was in the fog, and I could hear and smell the lather. Maybe I was something like a camerawoman. I think because of this sense, I watched without flinching or giving any impression that it was unusual for a stranger to arch and pat himself in front of another stranger. The fact that he was doing this told me that he enjoyed having me watch, and that his behaviour was acceptable, or maybe that he knew I was open-minded enough to accept it. He took his time. When he was done, he asked, "You mind?" while pointing to the stairs and sat next to me. His legs spread until his knee came to rest on my shin and from there on in its weight was all I could focus on: the pressure of his wet denim against the damp skin of my leg, its transgressive quality exaggerating the actual, true weight of that knee, my excitement exaggerating the actual, true weight of that transgression.

He gave a low grunt, stuck his fingers in his eyes, rubbed for a while, mumbled a delayed thanks, and brought his knees together. I immediately missed that weight. He leaned back to a near-lying position so that he could grab his jacket from where he'd thrown it, behind me. "Sorry," he said as he folded the jacket on his lap, "did you want to be alone? This looks like a nice place to be alone. If there's one thing I get right now it's not wanting to be around anybody."

"I did want that," I said, "but not anymore. You've got great timing." It was only honest, but I could tell it sounded smart. Sometimes these things slip out, a sentence like a line in a script; people tend to treat them as a door, an invitation.

"I've got good timing? That's good to hear. Thank you," he said, accepting the invitation. "So, when did the feeling change, you wanting to be around no one to you wanting to be around someone?"

He'd taken a couple of steps past the threshold, and I knew I could retreat at this point. It would've been so easy to stand up and walk away, but I was having a good time. "Just now," I said, "the exact moment you got here. If you'd come a second earlier, I would've stood up and left." I'd kept going, the gate was fully opened. Why not? I made it deadpan because I could tell he had a sense of humour.

He responded with laughter. It came easily. "Shit," he said, wiping his lips. "What luck. That's awesome. I'm glad it worked out for us." He looked away, into the distance, which was just rain, and happily shook his head.

It felt nice to have made someone glad with nothing but my wit, not even something that took effort. I believed it was real, that that's exactly what had happened. I'd impressed him and turned things from bad to good. I had unique qualities that somehow met a test I didn't even know I was taking. Before I could ask his name, he started talking. "This is crazy. I flew in from New York this morning. First I thought I was going to die from the heat. Then I'm nearly struck by lightning." He rearranged himself, leaning farther back on his elbows. "I went to sleep as soon as I got to this apartment they gave me, and got out of bed twenty minutes ago, to go to *this thing*." He waved his hand to the left, at some buildings. "Whatever," he said, not finishing his story.

We sat in silence, him staring into the distance, squinting at something he could maybe make out, and me trying to steal glances in the moments he seemed especially distracted. I could see he hadn't shaved in a while. Grey hairs sprouted from the temple that faced me and snaked through his slick-back. His lips had a pucker, a bit like a woman's. His nose was shaped like a small, bumpy potato.

I was able to keep observing for a while. I liked that he was close enough to see in detail, but I wasn't feeling anything like attraction, maybe not even true interest. I understood that I'd been bored that day, and in the months leading up to it. My boredom was so extreme, I'd come to believe my friends when they said our disappointment in what the days had to offer could trigger a transition to something beyond the perceptible. I'd started tracking cloud shadows and kept a notebook on the subject. Anything would do now, I thought, looking at the nose of the man sitting next to me. It's just good timing and some company in the rain. And then he turned his head and looked me in the eyes, hard, as if he'd heard me think, his mouth softening but not smiling, like he was hurt by what I'd just said about him in my head. "Don't take this the wrong way," he said, "but these are the best five minutes I've had in a long time. You know how to just *be*. You don't demand." He gave me a tired smile. It was honest, with nothing of the screen adults usually propped up before their emotions when talking to me.

I smiled back. Maybe it wasn't just about good timing. I looked over his boots and jeans. My thoughts turned back on themselves. I'm happy, I started thinking. This scene is unusual. Where did he come from? Why did he come to me? Whatever it is, it's not nothing. I took a closer look at his outfit, trying to gauge if he was faculty, someone who'd be teaching me come September. But he didn't look like most professors I'd seen strolling between the campus buildings. His jeans were fitted and black, faded to grey at the knees. His shirt was black, too, with sleeves rolled to the elbows, vintage Western style, with piped yokes, the top three buttons unsnapped, and a pointy fang-like collar with red roses embroidered on its tips. "So, you'll be teaching here in the fall," I tried.

He said, "No way," he said, "I'm sure they'd *love* that," but he'd only agreed to do a summer thing. "Now I've got all this other shit that came up back home. Whatever. I'll manage. I'll fly back on the weekends. These people, though." He spoke as if I already knew his work schedule, his life story, his name. "Already at that thing," he continued, vaguely waving his hand in the direction of the buildings again, "the guy who invited me brought all this stuff for me to sign. I could see the other professors laughing at him as he's following me around with a stack of books. Anyway, I left after three minutes. I can already tell this class is going to be chaos. I mean, the adoration—it's flattering. But I don't love it. I don't love these people, you know?"

"People are very hard," I said.

He shifted on the steps to face me. He was already smiling. "I love that! That should be the title of something. 'People are hard,'" he repeated. "You get it. People *are* hard. Tell me other things, please. Just talk on any subject while this rain just floods out the human race."

I've always done poorly when put on the spot, and usually Alex and Christopher saw to it that I was not put on spots. All I could do was shrug, there was nothing more to say about humanity, the futility of life, et cetera. But he liked that, too. "That's it exactly," he said, not disappointed. "There's nothing to say."

The raindrops grew to their biggest yet, sparse but extra large. They drummed the stairs below us. It seemed he wasn't going to ask, so I offered, "I'm going to start classes here in the fall."

He nodded thoughtfully. "This is where you want to be?" he asked. I shrugged, one side of my body this time. I said I didn't know, which I thought would make him laugh, that it was part of this whole world-weary, loose thing we were acting out, except he started nodding with an even more serious expression, like he was in pain, my pain. I saw his pupils dart from my nose to my lips and back to my eyes. I didn't flinch.

I said, "I guess it's just what one does. I've lived here all my life and have never been anywhere else. My mother moved here from a smaller town because her parents were terrible to her after their younger daughter drowned in a lake. She went to university here, then got a job at a library and cleaning offices. I just finished high school last week and didn't apply anywhere else."

"It's selfish," he said matter-of-factly. "Parents can be so selfish, with girls, especially. They want to keep them around. They encourage their domesticity. I'd be bothered by that, too." His eyes were still on me. I knew he was waiting for me to keep spilling, to drip to the last drop, but I was done. So he kept going: "Apply to transfer after your freshman year," he said. "Anywhere you want to go. Bring a reference letter from me to any department in the world and they'll beg you to come. NYU, Columbia, Juilliard. They just need to hear my name." He paused. "What do you say? Yeah? Let's get you outta here."

I looked again at the roses on his shirt collar, trying to square the roses with the power to get me accepted anywhere in New York, which is to say the world, the place where all art-inclined persons travelled to forge a better version of themselves, and to meet others with that same goal exactly. But the roses said nothing. I moved down to the worn-out jeans and worn-out boots. Nothing. I had no idea who I was sitting next to. The rain softened just then. First one and then a second cloud broke apart. The sun snuck through the fissures and the first-year residence building reappeared. We fell into a silence. I couldn't tell if it was the good kind.

After a while I thought it might be my turn to speak, that that's why the silence was upon us. And it seemed Jeremy, my first boyfriend, was the right topic for this moment. Jeremy had revealed to me on our second date that soon he'd be off to New York. We'd just finished watching a matinee screening of *Symbiopsychotaxiplasm* and engaged in some furtive hand-holding on the sidewalk in front of the theatre. He delivered the New York news so casually I didn't even think to understand it. I supposed the very quality that made you able to pick up your life and leave for New York also caused you to think it was nothing worth talking about at length. Jeremy then told me he played drums—the first I was hearing of it—and that his friend's band needed a touring drummer, or maybe someone they'd keep on for good. I was about to tell the man sitting next to me, "My ex recently left for New York, to play drums in a band," when he started speaking. "Besides, you're one of the smartest people I've met," he said, continuing his earlier thought, as if there'd been no silence at all, nothing I needed to have worried about filling. "I can already tell. You don't need reference letters. What's your name?" he asked, and when I told him, he said, "It's a classic name," in a reassuring voice.

I told him my mother liked Judy Garland and had written to her fan club. I wanted to say that she also had strange compulsions, was unusually brittle, with no sense of composure, and that Judy was her younger sister's name, so that naming me was a bit like bringing her back from the dead, which was an odd thing to do to your child. And that more than any particular city or university, I'd like to go to a place where I wouldn't have to live down the hall from her or be a parent to her. But he seemed to already know this. "My first class is Wednesday at noon, they run Mondays and Wednesdays," was all he offered as his own introduction. He scoffed like it was all very dumb. "Come to it. It's in there," he said, lifting his hand toward the building that looked like a fairy-tale fortress. "I want you in the room with me. Actually, I need you there. Hell, you should probably be teaching this poetry class. You'll keep me sane. Everyone's just going to want me to talk about what it's like to hang out with Patti. That's sort of as far as mindsets go these days."

I said that was awful, even though I didn't know who Patti was and whose mindsets we were tearing into. "You should visit New York, too," he continued. "It's wrong that you've never been. It's your kind of place, I can tell. It's a city for people like you."

I was about to answer with something nonverbal and modest, to hide that, yes, a trip to New York would be nice, might turn my life from nothing to good, like it probably had for Jeremy. But the sky let out another bang just then. What seemed to have ended wasn't over.

He stood up. "I have to go now," he said, looking toward the spot he'd come from and brushing his hands through his hair one more time. "Are you free in a couple of hours? Should we grab some food later on?"

"No," I said. I regretted it as soon as I said it, but he only smiled. He liked my no and how quickly it'd come out of me. I could do no wrong with this person. He said, "Okay," and "see you." He jogged away, into the rain that'd started up again. I'll see you Wednesday for sure, I wanted to yell after him, and he turned around immediately, as if he'd heard, as if already we'd graduated to telepathy. I saw his lips move. I bunched my face to say, "I can't hear you." He was walking backward, the leather jacket hooding him and falling across his eyes. Whatever he said next was muted by more thunder. I saw him happily shake his head. "We can't win," the shake said. This weather! This *Rashomon*! He wrapped the jacket sleeves around his shoulders so that it looked like a little monkey was clutching his back. He mouthed "bye," then turned around and ran, back to the spot where I'd first seen him, disappearing between two buildings.

4

The following morning, I awoke in one of the mother bedrooms. I could tell it was late by how well rested I felt and yet the room was dark, as if the sun hadn't risen that morning. I sat up to see better. The rainstorm from the day before had left a dense cloud cover in its wake. The clouds were *cumulonimbus calvus*. A phone rang, far away, and I stuck my head out the window. I saw Alex on the lounger, wearing long pants and speaking into the cordless receiver. He said, "The swimming pool, uh-um. Sure, yes, okay." My cousin lay stomach-down on the cracked ceramic tiles making up the pool deck. He'd lowered his head and bare arms into the pool and worked away with quiet concentration. Using the rose pruners, he snipped at the bushes that grew out of the concrete walls, then brought each branch up, to place on a pile at his side.

I watched them for something like five minutes, way past when Alex hung up the phone, let his cheek fall on his shoulder, and lay in this lopsided way, staring at Christopher, who went on clipping. The scene was almost Italian countryside film, missing only the light of a golden Mediterranean sun. The frame of my window's view was perfect, capturing just the right part of the side and back lawns, the pool, those two clowns, positioned in the left third of the rule-of-thirds grid, and the birch with its snow-white trunk playing off the grass, now revitalized and bright green after a heavy watering.

I think on that morning I started to conceive of them only as elements of a picture, specifically, a picture to give to the man from the rainstorm—an entertainment. Yeah, I'd tell him, I awoke in the mother bedroom, I got over the shock of a sky being grey for once, of the air not trying to slaughter me, not squeeze me like a lemon, and out the window I see the Brothers Slick and Slack, the Brothers Pushmeofftheearth, up to their latest nothing. The man from the rainstorm would laugh, catching the reference to Jean Rhys, and I'd confirm that yes, I'd been reading *Voyage in the Dark* that week. While sitting on my lounger, looking for signals in the sky, entangled in a metaphysical escape plan, I'd been reading Rhys's best novel. And then an impossible heat arrived, followed by a storm, and you and I met, like characters in *Rashomon*.

Upon hearing that, he'd laugh again.

AFTER THE MAN from the rainstorm had left me on the library steps, I'd used a nearby pay phone to call Christopher and ask him to pick me up. He arrived on campus looking shaken, saying what a day it'd been, with the mystery morning phone call that they thought was me ("No," I said, "my line's broken."), their AC giving out, and then the storm, which brought down an aspen right on top of the wooden shed behind the coach house, halving it like a walnut. At first they thought, well, if this isn't the arrival of the Big Shadow, what is? But then the violence of the lashing rain and the groaning thunder, the way the wood had split, and how they were removed from it, watching from a window, nothing feeling welcoming or transcendent—and worse still, my absence when I was meant to be a part of it—well, that told them it wasn't *it*, right? That told them: this is only a summer storm.

It'd been easy to tune him out during the car ride. I looked out the window, registering only fragments of the glossy highway lanes and, beyond them, the tile, countertop, and hot tub stores with their empty parking lots the size of airports. All I heard was the conversation with the man from the rainstorm, playing on a loop and slowing during my favourite moments. Once we arrived at the countrystead, I called my mother to say we were well and alive, after eating ice cream and getting drenched in the downpour. Then I said to Christopher and Alex that I needed to go to bed, that I too had had a draining day. Alex spoke cautiously, almost like he didn't believe me. "That heat was strange, wasn't it?" he said. "You sensed that too, huh?" And once I'd turned to walk up the stairs, he added, "You won't dash off in the middle of the night again—or should we leave the car running?"

I said, "Sometimes there are things I need to do, and sometimes there aren't. I guess we'll have to wait and see," and continued to climb up to the mother bedrooms, without looking back at him. Once in bed and removed from those two, I had trouble falling asleep. I imagined the story of me in New York, attending Columbia University or an art school. In between classes, I could meet up with the rainstorm poet. He'd help me settle into a routine in the city, and in return I'd provide him with my brand of light entertainment, the kind I'd offered on the library stairs. With more time on my hands, I could properly start writing essays and smart articles, capturing my fleeting observations and perhaps turning them into documentaries. Anyway, once the tale of me in New York City played out in my mind a few times, with all its tangents and alternate endings, I fell asleep no problem.

THAT MORNING ALEX and Christopher were so immersed in the task of brush-clearing that no one came in to check if I was up, or to ask me to come outside already. In the kitchen, downstairs, I called my mother at work, to tell her I'd be spending the day at the countrystead but would return home for dinner that evening. She spoke to me for a while, about last night's storm. She said that at one point during the rain she believed, with a true belief she described as "educated," that the world was ending, and she'd gone downstairs to knock on the neighbour's door, except that no one answered, though she did hear the sound of the television. She said she'd then called the countrystead, wanting to speak to me about this feeling, but no one had answered there either, and she figured we were still in the city, having ice cream and waiting out the rain.

After hanging up, I placed a call to the campus library, to my mother's old desk number, which I still remembered. The woman who picked up might've been one of the instigators who'd gotten my mother fired, but she was friendly enough to me, saying I'd reached the wrong number but that she'd look up the English Department office, to save me the trouble of having to search myself.

The woman who picked up at the English Department had the voice of a young person. She made empathetic sounds when I listed off the only clues I had: I was interested in registering for a certain course, the course starting tomorrow at noon, taught by a poet from New York City who was only there for the summer.

She knew straightaway—Maurice Blunt's "Poetry and Rock 'n' Roll: Verse in the Era of NYC Punk" had filled up in under a minute, she said, many months ago. She explained that the summer course selection was especially limited, and that there was a waitlist the length of a book if I remained interested in signing up.

Inside the coach house, I approached Alex's shelves, the poetry "B" section. Sitting between *Songs of Innocence and of Experience* and a Leonard Cohen was a purple-spined *The River That Rhymes with Insane, Not Sex* by Maurice Blunt, published by Wet Coaster Press, eighteen years earlier, in 1980. The author photo on the inner back cover showed a slimmer, grainier version of the man from the rainstorm, slouched in a murky stairwell, dead arms at his sides, and on his face, an expression perfectly balanced between blankness and disdain. "Legendary musician," the bio called him. The author of two other books of poetry. Born in Ohio.

Alex's music shelves were of imperial dimensions, a couple thousand records at least. Like the books, they were his father's, yet Alex could tell you everything about each one, as if he'd recorded them himself. He had nothing by Maurice under "B," it turned out, neither in the records nor the CDs. By the time I finished checking, Christopher was at my side, asking me to come out and be with them, and why was I being so distant? He was taking a break from the pruning. His arms were criss-crossed with raised pink lines, some tenuously bleeding, and I wanted to tell him to put on some long sleeves already, how stupid can you be?

Instead, we stood staring each other down, perhaps the standoff that'd never happened on the ramp. I really had no idea what to say. He seemed disappointed in me, but was too much of a shadow of Alex for it to manifest like it would in a normal human.

He was only projecting the disappointment of Alex, and wasn't that good at it. It was possible he was perfectly all right with how I was acting, and that his biggest hope was to get away from the countrystead as well, and come live with me in my mother's apartment. Finally, I said, "Go outside? Are we going swimming in the new pool? Should I have brought my bathing suit and goggles?" Still, his depressed, shuffling walk guilted me into following him. We crossed over the grass, which was spongy from the rain, and stopped at the foot of the cracked shed, with the trunk of the aspen, sure enough, in its centre, making the cleanest cut.

I suppose I was impressed, I think by the precision. The shed had broken in a symmetrical way, the halves falling to either side so efficiently that the items on its shelves hadn't had time to shift. There were tubes of shuttlecocks, cans of paint and paint thinner, a weed whacker, some coiled skipping ropes, and a decommissioned birdhouse. About two years earlier, I'd been very interested in photography, and this was the type of thing I would've devoted a day to documenting. I'd been into Cindy Sherman, especially, though it didn't matter now. "So what?" I said, gesturing toward the shed.

"So things are strange," my cousin said, widening his eyes.

"So?" I said, and Christopher shut his eyes for a few seconds, opened them, crossed his arms, and stomped away.

A POETRY BOOK doesn't take long to finish. I had read Maurice's book six times by the time Christopher had trimmed away enough green to make a tunnel to the pool's bottom. At some point, I'd gone back in the house and retrieved my cloud notebook from the drawer with the old bras, to keep up appearances. I looked at the sky now and then and made a few notations, immediately feeling more at ease, like my presence couldn't be questioned. Alex was still on his lounger, also looking at the clouds, and for the most part silent. I understood he was upset at me for having left in such an unusual way two nights before, but I didn't care too much about that. Christopher was in my peripheral vision, then suddenly slipped out of view as if sucked into the earth. He'd made a quiet *yeep* sound when he'd gone.

Alex lifted himself off the lounger, and I stood up too, leaving Maurice's book and my notebook on the deck. We both approached the edge of the pool, at the spot where my cousin had last been, to look into the hole he'd gone down. "I have a thousand thoughts this morning," Alex said, "and now there's this hole." He looked weary and beaten, and I actually felt bad for him for a moment. I felt like I was looking at an exhausted father with a family under his wing, and nowhere to go, and something gnawing at him, likely the family gnawing. I could hear my cousin's rose pruners, snipping away under the canopy that still covered ninety percent of the pool.

"Are we supposed to join him down there?" I asked. I think for once my tone was unironic, because of the feeling of pity, and Alex responded with something approaching that awful melancholic sincerity I'd only heard in my mother and Christopher.

"Well, do you want to? Are you still interested in getting out of here with us?"

I shrugged, or perhaps I nodded and shrugged at the same time. In my head, I was thinking of Maurice, how peculiar he would think this all was, and how much pleasure I'd take in setting it all out for him, the way the trees swayed dramatically in the new cool weather, the way the hole seemed infinitely deep and had made me think of Lewis Carroll.

I think Alex took my gesture to be my one-half of us making up. He grew animated and said, "Of course, let's go down there, for sure!" which was his half of us making up. From then on, he wouldn't shut up. He had a sense, he said, that we needed to explore all the ways in which we might need to position ourselves, vis-à-vis the landscape, as we awaited the Big Shadow. That this pool might be *the thing.* "Water!" he said, simply. He started talking like people who knock on doors with Bibles or collection boxes in their hands. He began deferring to me, when I hadn't even presented a position. "I can see why you picked up and left in the middle of the night," he said. "I understand it. Sometimes one gets a sense and one has to follow it."

I started to feel embarrassed. It would've been the perfect moment to say to him that I was only there to check for books by the rainstorm poet; that he was only a library to me. But Alex didn't leave me room to enter. "There's this way out we're supposed to be taking, but I can't fully figure out how yet." He looked me in the eyes. "I understand your impatience. And I respect the way you follow your nose," he said. He seemed to be wanting affirmation, or maybe help, when I already felt myself removed from those two and released from any responsibility. Anyway, our interaction had turned saccharine and strange, and I didn't think Maurice would ultimately want to hear about it. I began to lower myself into the hole and Alex held me by the wrists, so that I wouldn't drop down with too much impact or pain.

Inside the pool, the feeling was overgrown labyrinth garden, or neglected Versailles greenhouse, or swamp-burrow in Louisiana. The storm water that had collected reached halfway up my calves. My sneakers and socks weighed me down as I waded through what felt like driftwood and beaver nests. Light made it in, but was heavily filtered and appeared dusty, I think from the pollen, which was able to float about, safe and unimpeded. Once my eyes adjusted, I saw Christopher, our canary, ten feet in, at work on expanding the tunnel. Alex dropped down behind me, causing a splash. There was no room to spread one's arms, but the feeling was not claustrophobic. I think the life inside, the green and yellow-green, the fat vines and all the bushes that had managed to flower even in this semi-shade, all that confidence and self-drive, they made it clear they had no intention of keeping us. Why would they? Who were *we* to inspire a keeping? "It's so beautiful down here," I blurted out, not thinking. And now I was like them. Now I was like my mother.

"Isn't it?" Alex exclaimed, mirroring my earnestness, indulging in it so much. I could see he was happy. I wished I'd not said a thing. "I think this place might be *something*," he said.

WHEN I TOLD them I needed to be home with my mother that evening, Alex offered to drive. Christopher came, too, but sat in the back seat, the spot normally reserved for me when the three of us were in the Honda together. Alex had said he understood if at any moment I felt I needed to be in a particular place, like my mother's, instead of another place, like the countrystead. He outright asked if he'd been too prescriptive, not giving me the range and freedom to assist in welcoming the Big Shadow on my own terms, for the benefit of all three of us.

I said I didn't know.

"You picking up that book, that's big," he said and pointed at the book in my lap, Maurice's *The River That Rhymes with Insane, Not Sex*, to clarify what he was referring to.

I spoke offhandedly. I said, "I was interested in reading some poetry, that's all."

And he said, "Trust me, when someone 'just wants to read some poetry,' the last thing they pick up is the poetry of Maurice Blunt."

By the time we parked in front of my home, I'd learned Maurice had been in a New York punk band called the Sateelites, in the mid-1970s. I'd heard of them, but had only registered the existence of the singer, a man named Mark Houde, who I remembered as being good-looking, a kind of stud in the scene. Maybe thanks to his physical appeal, Houde had gone on to be more famous in his various post-punk projects. Maurice had done some solo work, Alex said, but it was nothing like Houde's stuff in terms of its reach or quality.

After walking me to the door, Alex stood on its stoop and gave the neighbourhood a sizing up. I was annoyed at how he was acting like there was more weight than usual in our goodbye, how everything had suddenly become so elevated, all on account of some bushes being cleared out of an old pool. Christopher watched us through the open car window, his mouth parted but his expression otherwise blank, generally looking like a smooth, white rock. Alex scanned the sky. Somewhere beyond that flat, grey sheet, the sun had started setting. He then examined the windows of the row houses across the street, all sectioned off into cheap, small apartments like how I lived with my mother. Even though we'd had our moment in the pool bottom and a whole history of many years together, I felt closer to Maurice, his ripped jeans and rough disappointment, than I did to Alex and whatever pathos he was conjuring. "But to return to your reading selection," he said quickly, sensing I was about to leave him, the way I leaned into the door. He pointed at the book again; I'd pressed it to my chest. "Each poem, I think four long poems in total, is about a different river, isn't it?"

I made a noncommittal gesture with my free hand. The book did indeed have four long poems about rivers: the Hudson, the Thames, the Moskva, and of course the Seine that was referenced in its title. At each riverbank, the poet-speaker met a dead poet or writer with whom he took a walk: Whitman, de Quincey, Mayakovsky, and Rimbaud. I wouldn't say I was strong at reading poetry, but my interpretation was that the speaker was disappointed in his current place and time and shared that disappointment with the dead writers, who in their own time had expressed their own version of that same disappointment through their art. The two disappointments anachronistically met to form one huge disappointment. It seemed a creative enough way to sum up the human condition. That we have more in common with those who share our brand of pain than those who share our time, our contemporaries. That really there are very few of us to get along with before it's time to enter the ground.

"Exactly—rivers, water! Water is something we need to pay more attention to. The pool has always been central for us, and yet we haven't really thought about it," Alex was saying. "Of course, it only gets filled, it only becomes a *body of water*, if there's a storm like last night's. That was spectacular. It really was unusual." Alex said water was everywhere, but it was also the most shifting substance; if we could see it shift in a number of ways already, in the normal course of life, imagine all the other transmutations it goes through that are out of perceptive reach. "You are primarily water," he said. "Upstairs, your mother is water. The brick veneer and the plywood underneath making up those homes, there are little pockets and veins in them, and they have water. The termites eating the basements of these homes are basically drops of sentient hungry water. The whole city is water! Think what else *we* can *be* then, the forms we can take on, the places that exist for being that form in."

I wanted to ask if that's what he ultimately wanted for us, to be rodents that eat away at houses, to live trapped in the hairline cracks of brick. But it wasn't an honest question, and there was no use in riling him. He went on, saying he believed that the way his mother had called to say the pool had to be fixed up was a premonition, not so much a genuine wedding plan. I wanted to ask if he thought maybe there was no wedding, maybe he'd imagined the call, or it hadn't been his real mother calling. Instead, I said, "So did you want me to stop looking out for clouds?" Here was an honest question; I wanted out of the cloud-watching job that I still felt unfortunately tethered to. "No, of course not," he said. "Clouds are one hundred percent water."

I pushed the door in a little, and a little more. I walked up the stairs, leaving him down there. Once in the apartment, I went to the window. I could see the Honda, climbing the street and leaving me finally. My mother had sprinted to the kitchen the second I'd walked in, to warm up our dinner. "They never come up anymore," she said, "they never come over to eat or watch a TV show." She returned to the living room and sat on the sofa beside me. "Soon I'll start taking it personally." Her sweatpants stank of beef stew and peppers. Since the age when one finally gets agency, when one understands that you can say "no" to older people who've spent your whole life saying you couldn't, Alex and Christopher stayed clear of her, it was true. And now that was serving me. "But I love how *you*'re spending more time here lately," my mother said, her hand on my leg.

"Oh, I don't know," I mumbled.

Her words plus the hand seemed to me a direct assault on Maurice, his promises, and the ideas that he stood for generally. His poetry was chasmically removed from my mother, our living room, and the reek of our apartment. One of the poems was dedicated to Peter Laughner, another to Robert Mapplethorpe. I figured Maurice had composed his stanzas in between sessions of drug-taking, as he sat on a fire escape with a pencil and a candle. It suddenly felt pointless—no, more damning than that: it was embarrassing—to have devoted the day to him, travelling to the countrystead just to find his books, then imagining myself as the next someone that he'd choose to walk alongside a river with, the next Rimbaud.

The microwave in our kitchen had a beep like a call to arms. It sounded like an announcement of impending murder. We'd inherited the microwave from my aunt Tamara when she moved into her new husband's house, which already had a microwave stuck inside its wall. My mother sprang from the couch so forcefully I actually felt it shift and shifted along with it. Maurice's book sat on the coffee table before me. Its cover had a black-and-white photograph of a light bulb, a large spider's web hanging over it, and no spider on the web. Perhaps the web's interlocking silk was meant to resemble rivers. I heard the microwave door open and shut. "The meat is ready," my mother said, "the meat is ready." She loved saying things in doubles, once to merely announce and a second time to celebrate. She said, "Let's eat on the couch today," already carrying two plates toward me, winking both eyes, and walking much too fast.

5

The way the desks had been arranged in Maurice's classroom, I couldn't find a place for myself. There were twenty-five spots, yet as soon as I approached any one chair, I'd see that it'd been reserved already, by the placement of a notebook or bag on top. It occurred to me that the number of chairs and desks might correspond exactly to the number of registered students. People milled around and talked to each other. They seemed to possess a mingling skill gleaned from an earlier university class. The room was not large, it was not a lecture hall, but it had tall ceilings, molding engraved with fleurs-de-lis, and grand, vast windows that overlooked the monotonous grey cloud cover still lingering two days after the storm. At the front of the room stood a massive wooden table that appeared screwed in place, right into the fat, lacquered floorboards. A grandfatherly man sat in the back row, reading a book of Maurice's poetry titled *Get Away*. I knew he was what was called a "mature student," pursuing coursework to stave off the boredoms of senior life. For a time, my mother had talked about wanting to become a lawyer, then decided she couldn't, that "mature student" had a ring to it that would ultimately undo her sense of self. I veered toward him, feeling we could silently bond over our shared outsider status. But once I sat in the seat next to his, having pushed its notepad and pen off, he shot me a disapproving look, then scanned the room ostentatiously, to scare me into believing he would actually report me to the owner of that pen and notepad. He quit after a few seconds and returned to his reading, but any confidence I'd talked myself into having that morning was gone. What a horrible old man, I thought. What a humourless, un-Maurice-like shitbag.

AROUND NINE THAT morning I'd been woken by a phone call. I heard an introductory sigh and knew it was Christopher, wilting on the other end. "Want to come up today?" he asked. I told him I was busy and heard him press the receiver to his shirt and tell Alex I'd said I was busy. "Alex just says to keep in mind the things he told you yesterday about water," he said.

"Okay, sure," I said, and hung up, then sat on the couch for some time until I experienced a proper realization that this was the morning of Maurice Blunt's class, that he and I would be meeting up again and having some sort of conversation. From that moment on, my stomach clenched, and I spent a while on the toilet, where I reread Maurice's poetry book. When I was done, I had the idea to do more research on him before class started. I got dressed and walked to the closest public library, a small postmodern building shaped like a clamshell, sitting near where Alex's original home had been, and where his father now lived with a new wife and two preteen daughters. Inside the library, I sat at the last empty computer and logged on to the library catalogue. There was nothing with "Maurice Blunt" in it. I opened the internet browser and typed his name into the search bar. A short list of links appeared. The first item was a fan page called "The #1 Maurice Blunt Fan Page." The wallpaper on the homepage was the CBGB logo, repeated in a mosaic. Below the title, and barely legible because of all the CBGBs, it said, "The most underappreciated genius to have come out of 70s nyc." And below that: "Enter."

I clicked on "Enter" and the cursor turned into an hourglass. Once the page opened, it displayed a black background with a yellow construction sign in the centre. "Come back soon," it said beneath.

I returned to the search results and opened the second link, an interview on the website of an independent record label out of Madison, Wisconsin, called Hectic Aura. They'd released Maurice Blunt's CD six years prior, in 1992. The interviewer asked Maurice about his influences. "So many," Maurice said. He ran off a list of names and I wrote them on the library's catalogue retrieval slip. Toward the end, the interview mentioned *The River That Rhymes with Insane, Not Sex*, which was being reissued by a new publisher, and the interviewer asked about the accompanying record Maurice planned to make and release with Hectic Aura. "Each poem has a song counterpart," Maurice explained. The songs were mostly finished. The book was made up of interlinked poems about his relationships to various artists he loved. Unprompted, he said he loved Rimbaud above all else. "He's my god. Actually, scratch that—he *is* God. Make that a capital G. Make that G fucking huge and fill the full fucking page with it [laughing]."

I knew Alex had plenty of Rimbaud, and it'd been stupid of me to not have picked some from his shelves the day before. The holes in my approach, my absolutely novice and unorganized way of preparing for Maurice, were becoming apparent. Once again, I faced the feeling of defeat, the pointlessness and embarrassment of me chasing after the notion that he'd seen a fellow equal artist in me. And yet when I rewound the reels to any single word he'd said, and his tone, and the easy way he'd professed to have just met someone unlike anyone else...

I checked for Rimbaud in the library catalogue, but it had nothing. I asked a librarian if there was any Rimbaud at the next closest branch. The librarian said yes, two books, but that branch was closed Wednesdays in the summer. The second closest branch was my mother's. I checked for the names on Maurice's list of influential artists: Joe McPhee, Michael Snow, Luc Ferrari, but the librarian had never heard of them. I decided to go back home, yet once outside, I realized I'd forgotten to check for the Sateelites. I returned and the librarian retrieved a book, *How What Happened Happened: A History of the New York Punk Scene* by Nixon Lowell, from the nonfiction/music section. "I hear this is the definitive account," he said. The book had five hundred and fifty pages.

Half an hour later I was on the couch, looking out the living-room window with *How What Happened Happened* on my lap. The day was ugly. It'd reverted to a spring chill, and the heatwave from two days ago seemed an improbable or outright false and made-up memory. I'd be seeing Maurice in less than an hour. I needed to leave my house in less than thirty minutes. I very badly wanted to take a bath, to relax myself, but there was no time, our water pressure was so low the bath took ten minutes to fill. I fanned the pages. I didn't know what part to read. By that point, I was like a junkie in need of a very quick fix, something superficial to tide me over, any snippet of cool, esoteric information that I could casually throw at him—about him—like it was an accident, falling out of a hole in my pocket.

"Blunt, Maurice" had three hits in the book's index, one of which said, "see: The Sateelites." The other two briefly mentioned Maurice's poetry, early bands he played in, the rocky friendship he had with Mark Houde, a conflict with another musician after Maurice accused that musician of selling his Gerard Malanga portrait for drug money, and a year-long marriage, at age twenty-one, to a much older woman, the co-owner of an art gallery. I started skimming around the parts that mentioned Maurice. The scene he'd operated in was studded with names, with cultural icons and exciting anecdotes. This was the fabric that made up the garments of the ensuing decades: the filmmakers, the musicians, the underground artists that had shaped our world. My stomach had tightened again in a bad way. I moved to the bathroom, shut the book, and placed it on the edge of the tub. I put a towel over it so that I wouldn't have to think about it, but I thought about it anyway and I lifted the towel, picked up the book, and opened it back to the last page I'd been reading.

I kept reading. Maurice, the Sateelites, The Neon Boys, Johnny Thunders, Richard Hell, everything, even Madonna. The phone started ringing. I should've left my house five minutes ago by that point, but instead I sat myself on the bathroom floor, leaned my face against the tiles, and closed my eyes. I let my ear rest against the toilet paper dispenser and stretched my legs to the far end of the room, not far. The phone kept ringing. The man who could have his pick of company, who could, if he wanted to, spend his days with Chantal Akerman, found me to be at least equally if not more interesting, found me undemanding. I let the thought spread, settle, and harden, so that my brain could never again argue against it. *What happened to me didn't often happen.* The phone had stopped ringing, but within a minute started again. When I passed it on the way out, I picked up the receiver and hung it up straightaway, but gently, so that Christopher, or Alex, or my mother would believe there was something irreparably broken with the line between them and me.

IT WAS A minute past when class should've begun. I casually remarked "It's so busy" to the old man, as a form of truce, but he didn't respond. I wasn't sure he'd heard me. People still walked about causing a racket. A girl, clearly older than me, made up with extreme precision—red lipstick, eyeliner like ink, everything like a prefabricated decal set on her face—and above the makeup, black hair smooth as a wig, approached the back of the classroom, looked around, then looked at me, and finally at her notepad, lying face down on the floor. She opened her mouth, that perfect red bow was real and functional, but said nothing and picked up her stuff. "You stole her seat," the old man whispered. He shook his head reproachfully. His breath was unbearable. On his desk, he'd stacked three Maurice books and a Maurice CD. I saw that he'd brought a Sharpie.

The extremely made-up woman—Bettie Page, I called her— found a chair that had no desk associated with it. She looked exposed, all the more so because of her screaming Bettie Page look. It served her right. She held her rescued notepad in her lap and glanced back at me a couple of times. I hated these people already. The last thing I wanted was to be like them: fawning, frantic fans, obsessed with a stranger, thinking of this class as their big break, the thing that would launch their poetry collections. It seemed a mistake to have come, on the off chance Maurice would pool me in with them, even subconsciously. But it was too late to leave the classroom. Everything had suddenly gone quiet and everyone still standing had started running for their seats.

Maurice stood at the front, paused just beyond the entrance. He'd not looked up since walking in, as if the room had no one in it. He walked the rest of the way in and threw a plain black technical-fabric shoulder bag onto the large professor's desk. He frowned and counted something on his fingers, unzipped the bag, and pulled out four books. He took a long time arranging them on top of the desk though in the end all he'd made was a stack. Finally, he walked around the desk and sat on its front corner. His legs were long enough that his boots remained planted on the floor. He drew a can of Coke from his leather jacket pocket and snapped it open. He set it on the table. He threw the jacket off. He picked the can back up.

"Cheers," he said, tipping the can toward the class.

The class was still and silent.

He took a long sip and smacked his lips. "Way better than New York cola."

The class gave him a short laugh.

"Hey, I like that," he immediately added, noticing a girl who'd sat on top of her friend's lap because it seemed we were one seat short, and it was likely my fault. "Very fucking familial. That's the way it ought to be, keep doing that. That warms my heart, right here." Maurice tapped his chest. The students laughed more openly now. The girl who was sitting on her friend's lap buried her face in her hands, so much glee and so much pretend-mortification. Some air was let out. The bodies around me relaxed. Maurice was in the same outfit he'd been wearing when we met: the embroidered red roses in mid-bloom on his collar tips, the strained threads in the groin and knees of his black jeans. He scanned the room and smiled, but the smile wasn't anything like what he'd given me on the stairs of the library. It was more self-aware and more self-referential, like the look on the inner cover of his poetry collection. It knew it had an audience.

"First there was Gilgamesh," Maurice started, then paused and raised his eyebrows. "I'm just fucking with you," he said, bringing his eyebrows down. "I wouldn't do that to you." Only the old man responded, with a hearty Santa Claus guffaw. I didn't know who Gilgamesh was. The door opened and two latecomers filed in, looking surprised at how little space was left in the classroom. They took a few tentative steps before Maurice suggested they sit on top of his desk. The stragglers climbed onto it, sharing a sheepish smile. Maurice picked up a book. He read us five of his poems.

By the time we got to Patti Smith and her crew, my discomfort took a new turn. The problem was we were halfway through class, yet I had no direction or plan for how I'd approach him when it ended. For the most part I worried that he'd forgotten who I was—one face in a sea of admirers—and I didn't want to have to remind him. It was anyone's guess what he'd gone through in the full day that I hadn't seen him. I imagined it involved meeting a whole host of people. And the transaction we'd initiated in the rain was so particular that its details—"You said you'd get me into a New York City college," "I am the favourite person you've been around in a long while," "I don't demand," "You asked me to come here and save you"—would be mortifying to say aloud, especially in a large and public room.

I fixed my eyes on him, dispatching silent messages, but one hour into Poetry and Rock 'n' Roll, he still hadn't looked my way. It seemed a bad omen. Nothing was the way it'd been in the rainstorm. The room had started feeling much too hot. The bodies, overcrowded and overexcited by the man talking about Richard Hell now, produced more heat than normal. Maurice had neglected to give us a bathroom break and everyone was too busy staring at him to think of cracking a window. Did he even need saving? I wondered. What does a person who is universally loved need saving from anyway? Too much admiration? People who follow you with a stack of your own books, wanting a scribbled version of your name and a handshake?

I had no idea why I'd trusted him. Was it only the context, the downpour, how alone we were in that moment?

I studied the sycophants around me. They were brimming with the same naive trust I'd felt just hours earlier. I scanned the backs of their heads, especially the girls. Bettie Page had heart-shaped barrettes on the sides of her head. The girl who'd originally sat on her friend's lap had relocated to the floor. Someone else had joined her down there, in solidarity, or was it in the hopes of impressing Maurice Blunt? "Let's all get down on the floor. Let's get closer to the fucking worms," he'd say if he saw them. I checked constantly for whether Maurice was looking at Bettie Page, but he wasn't. I looked at the clock hanging above the door and there were ten minutes remaining in the class. The old man shifted to show he was annoyed at my restlessness. "Sorry," I whispered, but that only made him shake his head. I think I was craving a confrontation, or the old man's attitude had compelled me to crave it. I moved my seat closer to the old man, to speak to him, but just then Maurice saw me. It was obvious that he did. He stopped talking mid-sentence and his eyes focused on their target, the back-left corner where I sat. He flashed a little smile, entirely private and mine. For that speck of a second, his face changed. Maybe it was only the eyes and a little bit of the mouth, but he became someone different.

His smile was almost pathetic. Everyone in the room turned to the back-left corner to see who'd made Maurice Blunt look pathetic. My face and ears started burning. The hot and the red spread down my neck and chest. I didn't know whether I was supposed to stand up and speak then, but Maurice resumed his sentence and I understood I should just stay as I was.

When I looked back at the clock, I saw there were four minutes left in the class. I knew what I had to do. I asked the old man for a piece of paper, borrowed his Sharpie, and wrote Maurice a note.

WHEN CLASS ENDED, the students ran up to cluster around him. Maurice leaned against the window frame and his body towered above the tallest of his admirers, conspicuous and separate as a landmark in a town with nothing else to offer. He pulled out a pen from his jean pocket and signed books and CDs. I walked past all of it. From his vantage point, as Maurice later told me, he saw me slip out of the classroom, neat and quiet, "composed and rock 'n' roll."

Before I left, I pushed my note inside the leather jacket he'd left thrown over the professor's desk. I made sure to not look back. I left the building, walking very quickly. I felt weightless and registered only the speed at which things were passing me by, not I them. I thought, I wish I could hit something right now, in the way men feel drawn to walls and glass, but for the hit to drain me of my excess happiness. I had so much happy in me I could barely think. Maurice Blunt remembered me! In his eyes I was distinct, separate as a mountain peak, smart, and undemanding. There was no one like me in his classroom, not the oversexed women with their careful, edited looks, not the punk and post-punk kids who could recite every Sateelites lyric. After a lifetime of that, he wanted something else. No excess or costumes. Just a friend, a normal someone who'd make him laugh in a rainstorm.

I took the least obvious path from the building and once on it, searched for a hiding spot. A bench, half swallowed by a lilac bush in the first week of its bloom, invited me to sit on it. I grabbed a handful of leaves and flowers, tearing them off their branch so that I could hold them on my lap. I lifted my knees to my chest. What would a person think if they saw me on that bench, all folded up, hugging leaves and flowers? I pictured Maurice reaching for the note at the first available moment. He'd laugh and throw his head back—a typically Maurician too-happy over-reaction. "Love it!" he would say to no one, though maybe someone would overhear. "She just slipped it in my pocket and left. She just slipped it in and left."

6

—

The note said, "Rashomon reshoot required. We need to find some stairs on which to discuss people and everything else," followed by my phone number and name. When pressed for time and in the thick of an exploding, life-altering moment, you write certain things and their direction is as random as a Roman candle. Or rather, you believe you've infused the message with your distinct essence, and that that is enough, and preferable to objective clarity.

While walking home I reread the note in my head, and with each reading, the words felt more and more clouded, as if a second someone were translating them into a foreign language and I'd come upon the translator in the middle of their project. First of all, Maurice had never actually referenced *Rashomon*; we'd never talked about it. And while the film was a staple of twentieth-century cinema and contained heavy rain scenes, there were people out there who hadn't seen it, or who had seen it but allowed it to drift out of their consciousness, so that even the word "Rashomon" could sound like a random scramble of letters, or a curse or joke. The thing was, I'd watched *Rashomon* a couple of weeks before meeting Maurice. It felt very much in the zeitgeist. And then the rain arrived,

and I assumed he'd just know. But now, halfway between his classroom and my home, I was no longer so sure any of it made sense,
even to someone with a loose, avant-garde approach to logic.

And was it clear that "reshoot" was an attempt at humour? Of
course Kurosawa was not actually visiting my town. "Rashomon,"
"reshoot," and "required" sitting side by side looked like a tongue
twister. And then there was the vagueness of the term "everything
else," which in the moment I believed made my note sound like
the title of one of my favourite novels, by Sarah Schulman, *Girls,
Visions and Everything*, a story set in Maurice's world, but which
now seemed empty as a hole and senselessly obscure.

At home I drew a bath, but rather than sit inside the tub as it
filled, the way I'd done all my life, I waited outside the door until
it was full and then ran inside to turn the water off, so that there
was no chance of the phone going unheard. Once in the tub, I
could swear I heard a faraway ringing, though nothing like how
our phone sounded, which made it all the more unsettling. The
sound was the thin and tinny squeal of a dentist's tool, and when
I let my mind consider it, really truly follow it to its place of ori-
gin, I came upon a clearing where a whole orchestra of noises
played: minuscule dinks, scramblings, and pings all hanging out
at the periphery of audible existence.

These types of experiences, moments when I came upon
something as yet undiscovered, only made me think of Alex and
his ideas about all the unknowable that floats around us, and that
embraces us, and sometimes beckons us to come be unknowable
with it. And so I tried to close my ears to the sounds, but no matter how long I waited, the ringing wouldn't leave. At one point I
couldn't be sure anymore, and I stood up and wiped my legs, all

rushed, and ran to the hallway phone, which sat completely mute, though that didn't stop me from picking it up. And then it so happened that I heard no dial tone, just a silence on the line, and that split second of dead air made me believe I'd picked up the receiver in the very moment that Maurice had called, outpacing his first ring. These fortuitous events happen now and then, though any time it'd happened to me in the past, it was of course my mother or Christopher calling.

After two seconds, the dial tone sounded; it'd been there all along, behind an invisible corner. I replaced the receiver and returned to the bath. I managed to read a little after that, though if anyone were to ask, I couldn't say what I'd read. I was too nervous to return to *How What Happened Happened*; its world felt too raw, too close now, since I was reading about my friend's friends. I flipped through my mother's *People* and *Good Housekeeping*. She'd earmarked half the issues while sitting on the toilet: articles about cold cases of murdered teenaged girls, diets involving forty days of eating only one type of food, an interview with Susan Sarandon. There was no intelligible tracking of any of her thought patterns, or rather, she did not produce patterns, like a speedboat gone loose. After the magazines, I lay with my eyes wide open for a while, then transferred myself onto my bed. Finally, I moved to the couch, where I'd be closer to the phone. Lying still was the only way I could imagine passing life until that phone rang.

SOMETIME IN THE early evening, with the apartment still empty of my mother, I heard a woman scream a silly-sounding word beneath my open living-room window. She repeated it over and over in a painful wail, as if she were losing her mind. By the time

I looked out, a number of other faces were pressed to their window screens, and a couple of people had stopped on the street to watch the woman break down. The woman was a neighbour, in the throes of despair, calling her dog's name because, as I gathered, the dog had sprinted away, down the middle of the street, disappearing over the horizon. I witnessed this scene as a picture for Maurice as well. It seemed I was no longer free to experience anything for myself, at least not anything that had a curious edge. I supposed this meant I felt my life had an element of the unusual about it. And I believed that Maurice would call me because he somehow knew that too.

When my mother came home, she immediately started talking about the dog. She'd transposed whatever pain the dog owner was experiencing into something that was legible for her unique and personal mania. She told me that when she'd first spotted the small crowd near the front of our triplex—and then remembered that on the way, she'd passed people who looked like they were on a search mission, with their heads turning side to side, getting down on their knees to peek underneath parked cars—she believed something had happened to me, not a dog but her daughter. There was no saying how she would explain why the search party was calling out the absurd word that was the dog's name, Taffy, or how they'd believe I could fit in the narrow flat space of a car's underside. I didn't question it; I didn't need to hear it. But I knew it was true because as I'd lain on the couch, waiting for Maurice's phone call, I'd heard her through the half-open window. With a wail as raw as that of the woman whose dog had disappeared, my mother had challenged anyone in our neighbourhood who dared be more deranged than she was: "Did something happen to my daughter?" she yelled at the sidewalks and its people. "*Did something happen to my daughter?*"

IN THE LATER EVENING, she and I were back on the couch, with me lying down and the top of my head pressed against her leg as usual. It would take a large couch to not make contact with her, a deluxe, peculiarly shaped couch like what Maurice likely had in his apartment. We watched a police procedural drama, then a late-night talk show began. At one point she left to change into her pajamas, and when she returned, I saw her breast through a seam that'd gone unstitched starting from the armpit. The breast looked like a floppy slipper that'd been thrown off a foot and onto her ribs. I hated seeing it, especially from the side. What a sad appendage to carry. And its only use was feeding me, a long time ago now, when a bottle would've done just fine, I wouldn't have known the difference. I could have cried whenever I thought of how superfluous everything that made her up was, the pointlessness and fleeting shelf life of everything about her. It was a terrible situation she'd gotten herself into by having a child, when in the end, that child would only want to lose itself, just like the runaway dog Taffy.

"Mom," I said, sitting up so we could look at one another. "I was thinking of signing up for a summer poetry class at the university." I'd decided I should start preparing her, to ease her into whatever my friendship with Maurice might bring.

She hit the mute button on the clicker. "Can an incoming student even do that?" she asked.

I shrugged. I told her it was part of a new program, for first-year students to get a taste of university life before university officially started.

"But we haven't even paid your first tuition installment," she said.

I hadn't really thought about how to explain things past that point. I told her I supposed it was an honour system, or an investment strategy—if the students really enjoyed their summer class, they'd want more classes come September, at which point they'd pay. She seemed uneasy. "Well, has this started? Have you already found this class you want to take?"

I shook my head and lay back down. I felt we'd travelled way past what a baby step ought to have been for her. She unmuted the television and put her hand on my scalp, but I felt her fingers rake me with a heightened tension now. From time to time, as we watched the host interview a celebrity guest that neither of us had heard of, she would mute the TV to impart some unsolicited wisdom: "The important thing is to not worry about impressing anyone—anyone but the professor, that is." Or she'd share a memory: "I never made friends with any classmate. When I think back on university, it's a dark tunnel that went on for too long."

At some point before the talk show ended, she stood up and left to go to sleep without properly announcing it. She looked downtrodden, and said I should also get some rest, making it clear she was insinuating something about the university course and all the energy it would demand of me.

I heard her feet pad on the floorboards, then the springs of her mattress.

"I wonder if they ever found that dog," I said, but in response I only heard the faint snap of her bedside lamp as she turned it from on to off.

7

—

I t's possible this made no sense, but on the following morning, the day after Maurice's class, I awoke feeling convinced that the only sensible thing was for him to call today, that calling yesterday was a complete impossibility and I'd wasted my time in not knowing better. Since Poetry and Rock 'n' Roll took place Mondays and Wednesdays, and Maurice had mentioned flying back home between classes, it was almost a given that he'd gotten on a flight home the afternoon or evening before. On this Thursday morning, he'd awake in his New York apartment, resetting to normal life, and get to any tasks he'd planned for himself, including the phone call. Where I was, the weather had finally turned to something properly resembling early summer. The sky was powder-blue and a lukewarm wind travelled in such a way that the smell of the blooms from the linden tree in the yard next door flooded the apartment. My optimism may have had to do with the weather. I sat on the couch for a while, then moved to the windowsill. Immediately, a passerby spotted me. He'd looked up at the sky, caught sight of me through the screen, seemed momentarily conflicted, then called out, "Have you seen a little curly-haired white dog?" lifting a printout with Taffy's photograph.

AT SOME POINT in the late morning the phone rang, but it was only Christopher. He pointed out the obvious, how the weather had taken a turn, finally reaching a happy equilibrium. More important, the sky was no longer an endless wall of concrete, but once again a bright, living canvas, full of scuttling message-carrying shapes that I was expected to read. When he asked, I told him I would not be coming to the countrystead that day. But I promised to be on the lookout. "You know how my living-room window is," I said. And in an uncharacteristic move, he countered me, saying, "No, I don't, actually. I haven't been over in a long time," using a terse tone that I pretended not to notice.

"Well, it's a very large window, with a very nice view," I said. I could tell the pendulum had swung and that those two had started to grow frustrated again with how little attention I was paying them, though once we hung up and I was alone with the silence of the apartment—which is to say, the audible notes of the downstairs television and the ringing that I still couldn't quite escape and the replay of everything Maurice had said to me on the stairs— I actually missed the distraction of my cousin's scrimpy attack. I even missed the idea that in his mind, I had a very important task at hand, involving clouds and their inscrutable shapes.

FROM AROUND NOON to five, I sat on the windowsill. I looked at the passing clouds, just in case, though I also held *How What Happened Happened: The History of the New York Punk Scene* in my lap and read from it now and then. Two o'clock seemed a nonde-script hour, ripe for placing phone calls, and the phone did ring around then, but it was only my mother. She was on her lunch break and chewed food throughout. She told me she'd shared with a coworker what I'd revealed to her last night, how I wished to effectively start university two months early. It felt like "a rug had been pulled from under her," she told me, re-creating the work conversation. She was expecting to have more time to get used to the idea of me "crossing the bridge of adulthood."

She said the coworker spoke with her in the library basement and offered her some perspective, but I didn't believe it. I believed she may have spoken to a person she worked with in the base-ment, but I didn't accept the perspective part. Before she could tell me more about it, I said I was needed outside, to help with the search party for little missing Taffy. And with that I freed the line for Maurice's call in something like four minutes.

THREE O'CLOCK SEEMED to me a time to ring up a person you'd describe as a new friend. It was a time both distinct, yet unlabel-able, just the clock stretching its arm to the left. By five, I couldn't understand what was going on. The whole situation had started to look like the days when I'd waited for Jeremy, after he'd left for New York, very soon after our second date. It wasn't clear to me if he'd planned a long-distance relationship for us, but because I'd asked for a postcard, he mailed me one, with his phone number squeezed into a corner. The content of the card was that the band he played drums for was doing great, as if this could possibly impress me when I didn't so much as know their name. Whenever I called to congratulate him, he'd only let the answering machine pick up. And no matter how many times I dictated my own phone number to the machine, I never heard back from Jeremy.

AROUND SIX O'CLOCK, my mother's impending return made me move to the bedroom. I prepared to tell her I had a headache and bundled myself in my comforter in such a way that still made it easy to throw it off in case I needed to run to the telephone. Taffy's owner must've had a similar work schedule as my mother, because around that time, her weak little calls returned. She was joined by another, deeper voice, out on the sidewalk, and the two of them went on, calling for Taffy for the remainder of the evening.

At dinnertime, my mother sat herself next to me on the bed and started eating off of her plate. I was still lying down, and from my low angle, I watched the sturdy horseshoe that was her jaw move up and down, then pivot as she looked around my room between bites, pausing on random spots as if seeing something new.

"I don't understand why you're not eating," she said. "I'm worried you're having a fight with Christopher. I *notice things*. You're spending less time with him." When she was close to finishing her food, she had a new thought. "You're nervous about this poetry class. I knew it wasn't the best idea. What's the point in rushing things?" After taking away my untouched plate, she brought me a steaming herbal tea. I drank it, taking long sips and considering how many minutes I could make pass between each burning swallow.

I LET THE SLOW dimming of the sun lead me to complete darkness. I didn't dare interfere by turning on the lamp or closing my eyes. The gradual darkening had a soothing quality, like the gentle descent of death, the way most people hope to pass. The hour was so late that a phone call from Maurice was now impossible. Maybe if I'd told him I lived alone, or with roommates, but not with a mother. The Taffy party had dispersed for the day. It was difficult to imagine that a creature that small would ever return and had not established herself in a new place, was already happier, and had no memory of anything before yesterday. I wished her well.

The release from phone duty was nice, actually. And the dark made me feel another type of freedom, a kind of rebellion, or carelessness. I was free from Maurice, not fully, but the tension was no longer as taut. I felt removed from his promises, and the burden of having everything detailed in *How What Happened Happened* read as if it were a textbook for my upcoming life, the complete opposite of my life as it had looked till now. I'd clearly missed a signal or misread a sign from him along the way. I'd believed we were tied by a thread that wasn't there. As long as I didn't think back on what he'd said on the stairs, which seemed objectively indisputably him saying there was a thread between us, I could convince myself that I'd had a momentary lapse, that no threads ever did or could exist.

Around eleven o'clock, I heard my mother open and shut the front door of our apartment. Any activity coming from her after dark, other than a shuffle to the kitchen or bathroom, or maybe a phone conversation with Christopher's mother, was highly unusual. It was possible she'd never left the house in the late hours in all the years I'd understood her to be a human with free will. She also rarely opened doors, even if someone knocked, believing rapists found their victims in this way, by approaching doors in the evening time. I lifted myself out of bed and called for her, and she answered straightaway. She sounded excited to realize I was awake and was now jogging toward my bedroom. "Something came for you," she said, opening my door and switching on the overhead light. For a moment I couldn't see a thing. Then I saw my mother and a padded yellow envelope in her hands that for some reason I believed could only be one thing.

There were ways of finding my address. I'd signed my note with my last name, and it was not a common name. He'd need only to look in a phone book, or press zero for the operator. His responding to my note with something equally whimsical, not a customary phone call, but a tactile missive, was Maurice-like exactly, and true to *How What Happened Happened.*

I forgave myself for doubting him and the vitality of our thread. I stuck my arms out, betraying my giddiness. My mother handed me the envelope and stiffly stepped back with a bewildered, questioning face. Of course she didn't leave the room or pretend to not watch me, though this was ultimately a non-issue since I saw right away that the grubby, crow-like handwriting spelling my name on the envelope was Christopher's. I tossed the envelope to the end of my bed, and that was enough to throw my mother into a frenzy. "Why are cassette tapes being left for you at our door?" (She'd felt up the envelope and identified everything before bringing it to me.) "Who just leaves something by a door and flees in the night like a gangster?"

She got worse after I told her it'd been Christopher. "So, he made the effort of driving from outside of town, parking, coming up the stairs, to the third floor, and then left, without even knocking or saying hi to his aunt?" Apparently, my mother had heard the rustle of the envelope brushing the grain of our door, her ears pricked up like a bat's. After she'd heard steps descending, she opened the door, and the envelope fell on her foot. I told her it was simply music copied from a CD, and she believed me, entirely distracted by the wrong of Christopher's insouciance. I pressed the subject; for my own good, it seemed a safe track to keep her on, being so removed from Maurice and New York. "Christopher's going through a rude and antisocial phase," I said. "He's got no direction in life. Hopefully it'll pass, but at the moment, it's a problem."

What could I have believed the envelope contained, if it had in fact been from Maurice? It didn't make sense. It'd been a product of my delirium. A Maurice missive was hundreds of times more improbable than a phone call, the effort it would've taken, the agency and investment. And yet there I'd gone, believing it completely as my mother crashed through my door with the envelope in her hands. What a hopeful idiot I was.

TRUE NIGHT ARRIVED and I must've fallen into a light semi-sleep. I remained in control of my thoughts, but they skittered in a direction I hadn't planned for them. So, in a way, my state was one of inspiration, not slumber. The result was a new and revelatory thought.

I hadn't listened to the tape, but I knew those two well enough to know it was likely a recording of Alex's voice, the type of wishy-washy instructional content that he'd delivered on my stoop two days before, about water. I suppose this set me off, or simply reminded me of what they called the Big Shadow. I realized with a new clarity that I might've missed a signal. And that the bigness of Maurice could in fact be the bigness of what not just I, but we three, had been waiting for.

I'd never known how literally to take Alex. Maurice was not a puff of condensation, and he'd not appeared in the sky, but he was *big* in a figurative and even literal sense: his height, his weight, the way he commandeered a class of twenty-five people. He'd also come out of the rain, and without a third-party witness I couldn't say for sure he hadn't actually materialized from it. I thought back to Alex's water obsession, the way he'd started on it the day after I met Maurice, as if sensing the significance of that very medium. Most important, Maurice had the power to bulldoze over me; he felt like a new dawn, something metaphysical yet personalized. I'd truly felt I was coming undone every minute since the minute we'd met. I hadn't eaten. By keeping him secret, I'd missed out on Alex's advice on how to handle his coming. The handling wasn't intuitive after all. My note about *Rashomon* may have been all wrong, though of course I was past the point where I could ever tell Alex the embarrassing, overthought language I'd used in it, how it'd scared Maurice off.

IT WAS AROUND two in the morning when I got out of bed and called the coach house. I used the kitchen extension so that my mother wouldn't hear. I believed that Christopher would pick up, considering the hour, and the way he sacrificed himself always. And with my feeble, accepting, sacrificial cousin, I would've come out and said the truth, because the truth would simply pass through him as water does through a sieve, so that the experience would be more about my relief, and there would ultimately be no consequence to anything.

What would you say if I told you that *Maurice Blunt* materialized from the rain for me, at the peak of a moment of absolute desolation, when I believed the world had nothing to offer me, just how you and Alex believe that too about yourselves. Yes, Maurice Blunt who played rhythm guitar in the Sateelites. Maurice Blunt who later put out solo records, and books of poetry, and who can be seen as a background, barely credited actor in some early 1980s films, from a burgeoning New York independent film scene of which Jim Jarmusch was a part. Maurice Blunt who was roommates with your favourite musician or artist, who famously shot up heroin by the cartload but denounced it after a time, thanks to which he's still around, here, among us.

What was he doing in our unmappable city? The rain was as thick—if I may—as in *Rashomon*. And Maurice had manoeuvred through a curtain of grey and wet, running from the fire of a thunderbolt, toward me, poised on a set of stairs like an altar. Upon finding me, he said I was unlike anyone he'd encountered. He said, in a sense, to "come with him." If we're looking for a messianic something, well there you have it: Maurice! I would likely stop revealing past that point, when I'd seemingly messed up our encounter.

But it was Alex who picked up the phone. There was a distracted, perfunctory quality to his hello, and he clearly hadn't been sleeping. He knew it could only be me calling at that hour, and I already knew he was upset with me. I simply asked how he was doing and said I'd received their cassette tape. "Good," he said, and told me he was holding a flood light over the pool and that Christopher was inside, snipping away at the bushes. They'd taken to working on it at night so that they could stare at the sky during the daytime. "We're very busy," he said, "so maybe call back later."

At that moment, the notion of sitting on the countrystead lawn, in the warm, fragrant night, with the crickets, the fireflies, and the two people who knew me best, seemed not only better than anything I could find in Maurice's world, but more properly mine. I asked if either of them would be up for coming to get me in the car, and Alex's tone immediately brightened. He said, "Yes, for sure, of course, we want you with us." Here was the opposite of Maurice, of being tossed to the side and forgotten. "We called earlier!" he went on. "We've been asking you to come be more a part of things for days now. I made you that tape!"

I could've cried. I supposed I felt a little like Judas, in whatever part of the Bible he's finally forgiven. "All right," I said, and Alex told me that they'd be there very soon.

After hanging up, I walked to my mother's bedroom and toward her sleeping shape. I gently tapped her highest elevation. "Mommy," I said, and she grunted and tensed, but then relaxed once she realized it was me. I said I'd be going to the country with Alex and Christopher, and when she asked what time it was, and I told her, she said, "What is it with you three, why are you doing everything so backward?" I answered that I didn't know, and that it was summertime juvenile thinking, which actually made her laugh even while she was still partly asleep. "All of you are crazy, and you're going to make me crazy too," she said, but with irony, then flipped to her other side. Her breathing slowed and her legs twitched, hitting the bed's footboard.

I climbed in next to her to wait out the time it would take for them to get there, thirty minutes in the middle of the night, when Alex could run all the red lights in the city, indulging in the thought that always seemed to drive him, that the world was or ought to be made in his favour. I fit myself in behind my mother, mirroring her shape and pressing my cheek to her back. I smoothed her T-shirt's fabric over her shoulder blades, then wrapped my arms around her waist, hard, but not so much that she'd wake. With my ear against her back, I heard everything. In my conch shell of a mother, I heard all the echoing, breathing, creaky, beating, flowing, blooming, the dying parts, and the regenerating ones too. I heard her catacombs; she had a whole world inside her. And I thought, speaking objectively now, with a conviction no one could argue me out of, not even Maurice: *this* world is what everyone should get down on their knees for. My mother, asleep on her left side.

8

In the story I imagined myself telling Maurice, I would say, "The pool as I found it that night reflected the moonlight." It was not the water doing the reflecting as one would expect, because the water sat hidden under the canopy of twisted green, which appeared black, though in turns also emerald, teal, and even yellow, almost the live gold of a fire, depending on how Alex moved the beam of his lamp across it.

I asked where they'd found the lamp, which looked like a very large aluminum flashlight, or a kind of light used on film sets, so heavy that Alex had to hold it with both hands and bend at the knees. It'd likely had a mounting rack and a stand at some point. It seemed impossible that it was meant to be held and carried around like a bowling ball. Yet Alex had fully taken to it, and the effort it took to handle seemed to add to its appeal for him. He said they'd found it in the shed, after the tree had sliced the shed open. He'd fixed the wiring in the back of the lamp, then connected a long, orange extension cable to a long, black cable, and a further grey cable that ran from an outlet inside the coach house, across the grass, to the edge of the pool.

He said the lamp was needed for lighting up Christopher's workspace as he continued to trim the plants that grew out of the bottom of the pool. And he said it really helped having a third person around that night, being the night on which they'd hoped to finally carve out the underside of the canopy. "Why tonight?" I asked, and he said, "Tonight's the night." I even held the lamp for a while and lurched this way and that as Christopher called out directions from underneath the foliage—"A little to the left," "Angle it down more"—though within minutes Alex took the lamp back. "You're going to fall into the pool and kill both you and Christopher," he said, "like in the final scene of *Deep End*. And then where would we be?"

Soon after, I was lowered into the hole, in the same careful way as before, with Alex holding me by the wrists so I wouldn't hurt when I landed, and with the lamp sitting on the ground, next to the pile of trimmed branches that was now several feet taller. Inside the pool, the water level was the same as before, reaching midway up my calves. With the lid of the leafy cover, the moderate temperature, and the humidity that characterized our area, the water had no reason to leave.

I walked down the burrow and entered the greater bowl shape that my cousin had cut out with the rose clippers. The space was not especially deep or expansive, but it was comfortable, and appeared planned for holding three people. It felt something like camping. The wet in the air made the plants release their perfume. I could live here, I thought. Here, I could be happy.

The beam of light began swinging, lighting my cousin and me, or portions of my cousin and of me, in turns and then leaving us invisible. The space looked like a private ball or discotheque. Alex yelled, "Just a sec. I need to prop this thing on the lounger at a good angle, then I can come inside."

After he got the beam settled and directed into the scope of the bowl just right, Alex joined us in the hole. Christopher set down his rose clippers and both he and Alex removed their T-shirts, in a sensible, nonchalant way that told me they'd done this before. "What's this?" I said, but they didn't answer. Each at their own pace, they leaned over to scoop water in their hands and splashed the water onto their chests and armpits. With the angle at which the beam of light shone in, anything protruding out of the wall or moving within the bowl space cast dramatic shadows many feet long. Alex and Christopher's scooping gestures were exaggerated in the translation to shadow to something much bigger than my two friends. I don't think I felt afraid. But I didn't understand what was up with the water.

At one point, Alex scooped some and splashed Christopher with it. The gesture came off as entirely utilitarian, not a romp or playtime; something two stoic apes would do in a television nature show. Neither had smiled or made eye contact. They'd also completely forgotten about me. At another point, Christopher squatted down and dunked his ass fully in the water. He took a scoop and, with his eyes narrowed, sipped from his hand as if he were drinking out of a little china teacup.

Both came at me without warning. Christopher crouched behind me when I wasn't looking and pushed my knees forward like you would do with a horse. At the same time, Alex tugged my arms, steering me sideways so that I had no way of stopping myself from falling. I landed in the water. The bottom was full of the disintegrating refuse of everything that'd lived, mated, and died in the pool all these years. My landing was entirely soft; I felt no pain, and for that I could give them credit. Still, the water was cold and disgusting. It seeped into my clothing, making me instantly heavy. "What is wrong with you!" I said and started crawling toward the opening. I thought, let me just make it out of the pool and up to the mother bedroom with the lock. But Christopher grabbed my ankles and dragged me back to where I'd started. We probably looked like mud wrestlers; you could believe we were having fun. "You've got to taste the pool of oblivion," Christopher said. "Drink it!" And relating this moment for Maurice, I could've made it the pinnacle of a drama or of a comedy, though that may be true of every strange thing that befalls us.

"So you're not having a drink?" Alex said after I sat myself between them, all unnerved, looking around. I couldn't think of how else to show them I didn't want to be there anymore. The water reached to my chest. By this point, I was nearly gagging from its smell. "Why did you even come here?" Alex seemed unusually offended. I didn't understand how agreeing to go down the stupid hole was connected to the activity of drinking standing water. What convention was I not grasping? Later on, I came to understand it was something I would have gotten if I'd listened to the cassette tape they'd given me. But as it stood then, I had no idea. Using his terrible, ironic tone, Alex asked if the countrystead was only a "default destination" for me, a place for getting away from my mother when we'd had a fight, or when I couldn't stand her, or a method for distracting myself on days when I was dumped by a boyfriend, or a place to grab some books to read while treating him and Christopher like chauffeurs who'd come and fetch me every time I made a phone call. The second to last point was ridiculous. I'd only had one boyfriend, and Jeremy had never formally said "breakup"; he more so left, in the way people are entitled to do—a compulsion I respected with a new understanding.

When I told them it was they who were lucky that I chose to hang around, they responded by calling me a flippant, arrogant bitch. In the moment, I said, "If you think I'm going to scoop this putrid water into my mouth, you're insane, which is way worse than what you just called me." And once I'd crawled out of the hole, skinning my knees as I hefted myself over the pool wall, I stuck my head back inside and yelled, "Enjoy drinking squirrel shit, deer shit, rat shit, gnome shit, worm shit, snail shit, and lots of other shits, because that's what that water is."

They yelled, "Get out!" in a voice I'd never imagined coming out of them, not at me. There was no question this was a termination, though what did it matter? I wiped myself down in the upstairs mother bathroom, put Band-Aids on my knees, and called a taxi company on the kitchen telephone. From the creaky mantle with a whole constellation of doilies, blown-glass pears, and one frightful bug-eyed ballerina, I pulled out the drawer that always stuck so hard I had to brace myself against the wall, where the cash for the woman who vacuumed and the men who cut the grass was kept. I picked up the stack of bills and waited for the taxi that took a while, but eventually came, crunching up the gravel driveway. The pool sat a ways from me, the heavy lamp casting a halo overtop, two lunatics splashing in its boggy bottom. Everything else at the countrystead was dark; the moon too had fled.

The taxi driver talked to me the whole way, even after I closed my eyes and started to silently cry. He talked about his wife, a daughter, and the city of Bucharest, Romania. He said that block upon block in Bucharest where he'd grown up is wrapped in a disgusting grey stucco that makes everyone who walks past want to puke into their own hands. Yet if you entered through a door, that is, if you knew where to find the door—not the main door, but a special alternate entrance to each building—you'd find very nice things inside, beautiful courtyards that made you think you were in France. "Very nice things," he said, stuck on that phrase as we passed the blocks of my own city, caught in the momentary limbo between night and another summer weekday. Here were its very nice things: my sleeping mother and the world inside of her, some vestige of Maurice and the energy he'd felt for me, and the Taffy posters that dotted our neighbourhood, their white glowing in the pre-dawn light, from every pole, tree, and newspaper box, looking like candles mourning an undoable loss.

9

—

Two days later, I walked into Maurice's second class and took my seat in the back. The old man asked how my weekend had gone; maybe something about my look told him it'd been the worst days. "I've had a terrible time," I said, and he nodded, not empathically but with a hard-boiled approval, as if that was precisely the precondition needed for absorbing Maurice Blunt's teachings. The old man opened his copy of *Illuminations* in a way that allowed me to read it too, and turned the page to the assigned poem. I made eye contact with Maurice each time he made a crack that sent the whole class laughing. I saw Bettie Page. She too had gotten settled with the idea of me; she glanced back only once, after Maurice paid me an extended look, followed by his characteristic private smile.

I pretended the unacknowledged note to him never happened, that the phone in my mother's apartment did not not ring. I was a director, cutting the one scene that had cast me in a bad light. Ninety minutes later, on my way out of the building, I waited for it. And sure enough, "Jude!"—I heard his holler, followed by the ungainly scuffle of a heavyset man nearing fifty. "Fuck," he said after reaching me. "I just remembered I completely forgot to call you the other day." He caught his breath. "All this stuff came up." He rolled his eyes and flicked his head, in the direction of the room we'd just left. "You being in this class is the only thing getting me through it."

Is that so? I thought. Just days ago, I'd been rudely excommunicated from a pool of stinking water and here I was, being chased down a hallway by Maurice Blunt after making his poetry class bearable to him.

Students filed out of the room and started passing us. Maurice fell silent. He hunched himself in my direction in a comically half-assed gesture of hiding and flashed an indulgent smile, seeming aware of how ridiculous he looked. "Let them pass us," the smile said. "Let's wait out the people who are nothing like us." Some of the students slowed down and actually made as if to stop, venturing a timid "bye" before realizing he wasn't engaging, that he wasn't for them. Bettie Page bounded past with her face turned away, as if intentionally averted. The old man trotted behind her, gave me a nod, and said he'd see me next class.

"Making friends?" Maurice said as soon as the hallway cleared. He laughed at his joke, and when I said, "Yeah, right," he laughed harder. "I love the tone you just used. You hate them all, don't you?"

I nodded, though I didn't hate them exactly. The hostility I'd felt on my first day had largely left me. The old man, I could even say, I actively felt pleasant around. He'd shown me something my own friends hadn't of late, the way he'd shared his book and stopped being judgmental. During a mid-class break, when Maurice had suggested everyone "take five and fucking relax," the old man told me he'd seen the Sateelites play in our town, twenty-five years ago, with a wife who'd since left him. I now knew that Maurice understood I had nothing in common with the other people in his classroom, and I almost pitied the old man for the way he seemed to revere Maurice when Maurice no doubt thought of him as nothing and, for some reason, thought of me as a lot.

Maurice started walking, somewhat fast and like he knew where he was headed, and I followed him out of the building. Once outside, he slowed and we fell into a natural gait. We didn't speak at first. I wasn't sure what the proper theme was for this encounter, so I didn't dare start the conversation. Very soon we passed the library where we'd met. Then we started on a loop around the oval lawn in front of it, becoming almost athletic in the way we lapped it with a silent determination.

"You find the class boring, don't you," he said at one point, but with a smile. I shook my head and that made him smile bigger. "I don't believe you," he said and gently punched my shoulder. For the next while, Maurice made gestures and semi-verbal expressions to convey exasperation, like an overtired toddler. I understood that this was all in reference to the class, and more generally his presence on the campus, and in my city, which couldn't compete with any world-class place he was accustomed to. I had no idea how to make it better. Since the summer semester had started, the paths had filled with groups of students, and that hardly helped. The lawn was mottled with friend-packs, sitting next to books, eating out of Tupperware, someone throwing a Frisbee. If I strained my ears, I could hear their inane exchanges. Maurice wore all black like the last two times I'd seen him, his jeans and a button-up shirt harkening to the Old West. He stood out, though none of the students looked our way. Maybe that made it worse for him. He seemed invested in playing up some aversion to it all, yet after each sigh or instance of imploring God, he'd let out a quick short laugh and look my way, assuring me that he wasn't entirely serious, that he wasn't quite *dying* because he had to teach a class.

I didn't find his mock despair funny in the conventional sense of reacting to a smart joke, but I laughed anyway. I laughed the way I would for a child who'd just performed a practised party trick. Which is to say, my laughter wasn't begrudging, it wasn't even not-impressed, but given the choice, I'd rather have found myself in a different situation.

When we started on our second lap, I realized it was I who needed to steer us out of that loop, or we might spend the rest of our lives walking it. "Maurice," I began, aware of how unusual, and for that reason striking, it is to invoke someone's name if the words that follow are ordinary chit-chat. "I think we should get away from this," I continued, with a jokey scoff that matched the act he was putting on. I knew he'd react, that he'd like the way I'd slipped into his one-man play, and sure enough, his affect changed, and he stopped and turned to me.

"Yes! I've been saying we need to get you to New York. Come for the weekend. It's your place. Come Friday. Get away from this. Get far away."

He waved his hand around and made a gagging face. I hadn't exactly meant getting out of town. I'd meant we should seek out a less public part of the campus, away from this hub of student activity. But he went on, "New York is the place for you. You'll feel at home"— though he didn't get more specific. "You can sleep on my couch," he said, "I've always got some artist friend crashing on it. Come, man."

The implication that I made art, or at the very least had an artistic bent, like the other people who'd slept on his couch, struck me with unexpected force. I had no immediate response. My face grew hot, likely because I wasn't sure I'd ever made anything that would qualify as art. But who was I to argue with Maurice Blunt and his assessment of me, Maurice who'd seen his fair share of professional artists? There was a passage in *How What Happened Happened* that described his collaboration with one of the members in the Talking Heads. I didn't especially like the Talking Heads, but that was beside the point. "Get a ticket, seriously," he said, then a ring emanated from somewhere on his body, and he froze and smiled a prankster smile, indulging in my confused expression. "Give me a moment," he said and pulled what turned out to be a cellular phone from inside his jacket pocket.

After a few seconds, he pressed the phone to his chest, mouthed "sorry," it was a friend who needed to talk to him. He said, "See you Wednesday" and turned around without waiting for me to answer, as if we hadn't just interrupted a momentous conversation, as if we hadn't been standing on a precipice before a fabulous drop: me, the artist, being invited to New York. A few faces turned to watch him walk past, the animated way he was talking into his invisible phone made him look like a madman. He hunched forward the way he'd hunched into me not that long ago, then disappeared in between the same two buildings as the first time I'd seen him leave.

FOUR HOURS LATER, I was at the dinner table, sitting across from my mother, feeling a vague happiness. I'd gotten more than I could picture wanting. I had an invitation more tangible than the hypothetical concept of transferring to Columbia University in a year. Yet that old discomfort had come and ruined things again. I felt two truths simultaneously: that Maurice found me fascinating like no one else and that, at the end of the day, I ranked somewhere near the bottom in the hierarchy of his wants, seeing how abruptly we'd parted, how he hadn't thought to make plans with me for the evening or for tomorrow.

"So, what's your prof like?" my mother asked. She loved setting the theme for each dinner's conversation the moment she stuffed the first forkful in her mouth.

"What do you mean?"

"Is he cool?" she said, her mouth full of chicken meat.

Instead of answering I tipped a tomato wedge on its side and watched its goop trickle out. The goop, with its sleepy, indecisive quality, reminded me of Christopher.

"Is he—what's the word—making the material *come alive*? That's the sign."

"The sign of what?"

"The sign of a gifted teacher, like in *Dead Poets Society*."

I didn't have the heart to tell her that *Dead Poets* was about boys much younger than I was, with family money that got them into boarding schools that hired men of the calibre of Robin Williams. After playing with my food for another five minutes, I left her at the table, saying I had a headache so intense I could barely keep my eyes open. In the quiet of my room, I rolled myself in my bedsheets and thought about Maurice, but it wasn't long till I heard her enter. The edge of the mattress collapsed when she sat next to me causing my body to shift toward her. Once again, we were touching. She started scraping at her plate, using the fork tines to collect any last trace of her chicken. When she said, "Is the poetry you're reading good?" I pretended I was asleep.

IN THE EARLY evening I took a walk under the pretense of looking for Taffy. I told my mother I had a peculiar sense, an idiosyncratic sort of feeling, that I'd be the one who would find her. Just a few doors past Jeremy's theatre was the travel agency, Sunset Vacations, with a sun for an O and a Sandals Resorts poster on its window so faded you could take it for a winter landscape. Inside, a young travel agent named Ivana told me New York was her favourite place to visit. She called it "perfect for weekend getaways"; she liked going with a gang of girlfriends. I considered telling her everything that had happened, the way I'd come to be where I was, with an invitation in my lap, and a stash of countrystead money in the little purse I carried, now so unusually bloated. Simply on account of Ivana being a woman and older than me, but not nearly as old as my mother, there was a chance she'd have, inside of her, the advice that would set me straight, that would level out my feelings to either one or the other thing I was thinking, but not this painful both. In the end I said nothing about my situation. I thanked her and walked out.

TWO DAYS LATER, after class, we did it again: my brisk departure from the room the moment his lecture ended, him running down the hall after me, crying out "Jude," claiming me with this diminutive I'd never given him permission to use. For a long time, maybe until the very end, I wasn't clear on where I stood with Maurice Blunt. I suppose I needed to intermittently test it and I suppose for the moment, in that hallway outside of Poetry and

Rock 'n' Roll, that test was viable and it was passed. "Fuck," he said as he caught up with me, "you're always out of there so quickly, and I don't blame you." He let out some breath and put on a jokingly gruff expression. "So, are you coming this weekend or what?"

I was afraid to look at him for too long. Sometimes you win a battle so fraught that the end is just a flat line, and there's nothing to do but simply lift your leg across it and say, "I've made it" to anyone who might hear.

I'd made it. I didn't know why, but Maurice had a look so expectant and excited. Even though he'd had his life depicted in the tome of *How What Happened Happened*, he believed *I* was someone special to live out more of his life around. I'd procured an exit for myself, something for myself, more easily and truly than what Alex and Christopher were attempting, more story-worthy than what Jeremy had achieved. It was all mine and a secret, a hot little egg to hold.

"You got that ticket?" he said. And after I gave an indeterminate smile, he said, "There are only so many weekends in the summer. Fuck, there are only so many weekends in *life*." Though, of course, in my head I was already saying yes. When one is offered a golden ticket, even the chance to buy a golden ticket with money set aside for landscapers and cleaning women, you grab it, you stick it into the ticket machine, you validate it, and ride it until the conductor kicks you out.

"I'll stop by the travel agency later," I said. "I've made friends with an agent who works there."

"Good," he said, taking me at my word, or perhaps not really listening, already digging in his satchel, pulling out a pen, opening the back cover of a book he'd been holding, his copy of *Illuminations*. He wrote his phone number on the inside. "I've got to run to a lunch, but call me with the flight details. I can maybe pick you up." He handed me the book. "I'll see you soon," he said, and then, as if the extent of what he'd gone and done now struck him, he staggered backward. "Shit," he said. "I just wrote inside my most prized possession. I just defaced my favourite copy of Rimbaud." He laughed once, a sole ruminating "ha," so taken by the extent of how much he wanted me in New York. How strange it all was. How singular.

10

Even with the cab window rolled up, I could hear what I'd heard in every film set in New York: the soundtrack behind the camera, but no longer a mediated transmission. If only sound were tactile, I could wrap it around me like a little coat. "Can I roll down my window?" I asked Maurice. Since I'd arrived, he had a look of quiet pride, as if he'd engineered all this and New York had been constructed under his direction in the days before my arrival. I understood that I was a compliment, in the way every tourist is, though he experienced it more personally. "Do anything you want," he said.

We'd exited the highway and were driving down proper city streets. The blocks were teeming with humans washed by the shadows of buildings I couldn't see the ends of. There was no reason to contemplate a sky or a pool of stinking water here, or to plan for strange exits. I could open the door at any moment—at the approaching red light, for instance—start running, and be gone, off to enjoy an escape more full than anything Alex could dream up. "You can open window," the cabbie said, sounding a lot like my Romanian driver. Maurice laughed. The situation was starting to get embarrassing. "Do it, do it!" he chanted. He closed his fists and banged them on his knees.

"Sure, okay," I said. I pressed the button that made the glass slide down and the city hurtled in.

"Very good," the driver said.

WE PULLED UP to a building and Maurice jumped out of the cab, not looking to see if I followed. His movements were more definitive in New York. They had the quality of a knife slicing through something with one go, and for that, the knife must be sharp, and the object being cut very familiar to the person holding the knife. I didn't think I moved in that succinct way back home, when I walked up and down the sidewalk, or between the kitchen and my bedroom. I didn't know if it was a matter of the person or the place, but I found myself imitating Maurice almost right away, and after the first little bit of being in New York, I couldn't imagine moving in any other style.

Maurice stuck his key in the door of his building. "For future reference, watch how I do it. You've got to ram it like this and jiggle it to the left," he explained. I nodded, indicating that yes, now I knew the secret way to open Maurice's portal. I didn't want to let myself believe the best version of what him wanting me to know this meant. While walking up the stairs, I complimented the tilework on the landings, but he was focused on the keys. "Watch closely how I open my door, too," he said. "This lock's even more messed up."

The first thought I had when we walked inside Maurice's apartment was that it was shockingly small. It looked the way a living space is presented in a museum, from behind a rope, so cramped it's indisputably artificial and only there to showcase a particular era of furniture and tableware. The end wall and tall windows were only twelve feet away from the entrance, a living room and kitchen somehow fitting in that space. There was a tiny nook with a bed, bedside table, and two-foot-wide computer desk to the right of the fridge. A door, presumably leading to the world's smallest bathroom, sat near the main entrance.

The second thing I noticed was the poster of a woman, taped to the wall in a place so central vis-à-vis the entrance that it was impossible he hadn't chosen the spot deliberately, for the effect it would have on anyone who walked in. "That's my ex-girlfriend Lexa," Maurice said, seeing, of course, that I'd spotted her. "She's the best. Go say hi."

Lexa was posted on the wall above the couch, not an artfully shaped contraption made for entertaining guests, but a beige, economically sized sofa with a darker spot on what was likely Maurice's default sitting cushion. She was wearing blue jeans and pointing a round beach-ball ass at the lens. My main thought was that I was impressed by her posture, and that her look had a quality that was loud and attractive, but not slutty. She was leaning all the way down while bent at the waist. Her head poked out from between her legs, which were spread wide, making a triangle. Her face hung upside down and her features were distorted by gravity just enough to make it clear something was off, but still keep her good-looking. Her hands, gripping her ankles for support, red nail polish showing, made this whole architecture possible. But leaving aside her posture, everything else was far from aerobic. She looked more '80s go-go dancer, some kind of strung-out Warhol muse, than gymnast. Her hair was stunned, woolly, and the colour of honey. It was resting like a sleeping pet on the floor between her heels. Lexa's makeup was garish: metallic blue all the way up the brow—or in this case, all the way down—and two screaming pools of blush on each cheek. Definitely not like how other jean models in other torn-out pages of magazines looked. But she wasn't modelling Calvin Klein or Guess, or even Jordache or Bongo. On the bottom corner of the magazine page was a logo, half thunderbolts, half cake frosting: Duxxy Denim, Est. 1985, it said. I'd never heard of it.

"It's a Japanese ad," Maurice said. He had the expression of a proud exhibitor, and I couldn't tell whether it was Lexa herself, the girlfriend she'd been to him, or her ad, the way she was captured for the imaginations of Japanese consumers, that he was so proud of. There was also the possibility that he'd never known her, the way we rarely know the people whose faces hang on our walls. I wanted to ask how long they'd dated, but the question seemed private and out of bounds.

"I like her," I said, meaning it.

"Oh yeah?" he said, grinning. He gave me a long, searching look and I didn't like that. When he saw my expression darken, he said, "Okay, okay, just checking," but he was laughing now, and I didn't like that either. I wanted this whole ghost of a presumption to be gone. That I had something against Lexa just because of that bold posture, which made her so unquestionably own the room, and because Maurice's apartment was painfully tiny, really, it was the whole apartment she owned, and maybe Maurice, too, because he'd wanted badly enough for her to remain in his life, and to dominate his tiny living space by means of her pointed butt.

I didn't mind one bit. Lexa could have the apartment, Maurice, and all of Manhattan. All I wanted was to be allowed to stay, to not be kicked out and sent home just yet.

"Let's go somewhere," Maurice said, but as he said it, he threw himself on the couch, under Lexa, swung his cowboy boots onto the arm, and closed his eyes. I stared at him for a few seconds hoping it was just a very long blink, but his eyes remained shut. He didn't seem to be sleeping. He was simply lying down, with his eyes closed. I didn't understand.

I turned to the windows. It was close to noon and the sunlight was reflecting off the railing of the fire escape, catching against the Christmas lights that'd been left coiled around the rungs. "Yeah, sure, let's go somewhere," I said, but Maurice remained as he was.

I let go of the backpack I was holding and let it hit the floor with force. I cleared my throat. Maurice stirred, one boot tip moved in an arc, but other than that—nothing. I sighed loudly and walked to the wall opposite the couch, to a simple black shelf unit with books, CDs, and a stereo on it. The stereo was old and not high-end like Alex's. Where a button was missing, Maurice had covered the hole with duct tape and a puffy heart-shaped sticker. Next to the stereo, leaning against a row of CDs, was a postcard with a naked cowboy lady wearing a bucket hat and an eye patch, her breasts swinging as she rode her stallion. I looked at the window again. The sun must have shifted because now its light reflected off the entire surface of the window, making a sludgy yellow cast as it mixed with the layer of dirt on the exterior pane. I saw a sock, lying on the floor just under the window, next to a tower of papers. In the end, Maurice's place didn't look all that different from my bedroom.

I turned back to the shelf and started scanning the book titles above the stereo, lifting paperbacks that had fallen on their sides and switching a few around so that they looked more organized. "Your shelf's messy," I said loudly. It felt like hours since anyone had spoken.

Maurice took a second to respond. "Your shelf's messy," he said, mocking me. "You want to arrange it all pretty for me?" I heard a grunt and the creak of a couch joist. I figured he'd flipped onto his side, to face me. It seemed like progress.

"That would be cool," I said slowly. "Like, say, on a rainy day, but not today, when it's so nice out."

Maurice made a sound, something between a yawn and a grunt. "You're hilarious. Yeah, we should totally go somewhere and not waste the day. Where do you want to go?"

I wanted to go plenty of places. For instance, to see Washington Square Park, the spot where Larry Clark shot *Kids*. But I couldn't say that exactly; I couldn't imagine anyone from New York saying it. I was about to suggest the Strand Bookstore, which seemed a more local answer, but Maurice yawned just then, long and indulgent. I heard the couch creak again. I looked behind me. Maurice was on his back, his eyes still closed, but his arms were over his head and spread like he was doing a jumping jack. I knew those arms were an invitation.

I turned back to the shelf and started arranging more books, pulling tall ones out and sticking them next to other tall ones. I picked up Céline's *Journey to the End of the Night*. "I like this edition," I said, though I'd never heard of the book. I was now seized by the worry that we'd never leave. It wasn't unthinkable we'd spend the next two days like this. Older people loved to lie on couches, especially on weekends, believing it to be their time off, especially when it was warm out and the sun crept in through a window with a dusty sheen, making everything muted and dreamy, as if half the effort of falling asleep had already been done for them.

"C'mere," he said. His arms were still stretched above him. He wiggled his fingers. "C'mere."

I took a step toward the couch with the book in my hand. I figured my choices were to either go to the couch, to his wiggling fingers, or keep checking if he was awake for the next two days— making sounds, clearing my throat, saying "it's a nice day out," as he lay spread, silent, and flat. I reached the edge of the couch and stopped next to his armpit. His eyes were closed, but his fingers kept moving. He smiled when he sensed my shadow come over him. I didn't like that my closeness made him happy. We were supposed to be running down the streets; he'd promised to show me the city. Instead it was couches, smiles, moving fingers. I didn't feel something bad was about to happen, but seeing how he'd smiled at my proximity, at the moment when my knee almost touched his side, I understood that more than I'd assumed would happen was happening.

I had figured we would sit around book-filled apartments, library stairs, and parks for the duration of our friendship, which would be a long time, until one of us died, Maurice probably going first. But we had a lot of good years left. I would tell him about my creative projects, come visit him after my classes at Columbia or NYU, wherever he got me admitted. He would tell me about his latest poetry collection. Lou Reed would sing "Jesus" into the night, and the only palpable energy between us would be the energy generated by our shared misanthropy, our love of Lou, our love of each other even, but not the kind that most men want. I just didn't feel that way when I looked at the person spread out before me.

"C'mere," Maurice repeated.

I wanted to tell him that what I felt was actually bigger, it was rarer and more special, not the obvious stuff, more like what you'd find in cult-status friendship films—*My Own Private Idaho*, *Thelma and Louise*. It was about a shared life philosophy, being on the same side, and criticizing other people. But it was too early to say all that to Maurice. It was only my first hour in his city.

"Okay," I said, still holding on to the Céline book. I placed a little of my knee on the half-inch of available couch space; I only wanted to take a seat. Maurice scooted over with surprising liveliness. He made two inches of space for me. I looked at the window. Then I looked back at the couch. I thought, the difference between sitting up and lying down is a matter of trigonometry, comfort, and pragmatism. I took the plunge and slid into the sliver of available cushion, my whole body. I lay down. Maurice wrapped his arm around my back, pulling me toward him. I rested my head in his armpit and placed the book on his chest. His arm locked me down, like a seat restraint on a roller coaster. His pits gave off a sharp odour. My shoulders tensed. I knew I wouldn't be seeing New York anytime soon.

"Want me to read this to you?" he asked. I nodded, my ear catching his T-shirt fabric as I signalled okay. I wasn't sure why, maybe it was how swaddled I felt, but Maurice reading to me all of a sudden became the thing I wanted most, more than any bookstore or Washington Square, like it was the thing I'd come to

New York for. It seemed so nice. It was the opposite of dangerous. Maurice used the hand that wasn't holding me to open the book, fumbling to gain a grip on the spine. He was no different than a parent, a loving someone wanting to read to you at bedtime.

Ferdinand Bardamu is on Place Clichy. He meets his friend Arthur. He's inspired to join the French army.

Maurice stopped at the end of the first chapter. "Want more?" he asked. I shook my head no. I wanted to save the remaining chapters for later. It was a form of insurance, a way of making sure we would do this thing at least forty more times. I could feel Maurice smiling. He put the book back on his chest. "I love that you brought this book over," he said. "You're so cool, man." Within seconds I heard his breathing lengthen and his nose start to whistle. The arm that held me twitched. I lay on him, captured, but not unhappily so. The ease with which I'd gone from one state to a whole other seemed impossible. Here I was, on a couch that was seemingly just a couch, a bunch of puffy cushions, some wood, springs, and screws, yet it was no ordinary piece of furniture. This couch had witnessed Maurice Blunt making art. All his friends had sat on it at various points in music history. Slept on it too, I imagined, sprawled in the same orientation we were in now, feet toward the dirty windows, head to the door. This couch was the exact opposite of my mother's couch—a place of worries, limitations, and bad TV. But I didn't want to think about her. I'd set a cap of one mother-thought per day and now I'd used it up.

THE DAY BEFORE my flight took off, I had crossed our apartment from end to end, making a show of packing a bag for a weekend at the countrystead. I watched a string of evening shows with my mother—dramas about savvy lawyers, more hosts interviewing celebrities—and during their commercial breaks, I brought up the weekend I would spend at the countrystead. On Friday morning, a week after I'd wrestled with my cousin at the bottom of the pool, I unplugged both phones in the house, took the bus to the airport, and boarded a Delta flight. The plane rose and climbed the first bit of sky. The pilots cranked something, steering us more up, more extremely. Through the window, I could see the spot where my mother and I lived and just to the left, the university campus, which appeared as a bright green tile. On that morning my town sat under a mass of *altocumulus* clouds, grand and distant. Yet as we pierced their soft underside and I braced myself for something great, their substance turned out to be sparse: a little spritz of aerosol, thin and embarrassing. Two seconds later we were surrounded by flat blue sky. The clouds lay beneath us, with the same dumb detachment they'd displayed when looked at from the ground. When we burst back out of the clouds an hour later, there were two million buildings under my feet. Then the plane tipped to a sharp angle and the sun shot through my window, blinding me, painting the thirty rows of the cabin with yellow-gold rungs, which made me think that if I were making a movie, this was how I'd depict someone's entry into a worthwhile place.

11

A forty-year-old Maurice in red lipstick, a vintage wedding veil, satin opera gloves, a red bustier, and his standard fitted black jeans walks into a store in what I assumed was Greenwich Village. The clerk shakes his head. "No, no, no," he mouths. He's a slim man in his early middle age. Maurice pleads with him, putting his hands together in prayer. All he wants is a pack of spearmint gum (we're shown a close-up of a pack of Juicy Fruit gum, which isn't mint, but it seems this discrepancy is intentional). In the next shot, Maurice is holding the gum package in one hand and a one-dollar bill in the other. "No!" the clerk mouths, more forcefully, and probably stomps his foot on the ground, judging by how his shoulder rises and falls. "C'mon, man!" Maurice appears to be saying. He tosses the gum out of the shot and picks up a Three Musketeers, except the wrapper (the camera zooms in) says "Three Mistakes." It's the name of the song that's playing, from Maurice's third solo record.

The bodega clerk does a cartoonish double take when he sees the altered chocolate wrapping. His eyes widen. Someone's been messing with his stock! Exterior shot now: Maurice is ejected onto the street, the chocolate bar noticeably absent from his hand. He stumbles but doesn't fall. He shakes his head at the storefront and curses under his breath. Next, it's an alley shot, and a Vegas style showgirl rubs Maurice's shoulder as he leans his forehead against a fire-escape ladder, looking forlorn. The song ends on a guitar fadeout and a shot of the Three Mistakes wrapper lying in a gutter surrounded by filth. If you look close—and know Maurice's oeuvre—you can see that some of the trash around it, more candy wrappers, a cigarette pack, a sugar packet from a coffee shop, contains the names of his other songs.

"Cool," I said, nodding. "I like it."

It was early evening. About six hours had passed since I'd arrived in New York and since Maurice had read me Céline. We were still on the couch, now watching music videos from Maurice's solo career years. "You really like it?" he asked.

I didn't know what to say. He sounded earnest. It wasn't rhetorical. For some reason Maurice Blunt cared whether I approved of his music video from eight years back.

"I do," I said. I looked into the distance like I was adding up big numbers. "It's got a campy element to it," I said. "It's unselfconscious. It's able to laugh at itself."

Maurice didn't react in his usual quick way—he didn't say "amazing." He scanned my face as if he were seeing my features for the first time, pausing on my eyebrows, my chin, my nose. I had to look away partway through it. I looked at the TV, where the last shot of Maurice's "Three Mistakes" video sat paused, the frame twitching. My stomach tightened just slightly. I knew I had either said something really right or really wrong. "You're amazing," he finally said and drew me in by my shoulder. "You know, I trust your opinion, really. You've got a great head on your shoulders. You're not like everyone else. You don't just say what you think people wanna hear. You don't give me bullshit."

I smiled and squeezed myself harder into Maurice's side. Maurice extended his free hand and pressed Play on the remote. The VCR screeched and started rolling. The tape had four more Maurice Blunt music videos. The rest were pretty much the same as the first.

"I'M GONNA SHOW you something cool," Maurice said. He flicked the TV off and jumped up from the couch. It was almost nine. I got up and followed him. He collected his keys and wallet. We were finally going out, I realized, into the New York City night.

When we exited his building, I tried to not look around me too hard, to seem unimpressed. Still, it took only two or three steps for me to understand why the world wanted to walk this town. I saw determined cyclists and the best-looking woman of my life. A shop that sold used military clothing and a restaurant interior criss-crossed with Christmas lights that descended right into plates and diners. Maurice walked quickly, veering between people and turning corners. He led me into a store.

"Hey, Mike! This is Mike." Maurice pointed at the small man behind the counter.

Aside from slightly droopier cheeks and an obviously self-administered dye job, Mike hadn't changed much since the "Three Mistakes" music video.

"Hello, friend," he said, shaking his head and grinning. "How are you today?" He wouldn't meet our eyes. He just shook his head and grinned.

"Good. I'm doing good. This is Judy!" Maurice said. He headed for the soda fridge.

Mike kept shaking his head. His store was tiny and had too much stock. The interior was the same as in the video.

"So, what's new, Mike?" Maurice yelled from the soda area.

There was another man and woman in the shop. I could tell they were tourists. They had backpacks on with the airline tags still dangling off them. They'd paused their shopping to watch Maurice and Mike interact. They were witnessing the real East Village: a man who was undoubtedly an artist, with artist-like hair that went past his ears and artist-like fitted black jeans, unselfconsciously talking up a bodega owner, just as an artist would do, especially if he'd lived his whole adult life in the city. With the artist was a girl, following the artist. To all appearances, she was just as much a New Yorker as him. She was probably an artist, too, or maybe studying to be one, at Cooper Union.

Mike didn't respond to Maurice's question, so Maurice went on. "I was just showing Judy our video, Mike. Your rock video debut!" he yelled. He was grabbing Coke cans out of the fridge, propping the door open with the tip of his cowboy boot, and piling them in the crook of his elbow.

Mike was still grinning. The way his face never changed made him look like a marionette. Eventually he started saying, "Oh, no," over and over. He reminded me of my mother.

"Mike, man, you've got to see this video," Maurice yelled. "It's crazy that you refuse to watch it."

"No," Mike said.

"I'll bring the VCR in here," Maurice yelled. "I'm bringing it over tonight! Judy and I will bring it."

"I have a VCR," Mike said. He pointed at the security camera mounted above his head.

Maurice started laughing. "That thing? Mike, you're crazy. That's not a VCR," he said.

I leaned against a Xerox machine and crossed my arms. From where I was positioned I could see everything: Mike, the tourists, Maurice in the soda aisle.

"No, no," Mike said. "There's a VCR. My wife would kill me."

Maurice laughed harder. "What do you mean, Mike? She'd kill you if I brought over a VCR?" I saw him drop a Coke can on the floor and heard the swoosh and slide of his boots as he ran after it. Mike laid himself across his counter so he could watch Maurice chase the Coke.

"Run, Coke. Run," Mike said in a loud whisper.

These people are nuts, I thought. I could do this every day.

I caught the woman tourist looking at me. She paused on my shoes the longest.

"This is Judy's first day in New York," Maurice said, appearing now, and setting the Cokes by the till. I checked if the tourists had heard, but they were busy reading the back of a box of cookies.

"Great news," Mike said and shifted a cylinder of licorice.

"You're gonna move here, right?" Maurice turned to me while arching himself to one side to dig money out his jean pocket.

"Totally," I said, jokingly sneering, to make it obvious it was obvious that I would.

Maurice loved it.

"Yes!" he shouted and threw money on the counter. "We're gonna make it happen. This girl's going to NYU."

Mike scooped up the bills. "NYU is very nice," he said. He still wouldn't look us in the eye.

When we left the store, Maurice said, "Your first Manhattan celebrity spotting. Mike the bodega guy. From my ancient, unself-conscious video with a campy element to it." We walked back home with Maurice's arm on my shoulders, each of us holding a shopping bag with Cokes, swaying like two winos, looking exactly like the Dylan album cover where he's with a girl and for once seems happy. As we walked, some people stared and others completely ignored us. I quickly learned that was the way to tell: the locals never looked at you. They'd already seen every version of everything there was.

AT AROUND ELEVEN at night we climbed onto Maurice's fire escape. He brought out a six-pack of beer with him and pillows from the couch for us to sit on.

"Cheers!" he said. "To your first night in the city." We clinked bottles. He took a long swig and sucked down half his beer.

Below us, Friday night unfurled. People walked in groups, girls talked unnecessarily loudly, guys strutted with their hands in their pockets. They yelled dumb, belligerent things at each other. I took a sip and set the bottle in my lap. I hated beer. I'd just wanted a Coke, but Maurice had never offered me one. We continued watching the street in silence, our foreheads pressed into the railing of the fire escape. The Iggy and the Stooges CD Maurice had put on was streaming out through the open window. By the time the album ended, I'd drunk about a fifth of my beer and Maurice was on his third bottle.

"Fuck people, right?" he said at one point. We'd just finished watching a couple end a long, awkwardly silent fight below us. The woman marched off down 9th Street, wobbling on her heels, and yelling "Go screw yourself." The man stood in one spot and eventually sat down on the curb, letting his head fall in his lap.

"No kidding," I said. "I guess people in New York suck too."

"People suck everywhere!" Maurice laughed. "That's why we gotta stick together. The real New York is this apartment. You and I. We've got all we need in here. We've got our favourite books, we've got the rest of Céline to read, we get to say who comes in and who stays out—like that woman over there, she's not welcome. Neither is her boyfriend." Maurice put out his hand to give me a high five. I returned one. I think he was a little drunk. I laughed. As if to seal our pact, the sky gave off a pop followed by a long, pitchy whistle and a boom.

"Firework," Maurice explained after taking another swig. "Some idiot can't hold it in till tomorrow. You know that passage in Kerouac?"

I only laughed some more. I didn't know what passage. Alex always said that Kerouac was for children. "Well, that's okay," Maurice said. "One day I'll read it to you." He wiped his mouth, examined what he'd wiped off, and burped.

I think because we were on the topic of people who'd offended us, all these passersby on the street, I thought to bring up my friends. I suppose what I wanted was to run the situation past Maurice, who seemed to have a sober, informed grip on human relationships. "I dread returning home," I said casually and lifted my chin toward the sky. "Everyone's always wanting something from me. They make living difficult." Maurice nodded but didn't say anything. Something like a whole minute passed. I worried he'd let my thread sink into the generic stew of complaints we'd been casting over the railing that evening. But finally he spoke. "Your parents, huh?" he said, and I quickly shook my head no, no, that wasn't it at all, eager to keep him hooked and feeling excited; the stories I'd been saving up, the way I'd pictured things through a lens meant for him, it was time to play the reels.

I told Maurice about the countrystead and the way it was a lonely place, though also striking and, in the right weather, quite beautiful and hard to abandon. Then I said Alex had wild ideas, and the thing about ideas was that the less detail you heard, the more likely they were to appeal to your senses or curiosity, or to mitigate a boredom. So, after a couple of months of hearing in detail about clouds and transmutations—and now the water!—I'd broken away from it, and from my friends. Though I also had nothing better to do with my days. "That's why being in New York is extra nice for me," I said, nodding at the building across the street. "There are no big shadows headed this way."

"Holy shit," he said.

I waited for more reaction. I was actually getting ready to continue. I had what I felt was my climactic gem of a detail: the pool of stinking water and what they'd done to me inside. But Maurice had stuck his head back against the railing and was looking at the sidewalk, searching for the next subject. I knew that if I let any more time pass, the thread would be lost forever. "Now they're excited about the old swimming pool!" I said. "And how it's filled with rainwater. They sit around *drinking* from it, and call it the pool of oblivion."

Maurice turned to me. "Ha!" he said. He grew animated, and I was so happy. He jumped to his feet. I loved the energy he was showing. He bounded through the window, into the apartment, and returned with a book very quickly. "This is my hero," he hollered, shaking the paperback. "The biggest hero in all of the Western canon." He bent to pick up his beer and chugged what was left in the bottle. "This is where your friends got the pool of oblivion from, by the way." He swallowed a latent belch. "Here, I'm going to read you my favourite passage, from my personal god, Milton's fucking Satan."

SOMETIME AROUND ONE o'clock the night turned hazy. The syrupy summer air had streamed in through the window all day and evening, filling Maurice's small apartment up to the rim. Walking across the living room felt like a waist-high wade through a river. He had a vintage lamp the shape of Saturn, with a flat ring like Saturn's, hanging over the couch. I lay down in its spotlight, fully stretched, with my arm underneath my head for a pillow and my face turned to the living room. The single beer I'd drunk had been strong enough to exhaust me. My eyelids felt heavy. With every blink, I fought off sleep. Maurice spent what seemed like hours pacing, all of it happening before me like a play. His tiny apartment was a stage and the couch the only seat in the house. He kept crossing the living room. He was looking through folders, moving books between shelves, stopping to write things down on pieces of paper, then sticking those pieces of paper in between pages of notebooks or between bigger pieces of paper. Throughout this, he managed to keep switching CDs, stopping albums mid song, and popping new ones in.

I looked behind me from time to time to check on Lexa. She was smiling, her eyes appeared closed, and her triangular architecture listed to one side then the other in time to the slow beat. Maurice changed CDs again, this time to Sun Ra. He was on a quest to find the perfect soundtrack for our night. Hours floated by and Maurice and I didn't exchange a single word. It was 2:30 a.m. according to the VCR panel.

I liked that I was no more than an accessory in the room. A permanent resident that needed no tending to, an old cat on the couch. The sounds coming in from outside—discordant honks, the lone offbeat drunken shout, another premature firework—weaved seamlessly into our music. Finally, he put on Devo. "Oh, man!" Maurice said, throwing his hands up. This was it! And when track eight of their debut came on, he pushed the repeat button so that it would stay on forever. Over and over Devo did "Gut Feeling." I'd heard it before, but never had it sounded this overwhelming. I wanted to crawl in between the bars of the song and convert before the altar of Devo's talent. By the time the third round of "Gut Feeling" started, Maurice was dancing back and forth across the rug in front of me, close enough to touch. He heaved his stomach and shook his hair. *Thump, thump, thumpa.* He stomped his cowboy boots and sang along, puckering his mouth into a tiny hamster snout and shutting his eyes so hard all that remained were two little slits, like staples.

I sat up on the couch, slowly, unsure of whether I should interrupt his solo act. Maurice's eyes were still shut, his face tensed and scrunched, the lines shooting out from the ends of his eyes and mouth exaggerated.

I decided to dive in. The worst that could happen was that he'd make it obvious somehow that he preferred me on the couch, watching him. I jumped onto the rug and started kicking my legs. There wasn't a whole lot of space in Maurice's living room but through some magic we never came close to colliding. We were like binary stars, these things that swing and dance with each other but never crash. I waved my arms up and down like a bat. At one point Maurice must've opened his eyes because he saw me and his kicks turned more springy. "Yeahh!" he yelled. "Judy! Dance!"

Encouraged, I started singing along with the song. My voice wasn't so bad. "You have a great voice!" Maurice yelled. He started singing too, except a different verse. I figured it wasn't accidental; he wanted us singing different parts for some kind of special chorus or syncopation effect. The words were barely legible over his laboured breathing. Then I realized that *I* was singing the wrong verse. Maurice and Devo were singing the same one. It didn't really matter.

WHEN I WOKE up the apartment was still. Even the city was still. It must've been five or six in the moning. The sky was brightening, filling Maurice's place with a muted purple light. I was on the couch and my arms were draped firmly around my stomach. A tightness was making its way up my digestive system. I bunched myself into a ball to put more pressure on my gut. I lifted my head and looked around, half expecting to find Maurice writing at his desk or collapsed on the rug beneath the couch, his legs still shooting outward in a dance move. But he was in the bedroom portion of the apartment, on the bed, turned away from me, the comforter pulled most of the way over his head but allowing two fronds of hair to escape and point up at the ceiling.

I tiptoed to the bathroom, shut the door behind me very quietly, turned on the light, and lowered my head into the toilet. I sucked in my stomach, hoping gravity would take care of the rest. I thought whatever was coming was just around the corner, was something easy and compact that I could flush and forget about, a secret for the sewers to keep, and my weekend in New York would proceed unstained.

But instead of a satisfying purge I let out a doggish hack, then a dry honk, and finally nothing. Strings of disgusting caramel-coloured spit floated into the bowl and clung to its walls. I waited, watching the spit slide into the water and start to swim in carefree, pretty formations. I lowered my head into the toilet a second time, as far as it would go so as to trap the sound, and tried again, squeezing my stomach with my hands this time like I was empty-ing a tube of toothpaste. I gagged and dry heaved, more painfully than last time. My throat felt skinned and my spit danced some more on top of the standing water.

The problem, I guess, was that I hadn't eaten since leaving my house the previous morning. Maurice had ordered himself a chicken Caesar salad sometime in the early evening. The salad was delivered in a brown paper bag by a man that came right up to his door and waved hello to me. I watched the man leave, understanding that my only chance at dinner had passed.

Part of it was I wasn't sure I could chew and swallow with Maurice Blunt watching. The prices, also, were out of my range. Maurice showed me the menu and asked if I wanted anything. A simple club sandwich with a side cost two hours of my moth-er's wage. I didn't know if he was paying, so I said no, that I needed to save up for future airfare, and Maurice shook his hair and said, "Yeah, Jude. You're always thinking. We need you in New York."

A new push started making its way up me. I dunked my head into the toilet and belched. Then I gagged and coughed. It was too loud and I would have given my life for Devo to be blasting right then or for fireworks to be whistling through the sky. As things stood, there was no chance Maurice couldn't hear. I felt desperate. I looked at the door. I snatched all the towels off the rack and wrapped them around my head. I lay on the floor, curled on my side like a spent little peanut shell, my back against the cold wall of the bathtub and tears collecting in my shut eyes. Ten or fifteen minutes went by. My stomach relaxed and entered some kind of peaceful intermission. Lying there on the fuzzy brown bathroom rug, I thought of all the people in rock 'n' roll history who might've trampled this rug, maybe just before puking into the toilet like I was trying to do.

Suddenly a new, more rapid spin seized me. I rose to my knees, let my turban fall to the floor, and stuck my face back in the toilet. My stomach roiled and finally drained. When it was over, I stood in front of the sink, but didn't dare look in the mirror. My T-shirt clung to my chest with sweat. My scalp was wet and my hair stuck to my forehead and the tops of my ears. I opened the door and looked toward the bedroom portion of the apartment. Maurice lay bundled under his comforter in the exact way as before, his contour unchanged, only his hair was now flattened. His body moved up and down in a rhythm that could've passed for sleep. There was a chance it was sleep. Outside, the city had grown several degrees lighter.

12

"**E**at this," Maurice said. He held out a plate with a bagel on it. I was sitting cross-legged on his floor reading a music magazine from the U.K. I suspected this was his way of addressing what went down earlier that morning, that I'd vomited after one bottle of beer.

I took the plate but couldn't look him in the face. The food plunged into my stomach. Things felt rotted in there. We didn't speak. Maurice shuffled through papers and phoned three people. Then three people called him. To the second caller, he said, "I love you" at the end, and "pick up some Echinacea. And liquids. And vitamin C!" and that he'd visit real soon, probably before Labour Day weekend, unless work got more crazy, but soon. He mentioned a woman's name, Liz, shaking his head, like Liz was someone he and the caller were equally frustrated with. I figured it was a sister or close cousin or aunt. "She'll be fine. We spoke yesterday morning. We've all gotta get our shit together sometime, Mom. For her, it's about time."

I watched guiltily from my place on the floor, flipping through more magazines. I was jealous of whatever it was that kept Maurice busy. Suddenly he'd grown adult-like; he had a mother and people who needed his assistance. I wanted him to put on music and dance in front of me like a crazy person so that I'd know everything was all right.

Then Maurice livened up. He laughed in his hearty, gruff way. He was on a new call. "Here, here," he said in a hushed voice and darted across the apartment while holding the receiver in his outstretched hand. He pressed the phone against my ear. Unaware it'd been passed over, the voice on the other end kept talking: "...I'm loving it. And yeah, we'll just keep trying, see what happens, keep trying, because I love you. I really really do. It's worth it to me. I love you..." Maurice took the receiver back and finished his conversation. When he was done, he said, "Know who that was?"

I looked him in the eyes for the first time that morning. I shrugged. "No," I said.

"Mark."

I shrugged again. I could've guessed which Mark I supposed, but there was more than one Mark in this world.

"Mark *Houde*," Maurice said, a little annoyed. "He sang in my band."

"Oh, nice," I said. I didn't know what else to say. The Mark Houde who went on to have new bands and solo records, who was significantly more famous than Maurice. If you looked in the right places, it was possible to find T-shirts and sew-on patches with his face on them. I doubted that a Maurice T-shirt had ever been made.

"Yeah, things are better between us," Maurice said wistfully.

I didn't respond. I only nodded like I understood that things had at one point been worse. I could tell he wanted to share, but I felt that asking anything would mean prying and coming off like a sycophant who was rooting around for insider knowledge about Mark. I felt embarrassed about how good-looking I found him, as he'd looked in 1976, that was. Maybe the truth was I didn't care that much why Mark was suddenly into Maurice again. By now Mark was fifty years old. He was older than my mother.

"Will we do something today?" I asked. I wanted to change the subject.

"I have to run out for a bit," Maurice said, "but here's a set of keys and—you know the city's just a grid, right? You can't get lost. But promise you'll be careful and here—" Maurice grabbed a pen and a piece of paper and drew a rough Manhattan. "Go in this direction, not this one."

As soon as the door shut I brushed the magazines from my lap and walked over to the window. I smiled and pressed my forehead into the pane until it felt like the glass might give. I was lucky. I was very lucky. I looked across at the windows facing me, expecting to see another eight of me looking out, just as giddy and full of awe, but the squares were blank and empty. I picked up one of Maurice's books and read it on the sill. After an hour, I looked at the map he'd drawn. I didn't understand it, but at the top of the map, he'd written, "Fuck yeah, Jude!" I assumed as a form of encouragement.

AFTER JEREMY AND I had met up at the theatre on our second date, the first thing he'd said was "Name a film with a scene that made you believe that the artifice of film is superior to anything you could find in real life. Go!" He asked the question very quickly, as if it were part of a game or challenge. We were getting ready to walk into the auditorium just then. Since I hadn't given Jeremy my phone number after our initial date in the alley, what had happened was that I'd walked by his workplace about one week later and saw him, crouched frog-style, washing the theatre's glass doors with a Windex bottle clamped between his upper thighs.

It was a quiet midday hour and he said his lunch break was just long enough to allow us to watch the matinee screening of *Symbiopsychotaxiplasm*, which had a running time of seventy-five minutes. Jeremy put away his cleaning supplies and let me into the theatre for free. And in response to his little game or challenge, I answered, "Fellini's *Close-Up*," when I meant Antonioni. And not "close-up." By the end of our date, as Jeremy and I and five other patrons slipped out of the auditorium, I couldn't take it anymore; I said, "Just kill me for the Fellini, I want to be dead." But even though he worked in management in a repertory movie theatre and he'd for sure known the correct title and director and that I'd botched it up bad, by that point, he had no idea what mistake I was referring to. He had a way of forgetting things, moving on very quickly. A film reference, anything that came out of me, I eventually learned, was a speck of lint, a little raisin to him.

I HADN'T PLANNED it, but twenty minutes after leaving Maurice's place, I was standing on 8th and 6th, close to Jeremy's apartment, according to the vague description he'd given in his postcard. It wasn't that I wanted to see him. I wasn't so stupid as to think he'd be standing on the corner when I arrived. His was simply the only address I knew, and no more a destination than any New York landmark. If anything, I wanted to make it quick, so that there was no chance he'd see me, even from a window. I wanted to show him, without him seeing me show him, that I was there too, that

New York was mine, and that the easy way he'd left our city and come here, well I could do that too.

Somewhere near Jeremy's place a man popped out of a doorway with a spring-loaded energy, blocking my path. "Can I buy you dinner?" he said. His cargo pants had stains around the knees, big and blotchy as if he'd been kneeling in a puddle. "Huh? Can I?" he said. I lowered my head and placed my hand over my eyes. The worst thing about him was that he had scars across his forehead, as defined and intricate as full sentences written by hand. "What's that, huh?" he said. "You don't like me?"

I walked away, down 8th Street or 6th Avenue, I wasn't sure which. "Hey, what's that?" he yelled from behind me, offended. "Don't wanna talk to me? Okay! All right!" His voice sounded distant enough that I knew he'd stopped following me. I looked over my shoulder and saw him lumber across the street, now most of a block away from me, walk up to a restaurant window, and yell into the glass. I stopped next to a vintage clothing shop. The window display had mannequins in outfits Bettie Page would've liked, a lot of black and violet. I thought about how, statistically, it was almost impossible that Jeremy had not passed this store and contemplated its window display. Even if he hadn't slowed in passing it, he had very likely looked at the exact same mannequins, in this rotation of outfits. I supposed this was as close as we'd get to anything like a third date.

I pushed the door open and walked downstairs to the basement. I assumed the cheaper stuff would be down there. The space had a low ceiling with exposed pipes. It was tightly packed with carousels. There was music blasting, a different song than on the main floor. I started pushing aside the hangers. The stuff was pretty nice and wasn't as expensive as I'd expected it to be. I thought, if I only got a job, I could probably afford New York. An employee walked into the basement. He had teased black hair, pale powder on, and eyeliner. He looked like he was doing interesting things with his life. I was afraid he'd judge me, recognizing it was my first time in there. But he only walked past and disappeared behind a "Staff Only" door.

I wondered where these people came from, how they got here. Whether leaving home for New York and scoring a job at a vintage clothing shop was easy, the way taking cash from a drawer and buying a plane ticket at a travel agency called Sunset Vacations had been. I was in New York like the rest of these posers. I knew deep down they all came from somewhere else, or if not them, then their parents or their parents' parents. I knew they'd arrived at Ellis Island by boat or from the Midwest in trains. They hadn't always looked like they did now. There was a moment in their lives when they were children, and embarrassing. I'm in New York and I belong here too, I said to myself. I stood still, not moving for a moment so that the idea could swell in me: I'd really made it.

A New York Dolls song came on and its quick tempo lent me a further boost. I felt equal with Jeremy, and with Maurice too, actually. I couldn't say whether Jeremy and Maurice were equal with each other—it was unlikely. But I felt level with each. I wasn't sure if that made sense mathematically.

I started flipping through hangers on a carousel filled with baby-doll dresses, these salvaged Courtney Love-style nightgowns. I lifted an AC/DC T-shirt that had been turned into a dress and put it back on the rack. Behind it was a Milli Vanilli dress with rhinestones glued over the singers' eyes. I brought my nail close and was about to scratch at one, just to see how securely it'd been glued on, when *wham!* I fell, or maybe "plunged" is the better word. Something gave out from under me and my knees went hot and buckled. It was like I'd fallen though ice, except there is no ice on the floor of a West Village clothing store basement. A few seconds passed and I saw that I was still standing. My hand gripped a hanger that hung off the carousel rack but no longer had a dress on it. Behind me, the man with the writing on his forehead made a full rotation around a clothing carousel with men's corduroy pants. When he was done, he walked away and proceeded toward the stairs with his dead, fixed march. I heard the brush of the door as it opened and the second brush of it shutting. We'd been the only two people in the basement and as soon as he was gone, I kneeled on the floor, to pick up the fallen dress.

Once I was close to the floor, I only sat down. It felt safe being low. I squeezed my thighs together. Things felt sliced and separated between them. It wasn't just how badly it hurt, it was that it was a new hurt I'd never before considered. The man with the writing on his face had swooped his hand down the back of my shorts, and in between the fabric of my shorts and my underwear he'd spread his fingers, curled them, and taken a generous swipe, ripping and mangling whatever he could, to get the most he could, in that short window of opportunity. I thought my groin might be bleeding and that the blood would make it out through the edges of my underwear. But my bigger concern was that the store employee with the black hair and pale skin makeup had seen it happen, watching through a camera eye in the "Staff Only" room. I wanted to get out of the store and out of this side of Manhattan as quickly as I could because of all the things that could happen to someone pretending to belong in New York, this was the most embarrassing.

I ARRIVED AT Washington Square Park and sat on the first empty bench I saw. It felt like my crotch had a heartbeat inside of it. The heat of the wood stilled the heartbeat. I looked around to see if anyone was looking. There was a group of teenage boys on a bench next to me, busy passing around a joint, two girls in their twenties deep in conversation next to them, and an old man with an orange terrier at the end of the line. No one looked my way.

I stuck my hand down the front of my shorts, into my underwear. I pulled it back out. I examined my fingers, front and back. I was sure I'd see a shocking shade of red, but there was nothing there. I was almost disappointed, I was in that much pain.

I DIALLED HOME from a pay phone and the phone rang once and then another time. I quickly hung up. All the quarters I'd packed into the machine rained onto the floor and I couldn't bend down to get them. I looked down at my money, spilled around my shoes, and the tears were already pouring out of me, falling to the ground, next to the coins. That was at least four dollars in quarters. I cried hard, and I didn't care. I thought of our phone back home, the broken extension that I'd unplugged in the hallway, the extension that I'd unplugged in our kitchen, spaces that no man with sharp hands could ever get into. And these thoughts, of course, made me think of just that kind of man getting in there, and I thought of my mother, of how offended I'd been at her during various moments in the past weeks and months, how resentful I felt, especially at the sight of her approaching me with food. The tears wouldn't stop.

I DECIDED TO KEEP walking, past Maurice's apartment, past 9th and 2nd. I needed more time to look like no one had hurt me in New York. The ten hundred locals who passed me didn't seem to mind that I was openly crying and wiping away my snot. And they didn't mind my limp and the funny way I dragged my feet. I liked that. The more blocks I passed, the more I liked it. That I didn't have to hide in a bathtub behind locked doors to be upset. I'd heard all about it. That you could be insane in this city, or perfectly sane, or whatever you wanted to be, and you'd fit in fine, people knew not to bother you. I felt like I was in a Sarah Schulman novel. One of those wonderful problem-riddled girls who just walks the streets and passes the same people I was passing.

I stopped crying around Broadway. The sun dried my face by 3rd Avenue. By the time I unlocked the front door of Maurice's building, jamming the key the way he'd taught me, I'd forgiven New York. And if asked, at that moment, I still would have said that I felt equal to Maurice, Jeremy, and anyone else who'd ever made it in this town.

MAURICE CAME HOME past one in the morning. I was asleep on his bed. I'd lain face down and put a pillow under my stomach to elevate my butt. Things down there felt almost normal again. Through my sleep, I had faintly registered the sound of Fourth of July fireworks.

"I've been calling," Maurice said. He sat down on the edge of the bed to pull his cowboy boots off. Sure enough, the phone had rung, but whenever it did, I'd give Lexa a quick look, which meant to ask if she was going to get it, and she'd give me a look that said "you get it," and in the end neither of us would, which is how these exchanges typically end.

"It was me calling. I wanted to ask if you want to come out and join me. Ken was shooting a clip for Elena, and we had to run around a room. You would have really liked it. I want you to pick up the phone here. Treat it like your own place. Do anything you want."

I gave Maurice a weak smile and turned back to the wall. I didn't know who Ken and Elena were. And what did it mean to "run around a room"? I was annoyed with how vague everything Maurice said was. The conversation felt no more appealing than speaking with Christopher and Alex. After that, Maurice started his usual restless browsing. Whenever I awoke I heard papers being moved or the quiet of him writing something. At one point, he put on a record. For hours he moved the needle back to a single point in a song. It had no words, just the odd screech of an instrument I couldn't identify, something gruelling and experimental, maybe made by John Cale. It lasted for about twenty seconds and then Maurice would push the needle back to its start. It felt like torture. The instrument screeched two hundred times. Finally the sun came up and Maurice quit moving the needle.

When I woke up, Maurice's leg was on top of my lower half. Worst of all, his foot, sockless and sticky, lay pressed into my naked calf. I tried shifting my body but couldn't. The leg was too heavy. It was like being pinned under a tree after a hurricane. I summoned all my strength and shifted harder. Maurice's leg retreated, quickly, like a bug shamed and scurrying after being found under a rock's moist underside. Once the foot was gone, I flipped over to face the wall and grabbed a generous handful of comforter. I fell back asleep.

"WE HAVEN'T BEEN anywhere," Maurice said as we ate our bagels on his couch. It was nine in the morning on Sunday. "And you're leaving in six hours."

"Four," I corrected him.

"Four," he said. "Maybe there's something good at MoMA," he said and looked helplessly at the window. "I messed up," he said. "I haven't shown you a thing."

Ten minutes later, we walked out of his building. The sidewalk was aglow it was so bright out. We were completely alone on Maurice's block.

"This way," Maurice said, turning onto 2nd.

I counted the blocks. There were ten exactly. We arrived at a set of dark doors, wedged between other murky shut-looking things, not meaning anything. We stood on the sidewalk, facing each other in front of those doors.

"Do you know where we are?"

I shrugged.

"Look in," Maurice said, pushing open the door. I stuck my head in. Inside was more dark, a long dark room ending in dark. "It's closed right now," he explained and let the door shut.

I looked at him blankly.

"CBGB, Jude, geez, know your history!" he yelled. He gave my shoulder a light, jokey shove. A man walking by flashed Maurice an annoyed look.

"Oh," I said. "Can I look again?"

Maurice pushed open the door. I saw a dark room ending in dark.

FOUR HOURS LATER my plane was tearing through the sky of New York. CBGB, Maurice's apartment, Jeremy, forehead writing-man, Lexa, all of it swam below me, slowly gaining distance. I watched them get left behind, feeling like I was being pried from a family that had just promised to adopt me, blemishes and all—theirs and mine. The flight attendant came by with a drink cart and handed me a little napkin. I pulled a pen out of my backpack and on the napkin I subtracted the sum of one plane ticket from the total I'd taken from the countrystead. According to the napkin, I had enough for at least two more flights to Mauriceland.

13

I was standing in front of the campus building that looked like a fairy-tale fortress. Who would've thought that spending the weekend in Maurice's apartment would make me feel like more of a stranger around him come Monday? I went to the classroom, pushed past the desks, and sat in the back row, next to the old man. I brought my feet up on the chair and pressed my knees to my chin to put pressure onto my stomach. I was nervous about our impending interaction. I didn't know if I should greet Maurice or pretend I didn't know him. When the old man asked how my weekend had gone, I only said that it was nicer than usual.

For an hour and a half, Maurice read his own poems to the class, some of them poems he'd read to us on the first day, a lot of them unpublished. Once it was over, I waited for the last student to leave. I approached Maurice. "Jude!" was all he said, happy it seemed. He looked tired, like he hadn't slept the night that I left. His hair had too much product in it. I figured he'd dumped it on too hastily, maybe in the airplane or a cab. We walked out of the building together without speaking. I couldn't tell whether our quiet was the quiet of closeness, of not needing to say anything because we knew everything, or whether it was the opposite, the uncomfortable realization that we had nothing to say and that we were in fact complete strangers.

Since coming back from New York, I was preoccupied with the thought of whether I would ever be invited back. He'd never made it clear that I was. I worried he was thinking about how I'd thrown up in his bathroom, focusing on that low point, forgetting the other, more fun parts of my visit. "God, I have to meet with so many people I don't want to see today," he finally said. This sounded like he was trying to pre-emptively stop me from asking him to hang out that day.

"Sucks," I said, trying to sound like I didn't care.

We passed by the library where everything had started, the first-year students' residence, the oval lawn. Maurice's cowboy boots clicked and clacked on the pavement like a set of women's heels. Their noise underscored just how quiet things were between us. I looked around the campus. I didn't know what to say. Suddenly Maurice stopped, spun around to face me, and put his head on my shoulder, pretending he was miserable. "I don't want to meet with a bunch of lame, grovelling idiots. Help me! Can you get me out of this?"

I started laughing. I patted his hair. "Poor you," I said. Maurice let out a single fake sob. I kept patting his head and with each pat, more of the sticky substance that made his hair glisten transferred onto my hand. A woman walking by looked at us curiously. Here was a man her husband's age, in a leather jacket, in black jeans and loud cowboy boots, collapsed and pretend-crying on a teenage girl's shoulder. She searched my eyes for an explanation and gave me a little smile, maybe sad, maybe just confused. "Why can't they all just go away?" Maurice went on. "I want it to just be us. Reading Céline on a couch, you know? Is that too much to ask?"

"I know," I said, still patting his head. For the time being, I was happy again. Ten minutes later, we were standing in front of Maurice's faculty housing building. The building was a Victorian mansion, sectioned off into apartments for temporary visitors' stays. He told me his unit was on the top floor. "It's decorated like my grandmother's place. Thank God I only have to be here for seventy-two hours at a time." Maurice, I learned, would fly out of town the minute his Wednesday class was over. He'd fly back in early Monday mornings. I looked up toward the top floor windows, nodding and uncertain if what he'd just said was an invitation, an apology for the place looking not-cool. I wanted badly to go in, to listen to music and dance, and redo our weekend a little. But Maurice was already backing away from me with a key jingling from his finger.

"How am I going to survive a whole bunch of days before we hang out in the city again?" he said.

"I don't know," I said. "How am *I*?" My words were a little choked. My weekend plans had just been confirmed; "the city" could only be one city—I was thrilled—but I didn't understand why we couldn't also spend that afternoon together. "You have a lot of work, huh?" I said.

He shrugged. "I'm thinking of taking a nap, actually." He smiled at me and put out his fist, to bump my fist. "See you Wednesday at noon, sharp," he said. "Do all your homework."

I said bye and walked away first, so that he'd know I'd had no intention of going into his visiting faculty apartment. I crossed the street and headed for the nearest path that took me back to the maze of the campus. On the rose-lined walkway from which I could already see the facade of the library, a familiar shape emerged, still partly eclipsed by a pair of hand-holding students. Bettie Page, my over-made-up classmate, was taller than them, on account of her high bun and purple foam platforms. When the students veered out of the way, I could see all of her, bouncing toward me in a black velvet minidress. We were the only two people on the path now, and the closer we got, the more her face hardened. There were so many lines there, so many shades of purple. We were twenty feet from each other now and I believed then that she didn't like me. I was the teacher's pet, the student Maurice left the classroom with. I braced myself for the impact of her disgust at seeing me; my jaw tensed and I defensively lowered my chin. Yet when Bettie Page was about to pass me, her face softened and she smiled in a benign way. I returned the smile too late and was afraid to look behind me. I kept walking, not wanting to picture her destination, so obviously the place from which I had just come.

AT HOME I SAW we had a message waiting on the answering machine. My thought was that Maurice had changed his mind about seeing me, but when I played back the very small tape, I only heard silence followed by a clumsy hang-up.

A few hours later, my mother came home from work. We went through the routine of her making dinner, *Jeopardy!* on the couch, and a walk for me in the pre-sunset hours, still on the hunt for little missing Taffy. This time I made something of an honest search, walking the nearby blocks a couple times over, even calling out "Taffy girl" the way I'd heard her owner say it. It was typical for me to conjure up Christopher whenever I contemplated anything vulnerable, small, and sad. He wasn't so badly off, and yet the walk left me feeling an overwhelming pity. I missed him, I supposed. I called the coach house as soon as I got home, planning to leave the line silent then hang up in the same way as I'd heard on my answering machine that afternoon. I was hoping it'd been a signal from him, and this would be me returning his coded message. But the coach house phone went on ringing. Without an answering machine, it could ring for all time. I eventually hung up and joined my mother on the couch. She was tuned to the police procedurals, and after that came the late-night talk shows.

A LITTLE PAST MIDNIGHT, the phone rang. Before bed, I'd turned the ringer off on the hallway phone and plugged the kitchen phone into my bedroom socket, keeping the unit under a pillow to muffle it. Across the hall, I heard my mother groan, but it wasn't clear whether she'd heard the ring. "I just had the worst three hours of my life," Maurice said without saying hello. He'd gone to some professor's house for wine. He said a grad student came up to him and asked him to read his manuscript of a novel in verse. I imagined Bettie Page had been there too, but there was no way to ask. "You should've seen this guy," he said. "He looked like Timothy Carey. He said that if I like his writing style, we should start a band together, God help me. How does that make sense?" Maurice started laughing hysterically, then let out a long watery burp.

I couldn't think of anything to say. I was worried my mother would be at my door in a minute. "Were you sleeping?" Maurice finally said, he sounded annoyed at my silence. He had a lot of energy that he wanted reciprocated. He seemed pretty drunk.

"No," I said. I was propped on my elbows, with my eyes on my bedroom door.

"You didn't go out with friends today or anything?"

I realized Maurice hardly listened to a thing I said. In New York, whenever I'd wanted to bring up the Big Shadow, I always stopped myself, having the sense that the subject had been exhausted, simply on account of Maurice having read me some Satan parts from *Paradise Lost*. I understood that the odd and eccentric friend-tales Maurice had accumulated during his years in New York's art scene likely eclipsed my own two friends, their clouds, and anything they could get up to in an old empty swimming pool.

"The only friends I have are people I don't want to see anymore. I've told you," I reminded him.

"Right," he said, sounding like he half remembered something. "They're into Y2K?"

"They think they can escape to another realm," I said. "Like Jesus. Not Y2K."

"Oh, man," Maurice said, laughing a little. "Right, I remember. The pool of oblivion. Escaping the tedium of existence. I hope you're staying clear of those nuts."

"I'm trying," I said. "It's not as easy as you'd think. Maybe it's like how you said your old band mates and all the people you've been hanging out with your whole life drive you insane but you keep coming back to them and you'd never move out of the city."

Maurice went quiet. All last weekend, whenever someone called him on the phone he'd hang up and sound exasperated afterward. He'd say, "Oh God, that was Liz or Tom or Julian," like

I knew who any of these people were and why they called. From what I could make out, it seemed these Lizes and Toms and Julians had problems, that Maurice had to talk them into something good or out of something bad. They called all day and night, like he was a hotline. And when he'd hang up, he'd say something like, "I don't know why I talk to them still. I don't know why they're still in my life, they're such narcissists, I need out of this," though as soon as the phone rang again he was on it, running for the receiver. It was clear that this was his life. He enjoyed talking to them. And as always, I'd just nod from his couch when he told me about them, making no remarks, not wanting to sound like I was prying into the lives of the rich and famous, or at least of the aging New York City '70s cultural scene cohort.

Maurice was still quiet on the other end and I grew worried. I worried that I had overstepped some boundary by comparing my odd, unfabulous friends to his significant and fabulous ones, that I shouldn't have brought up the people he knew because I, after all, didn't know them. "Maurice?" I said.

"Yeah, Jude, I'm here," he answered. After a pause, he said, "It's just that I don't know how this happened. I understand what you're saying. It's hard to shake these people. They're part of you and you're part of them. It's all so fucked up and intertwined. You and me, we're so alike, with the things we're dealing with. We're soulmates. We were meant to find each other. To save each other. From everybody else. 'People are hard,' remember how you said that to me?"

I smiled into the dark of my bedroom. Of course I remembered. It was a good line.

"You've just gotta move to New York. It's the place for you.

Enough of this flying back home bullshit. Enough of hanging out with crazy friends and planning space travel. You belong at my place. It's Mauriceandjudyland."

"I know," I said, no longer worried he didn't want me there next weekend and the weekends that followed the next. I let my head fall on my pillow and laughed, just like a teenage girl getting what she wants in a movie would. Then I said good night to him and returned the phone to the kitchen so that come morning my mother would find it in its proper place.

14

I t'd been a week and a half since the pool incident, and I hadn't heard from Christopher and Alex. After my one hiccup of trying to reach Christopher at the coach house and communicate with him through answering machine silence, I barely registered that they were no longer in my life. The day in between Maurice's classes, I was woken by a knock on the door. It was ten in the morning, and the only people who I imagined could come over that early were them. Through the peephole I saw a man in a uniform that had a vaguely familiar logo and colour scheme. He turned sideways so that I could see the large leather satchel on his shoulder with coils of wire hanging out. He said he was from the phone company, and I opened the door. Once inside, he examined the parts of our phones and the wall where cables came in and out. He told me the ringer had been turned off on the hallway unit, with the little sliding switch, did I see that? I lied and said I had not. He placed test calls from a cellular phone and each time, the phones in the apartment rang just fine. While he worked, I found a note from my mother on the kitchen counter. It said the phone company would send someone between ten and five that day, and could I be home to let them in.

When he was done, the phone man walked out with a barely audible bye. I hoped he'd make a notation somewhere in the system, saying to ignore or treat as low-priority any future complaints from this particular account holder.

AROUND NOON, I decided to take a walk to the campus. I had a hard time imagining what Maurice was up to on the one free day he had in my town. If I transposed his New York persona onto the environment of my city, the only thing I could picture him doing was sleeping through the day, like an animal taken from a jungle and placed in the tundra. I walked every conceivable route, including right by his housing. I wondered if the faculty apartments came with individual telephones. From the pay phone in the campus library's atrium, I called the coach house, but no one picked up. I wasn't sure that I planned to say something if they answered. I called the main house and no one picked up there either.

A few blocks away, about halfway between my home and the university, I came upon another pay phone, and I again called the coach house and the main house, and then the coach house once more. The inside wall of the phonebooth had a Taffy poster taped to it. I thought how wonderful it would be to be the person dialling the number on the poster, how your fingers would barely manage to hit the right buttons as your entire body shivered from the anticipatory thrill of being able to say, "I've found her. She's here, next to my foot!"

By the time I got home, a shift had taken place. I'd had a whole walk of nothing but time to think, and Maurice and Christopher and Alex had become an equal concern. The week and a half I hadn't heard from them now seemed an absurd length of time for any two parties to not give the other a sign of life, even if the parties didn't particularly get along. It seemed negligent. When the phone rang, I hoped it was Christopher, but it was only my mother, calling to ask whether our line had been fixed. I told her there was nothing fixable about it, and when she asked what that meant—what about the fryer sounds and the way the line was dead half the time she tried it—I said, "I'm only the messenger repeating the repairman's words. There's nothing to be done for our situation."

I ran myself a bath right after and brought *How What Happened Happened* in to read. Yet the moment the water closed in around me, I became distracted by the noises again, trills and a whistling, and still, something so much like a phone ring. I pressed my ear to the cool enamel of the bathtub, where the sounds played on in a proper amplified way. If my cousin and Alex had gone away—in any definition of "gone" that the universe allowed—I'd be the only person to know, and then the ethical dilemma would set in, and it would start haunting me as I tried to sleep, eat, or start a life in New York. Would I say something to Alex's or Christopher's mother? Would I call my mother's brother in British Columbia, in the new home he'd made for himself after leaving his wife and son in a way so swift and easy it was actually quite admirable. "Not sure if this interests you, but your son is gone, in a peculiar sense of gone." I supposed I wouldn't tell anyone, except for Maurice. "Where have they gone exactly?" he'd ask. And I'd say I didn't know. They could now be the water that fills the empty space of the bathtub. "How do you know they're gone?" "I don't know that either," I'd have to admit.

IN THE EARLY EVENING, I left a message on the main house answering machine vaguely mentioning wanting to pick up some clothing, which was really never mine, but Alex's mother's, or his mother's sister's, or that of other women who'd passed through the country-stead and shed what they no longer wished to wear into its several dozen drawers. After dinner, Christopher returned my call. It'd possibly been the longest I'd ever gone without talking to him. "Which clothes specifically and where can I find them?" he said, all curt and impersonal, sounding like he was holding a clipboard. "We want our cassette back, by the way," he said, and I told him that I'd never even listened to it, which I realized right away was the wrong thing to admit. "Of course you didn't," he mumbled. "Anyway, the last thing we need is for it to end up in the wrong hands." He said to leave the tape in a bag on the doorknob of my apartment and in the morning he'd exchange it for a bag containing my clothes.

I HOPED MAURICE would call that night, but he didn't. The hours felt unusually long, and I had trouble getting to sleep. Christopher's cold tone and the way he seemed to want to keep his distance from me was something worse than a lesson, it was a flagellation. And maybe it worked, and here I was, a wayward nun starting to see sense again. All I could think about was how it hadn't really been wrong to put me in that hole in the pool, the way it was quite beautiful in there, especially in the daytime when the green could be seen, the pollen and spores and little flies. I thought about how the floor of the pool was soft as a pillow, how falling hadn't hurt in the slightest, and how what I said to them was disproportionate, all things considered, though what they'd said to me was also inaccurate and crass.

From Maurice's reading of Milton, I understood the pool of oblivion was shorthand for the mythical River Lethe, a body of water where preparation takes place, where the last rites occur before a person goes from A to B.

I picked up my tape deck and found an old tape to record over. I made a copy of Alex's tape, half listening as it recorded, and put the original in a plastic bag for my cousin. Sure enough, Alex rambled on the tape, about this preparation, the way the pool was there to get us ready, to sit in and wait as one would in an airport lounge, ears perked for a boarding call. "We will sit, we will sip, we will await the shadow." He was unnaturally excited about the idea, or discovery, of what the pool meant for them. "The clouds gifted us a benediction, they filled the pool, and now we will await the next cloud, from within the basin called the pool of oblivion. It all comes down to water." He invited me in a wholehearted way, to see their actions as preordained and mine as petulant, to give them a call when I felt ready to come by, to come and taste the pool of oblivion.

IN THE MORNING, I awoke early. The nerves of a Maurice class and Christopher's visit combined had me up before the sunrise. My mother was readying herself for work. She paced the apartment in her bra for a while. "I like how this poetry class is getting you out of bed early," she said while tugging at the underwire so emphatically it looked like she was pulling a blade out of her heart. I believed all her bras were very old. They were also the wrong sizes, leaving the tops of her breasts looking choked. As soon as she was gone, I placed the bag with the cassette tape on the outside knob, though I also placed a sticky note on top, saying, "Come in. I have something to tell you!" An hour later, my cousin let himself in. He looked around, though nothing had changed, of course, in the few years since he'd last let himself enter. I told him my mother wasn't home, to not worry, and he said he'd figured she wasn't, and sat down on our couch. The shopping bag with the clothes was left in the hallway.

"I signed up for a summer poetry class at the university," I said, and he reacted by rubbing his eye and ironically asking if that was it, that was my big announcement. I knew there was a way for me to wear him down, that if I wanted to, I could destroy him and his insolent act in minutes. But there was no point. As I walked him back to the door, I said, casually, "Would you mind monitoring the coach house phone this weekend—and if my mother calls, tell her I'm there with you?"

This of course made him stop, and I went on, perhaps ultimately only trying to impress him, to show him that I was bigger than Alex, because while Alex talked on tapes and engineered holes in pools, I actually went places. "I'm going to New York for the weekend," I said. "Not to see Jeremy or anything, I—" but Christopher interrupted me here.

"Yeah, fine," he said, "I don't want to hear any more." I took this as more of his insolence, and a petulant show of his hurt. Yet what could I do? I needed him in that moment. I said thanks, not ironically. There was no way to get through another weekend of an unworking, unplugged phone when my mother had set her mind on fixing it. From the window, I watched my cousin shuffle from my front stoop onto the sidewalk, stop to remove the Taffy poster someone had stuck under his windshield wiper, fold the poster, tuck it in his back corduroy pocket, and drive off without once looking my way.

15

The next day, after he returned to New York post-class, Maurice called me at one thirty in the morning. I picked up my bedroom phone—I'd again moved the kitchen phone into the bedroom for the night—cutting it off in the middle of the first ring. "Hey," he said, "just needed to talk to you." There was a new urgency to the way he said this. Ever since I'd told him about my attachment to Christopher and Alex and compared my predicament to his, I'd tightened our odd bond.

"I was at the stupidest thing. I just need to talk to a sane person for a while. Sanity!" he said, sounding pretend-frustrated. I could hear the city behind him.

"All right," I said. "Go on."

Maurice told me about another party he'd just come back from, and I realized, after he burped again, that he was probably a little drunk. The place was full of artists who had made it and moved out of Manhattan to L.A. or Berlin. Of course, they still spent a lot of time in New York City. "I wanted to jump out the window," Maurice said. He described a guy who'd followed him around the living room, onto the roof, back inside, through the kitchen, into the bathroom even. He wanted to make a movie with Maurice, starring Maurice. A short film shot in New Orleans. He said he had the funding. "Do it," I said. I hadn't meant it entirely as a joke, but Maurice started laughing. "Do it," he imitated me. I could tell he'd said it through a smile. A pause followed. He sucked in a bunch of air and breathed it out. "We're the ones who should be making a movie. Can you handle a camera?"

I believed I could handle a camera. Christopher's mother had the JVC camcorder my mother loaned her to make movies of Christopher's half-brother, Baby Marco. Marco was no longer a baby and she'd never returned it. Alex had a real eight-millimetre Kodak Instamatic that had belonged to his father. I told Maurice about it. "Let's do it, then!" he said. "Bring the Instamatic to New York. I wanna see this thing."

"But I'd have to interact with Alex, and explain why I need it, and make a trip to the countrystead to pick it up," I pointed out.

"Right," Maurice said, and I was happy to hear how grave he sounded, that he finally understood Alex's was the last place I'd want to go if I could help it. "Yeah," he said, "you can't be going there, you might get sucked into outer space."

We were silent for a moment, thinking hard in our respective places in the world. "I can just borrow a camera from someone here," he finally said. "You're coming this weekend, right?"

"Obviously." I said it coolly. We were collaborators, making art, now. My visits to New York were a default.

"That's what I like to hear. Yeah. Let's shoot *a movie!*" he said.

BASED ON HOW things had gone so far, and what I knew from knowing Maurice for two weeks, I didn't think he'd bring up movie-making again. But when I arrived in New York two days later, he was still on it. "So did you make any notes?" he asked as soon as I shut his apartment door. "For our movie," he added, seeing I had no idea what he meant. "Did you bring the Super 8?"

"It was an Instamatic, and no," I said. I felt my face grow hot. "I thought we decided you'd borrow one."

"Really?" Maurice said. He looked at the floor, thinking for a while. "I guess I forgot. Okay, I know what we'll do." He placed a quick phone call, hung up with an exaggerated gesture, grabbed the keys from the kitchen counter, and stuck his feet inside his cowboy boots. "You're gonna meet your new favourite person. Get ready," he said.

I set my backpack on the floor and followed Maurice out the door.

DANA MILLER'S BUILDING had the feel of a haunted house and if only the lighting had been better, I could have said why the lobby floor felt sticky and maybe identified the source of its graveyard smell. But once the elevator took us up and opened its doors directly into a bright room the size of a gallery, I saw that this was the home of someone significant, likely a professional artist.

Room one was bare and spotless, with floor-to-ceiling windows looking on to more windows just like them across the street. Room number two had brown paper spread across the floor and taped to the walls, some photography equipment, a portable hot plate in the corner, and next to the hot plate, a package of Wagon Wheel cookies and a couple of mugs with coffee-stained rims. Room three was smaller than rooms one and two. Dana Miller was sitting inside it, perched, with his legs primly crossed, on a plastic lawn chair next to a mattress with some sheets mussed on top of it. He was tying hemp rope around a square package wrapped in butcher's paper. A cigarette dangled from his mouth.

"Oh, hi," he said distractedly, not looking up. He bent down to set his cigarette on an ashtray, just next to his foot. "Don't ask," he added, as soon as Maurice wandered to his side and looked down at the package. "Don't ask, don't ask. Don't ask. Do not ask," Dana said, trying to get a grip on the string and twisting his lips as he tightened the knot.

"This is Judy," Maurice said, throwing his arm in my direction.

I was still standing in the doorway.

"Hi Judy," Dana Miller said, keeping his eyes on the package. "Don't ask," he said, maybe to me now that we'd been introduced. "Don't ask what the fuck I'm doing. Don't ask, Judy. Don't ask, Blunt. Don't ask, Judy," he went on. I did not like Dana Miller.

"Judy and I came to grab the camera," Maurice said, sounding a little shy. I wondered how good a friend Dana was. I'd never heard of Dana Miller, but the way Maurice was acting suggested he was someone big.

"Oh, yeah, over by those," Dana said, pointing his face to a corner where a stack of paper tubes lay next to a filing cabinet.

Maurice walked across the room, his cowboy heels embarrassingly loud on Dana's bare floorboards. Dana paused his work and watched Maurice with an impish expression, like he'd just directed him toward a booby trap. Maurice started digging through the tube pile. "Where?" he said. He was bent in half and his voice was strained. Sections of his hair came unstuck and fell over his eyes. "Where is this thing, Dana?" Dana didn't answer.

The tubes were falling, tumbling like logs, crashing into Maurice's legs, and unfurling on the floor.

"Dana, where?" Maurice said again and looked back to flash me an amused look which said, *That Dana. Always so hard to get him to clarify.* I nodded once as if I agreed.

"Keep at it. Getting warmer," Dana said.

Maurice kept digging.

"Cooling down now, Blunt." Dana took a puff of his cigarette, tilted his head back, and blew smoke toward the ceiling. "You're in Alaska," he said, still staring at the ceiling. "Fucking celebrating Christmas."

Maurice found that funny. "Jude, help me," he said.

"Don't even think of it, Judith," Dana said. "Blunt's got to learn to persevere. He's got to burn some calories." Maurice told Dana to fuck off and Dana told him to watch his language. I stayed where I was. I wanted to leave Dana's so badly. Two minutes later, Maurice unearthed the camera, a shitty Panasonic camcorder covered in splotches of paint. It had been nowhere near the tubes and the filing cabinet. "The Equator in July," Dana had said when Maurice finally found it. "What are you going to film, Blunt?" His expression was a sociopathic flat.

"We'll just roll with it," Maurice said. "We'll go with the flow and see what happens."

WE LEFT DANA'S and walked back toward Maurice's place. "Dana's pretty crazy, huh?" he said and smiled in a distant, slow way, like he was reminiscing about a beloved monarch.

"I guess," I said. The only thing he seemed like was self-involved, which had nothing to do with craziness.

"Yeah, he's the best," Maurice said. "Wait. Is there tape inside? Is it charged?" he asked, stopping suddenly in the middle of the sidewalk.

I looked at the camcorder. I'd been cradling it in my arms since Dana's. I pressed the power button. A green light came on. "I think so," I said.

"Great!" Maurice said. "I'm gonna run in and get a coffee." He pointed at a store whose windows were covered in candy bar advertisements. A sign made with markers and cardboard said Snacks and Keys Cut Inside.

"You film!" he continued. He took a step toward the store and turned around, his hair in his face. He was excited. He looked nervous too, like an actor who'd been called in for his big audition, out of the total blue. "Can you get an angle from the entrance looking in, or whatever you think works best, actually. You're the director here. Just get me buying a coffee. Just me being me." Maurice waved his hands in the air as he said the last part, then bolted into the shop. For thirty seconds I stood unmoving, the camcorder still in my arms. I looked around, at the cars, the people, and the buildings that knew nothing about Maurice and me, about where I'd come from and what I'd been doing since the rainstorm hit my city two weeks before. For the first time, I felt something that I'd only ever felt in the company of my mother— an embarrassment so deep it shamed me to feel it even in secret. I felt it in my chest and in my guts. I wanted to set the camera on the sidewalk and run.

I looked down at it, at its mocking green light. I wished the battery would die suddenly. I felt burdened by this machine, the way it implied a whole job for me to execute not on my terms. "Okay," I called, lifting the camera to my face. "Here I come."

I walked into the store with the viewfinder pressed to my eye. There was an old man sitting behind the counter. He had deep creases around his mouth and a tiny electric fan directed at his head. As I crab-walked the length of his store, he followed me with his gaze, but said nothing. He didn't ask me to go away. I wedged myself into a corner of the shop, next to a tower of flattened cardboard. I filmed as Maurice sauntered toward the counter. He looked casual. I hopped forward to get the old man in the shot too. Then I took a few steps back. I panned from the old man to the back of Maurice's head, doing an extreme zoom on his hair so that all I saw for a second was a wobbly dark field. Then I zoomed out and panned back to the old man. For some reason, the old man never looked into the camera lens. It was like he'd been trained in this, out in Hollywood.

"I'll have a small coffee," Maurice said, sounding oddly stilted.

The old man set a Styrofoam cup next to an ordinary Black & Decker coffee maker. It was the same kind my mother used in our kitchen. He poured coffee from the drip pot into the cup and handed it to Maurice. "It's not very hot. You want it hotter?" the man asked. At the same time, Maurice tossed two singles on the counter.

"Huh?" he said.

"Not hot," the man raised his voice. "I don't have it hot because it's pretty hot out." When he finished, he stared directly into the lens, looking unhappy. The camera kept rolling. In the foreground, Maurice turned around and walked past me, without looking at me, and out the door.

WE WERE STANDING on a street lined in yellow-brick townhouses interspersed with brown-brick townhouses. Maurice had taken me to a new part of town. The houses seemed grimy, in an exciting way. Air conditioner units dangled precariously from windows and garbage containers sat crookedly arranged by the stoops. I saw people my age huddled on stairs, everyone looking in opposite directions, a girl on another girl's lap, a boy rubbing his face. They paid no attention to us.

"Okay, now!" Maurice called from across the street. He had his hands in his jean pockets and stood at the edge of the sidewalk. Just next to him was a plain-faced building with the words Iglesia Cristiana. Maurice looked to one side and had an expression like he was lost deep in thought. He looked to the other side, still with the same expression. He looked like an explorer on the verge of a new frontier. A hunchbacked woman with a cane and a kerchief tied under her chin entered the frame. She'd come out of the Iglesia Cristiana. I pressed Pause.

"I think we're done at this corner, yeah?" I yelled. Maurice gave me a thumbs-up and scuttled toward me with a big smile. The teenagers were still distracted, not minding us from their stoops. I wondered what this part of New York was called.

WE WERE STANDING in front of a chain-link fence. We were right next to the riverbank, and I could see the Statue of Liberty. It was my first time seeing her not from an airplane window and not on TV. I knew that feeling this way about someone so famous was pathetic, that I was no different from the students in Maurice's rock 'n' roll poetry class now, but I couldn't take my eyes off her.

Something about her colour was unreal, like it wasn't colour, but light, glowing from the inside.

"Now!" Maurice yelled.

He leaned against the fence. He looked to one side. The wind blew a frond of hair onto his face. He brushed it away and turned in the opposite direction. The wind blew more of his hair forward. He looked down and rubbed the toe of his boot in the ground like he was mashing an insect. More hair flew forward. I made sure that the Statue of Liberty was in the frame.

"My stupid hair," he said, patting his head when we were done.

"You looked great," I told him. "Nothing to be worried about."

MAURICE WENT OUT in the evening and returned home around ten. We hooked the camera up to the TV and sat on the couch together. He cracked open a beer. I sat so that I wouldn't block Lexa's view. I knew she'd get a kick out of this.

The first scene—Maurice Blunt buys coffee—came on.

"You've totally got an eye for film," he said and turned the volume up a little. "This looks amazing. Kind of gritty, like Jarmusch."

I leaned toward the TV. Jarmusch was one of my favourite American directors; the frames *did* look good. "I think we should've shot these in black and white," I said. The camera had a setting that turned the image to black and white. I moved from the couch to the rug, to be closer to the screen. I needed to get a good look at what I'd created.

"You think? Yeah, I can see that. Good idea. Make a note of it," Maurice said. "But seriously, this is amazing. You get light, you get composition..." Onscreen-Maurice looked to the right and winced from the sunlight. "I know so many people, musicians, artists, who would love for you to do this for them. To make beautiful footage like this. You obviously *get it*," real-Maurice said. "You should start doing this shit full-time."

I narrowed my eyes at the TV, but I was no longer seeing anything on the screen. I gave a slight nod to show I'd heard him. I was too afraid to look back or to respond in a real way. This was the moment, I knew. The moment that passes by with the speed of any other, but is later slowed to a stop and dissected in the pages of a book, magazine article, or your own autobiography, even. "This is how I started out," I would say one day. "I made a video. For a good friend. We were just messing around, using a camera we'd borrowed from another friend, I think Dana Miller. The camcorder was something shitty. Panasonic, if I remember right, and covered in splotches of Dana Miller's paint."

I waited for Maurice to elaborate just how I would become a film director, a videographer whose gigs earned her enough money to pay rent in New York. But Maurice was silent. He was mesmerized by the video. He'd moved on. Onscreen-Maurice turned to the left. The Statue of Liberty was behind him, looking me right in the eyes. The room filled with the crunchy sound of wind barrelling at us off the Hudson. "Ugh, my hair," Maurice said. "Stupid wind."

"You look great," I said.

As soon as the film ended, the phone rang. "Tonight? Nah, we're staying in," Maurice said. "Just watching Judy's movie... yeah, she's a total filmmaker. We shot this afternoon. You should see these shots we got...huh?... On Canal...Next to that place you suggested...maybe..."

"That was Mark," Maurice said when he hung up, but I already knew. As he'd talked into the receiver, I'd gotten off the floor and walked over to Maurice's bookshelf. I ran my fingers on books I'd already touched and flipped through more than once: Bukowski, Céline, Henry Miller. I stared at the records. I smiled at Lexa. I knew everything by heart, yet everything remained as exciting as yet unseen.

"You seem deep in thought," Maurice said. He started walking toward me, slow at first.

"I was just thinking about how much I like it here." Something was exploding in my stomach, good this time. I felt overcome with emotions. Everything was the opposite of wrong. I was so far from my city, the countrystead, my mother, holding on to the cheap plywood of Maurice Blunt's bookshelf, standing on his rug. I couldn't believe I'd made it. The apartment was vibrating with the sounds of the city. He'd loved my camera work. Mark Houde knew me by name. I'd made a film.

"Good," Maurice said and took the final step toward me. His voice had dropped and became fuzzier. He cupped my elbows and pulled me into his chest. We stood embracing, me on my toes, my head peeking over his shoulder, his hair scratching my forehead. I saw the unmade bed, the little bedside table, the little kitchen, a silver tub of Philadelphia cream cheese that Maurice had forgotten to put back in the fridge after breakfast. I wanted this freedom, the apartment, and its mess for myself so badly.

"Good," he said again, releasing me. I went on smiling. I could feel it was a dopey smile, but I couldn't shut it off. Maurice leaned closer, hunched himself, and cupped his hand on the back of my head so that I couldn't move it sideways or back, like Malcolm

McDowell trapped in *A Clockwork Orange*. He put his finger under my chin to tilt it up by about an inch and stuck his lips into mine. His lips gyrated a little. My lips didn't move. Eventually Maurice let go of my head and took a step back. He pivoted on his heels to face the shelf with CDs and began crashing their cases together. "*Exile on Main Street!*" he hollered, pulling one out. Within minutes he was kicking his boots in the air as I sat on the couch, watching him. I watched Maurice dance with my flat rock 'n' roll composure—cool and carefree, whatever, who cares. After two trips to New York, I had it down.

I GOT THE edge of the bed that night. Maurice was pressed against the wall even though he'd gotten in second. He'd climbed over me, said, "Night, night," and started snoring within a minute. The smell of the beers he'd had that evening filled our small sleeping space.

My eyes were open. I'd been waiting for Maurice to pass out. With his dancing, his unceasing chatter and movement, his holler and boom, I hadn't had the peace to sort out how I felt. Sometimes people walk away after a crime. They suck it up and their embarrassment is an armour; the entire bad incident is a good lesson learned. Other times, people scream murder, collapse, call 911. I knew that what had happened between us—how he'd stuck his mouth on mine—didn't warrant the second kind of response. I wasn't entirely sure if it even warranted the first.

I looked at the Philadelphia cream cheese, still out on the counter. It glowed a little, reflecting the light from the microwave panel. I thought how the last time I looked at the Philadelphia container was before Maurice had stuck his mouth on me, and now it was after. The Philadelphia was a testament to whatever that was. It was a witness, but unfortunately, not one that could explain Maurice's actions.

I wondered whether I should get out of the apartment and flee into the night. His snoring seemed deep enough; it was believable. I could wait out the two days until my flight by sitting inside Penn Station or walking around Central Park. There was enough countrystead money in my purse to feed me for a few days, maybe even book a hotel. I couldn't tell whether I was being reasonable or adapting the plot of *The Catcher in the Rye*.

"What's up?" Maurice mumbled. "Can't sleep? You're flipping all around," he said. He rolled onto his back and lifted his arm, the jumping-jack pose again. "C'mere," he said.

I'd started something. I was the star of a movie in mid-production, at a point when you don't back out, for fear of shame and inconsistency, and the shame of inconsistency. So I slid over and laid my head on his armpit. He brought his arm down, wrapped it around me, and gave my elbow a gentle rub. The rub was no more than what my mother would give me if we found ourselves on the couch together watching *Jeopardy!* or the news. I was waiting for its radius to grow, to become more than just motherlike, but it remained as it was. A rub. Just a thumb and its little movement, wanting no more than a life of lying around in beds, making movies, reading books.

"You know you're the coolest, right?" Maurice said.

I said yes, like he'd convinced me, just with those words.

"Don't worry about what people say, what people want. You're going to come upon so many assholes in life. Just do your own shit. You know what's right. It's your life. You're *smart*."

"Okay," I said. I was pretty sure this was an apology for what he'd done. He did wrong, and I should be calling the shots, he'd said, effectively. It made sense. It was protective. Everything started to feel normal again, it felt safe, like when he'd read me Céline on my first day in the city. What happened by the book-shelf never happened. It was a failed multiple-choice test. A or B? It was B, not A, turned out, and Maurice had failed the test—but no matter. The test was done. We'd moved on. We were friends and friends forgive petty failings.

"Good. We're best friends, man," he said, as if he'd read my thoughts. "I don't know how we managed to find each other. But we're gonna rule New York."

I said okay, and I believed it.

"Now go to sleep," he said.

With that, Maurice's breathing lengthened, his hand fluttered, a grizzly snore followed. New York City beeped and honked through the open window. I closed my eyes. Eventually, I fell asleep and dreamt something long involving Christopher.

16

"I've always wanted to see Coney Island," I said to Maurice the next morning. I was sitting on his bed cross-legged, with the covers pulled up to my waist. I was no longer afraid to show interest in unoriginal destinations. I felt like I'd proven myself and could ask for pedestrian things.

"Okay," he said, sounding pretty excited, actually. He was next to me, sitting against the wall in his boxers and a Michael Jordan T-shirt, his bare, hairy legs stretched out past me on top of the comforter. He reached underneath the bed and pulled out a small silver radio the size of a sandwich. "Let's do this old-school style."

He flicked the "on" switch, pulled the antenna up, and twisted the tuner in search of the news station. "Rain. Perfect!" he shouted after hearing the forecast. He held his free hand out for a high five. I gave him a high five. "Best time to go to Coney Island. It'll rain all the losers out." But instead of getting out of bed, he tugged on the comforter to get underneath. "I haven't been to Coney Island in fifteen years probably," he said. "Not since I took my nephew and niece out there. Of course, *you'd* be the one who takes me out to Coney Island after fifteen years."

I smiled. I took that as a compliment and show of strength. His leg touched mine underneath the covers. I had my jean shorts on. I couldn't bring myself to wear pajamas in Maurice's bed. Pajamas in New York seemed worse than wearing clothes to bed. Maurice turned off the little radio and stuck it back under the bed. "So, what are we waiting for? Let's go," he said.

AROUND NOON, the phone rang. I was on the couch, sitting cross-legged, chewing the cream cheese bagel Maurice had made me for breakfast. I sat sideways so that I could still see Lexa as I ate. "I'm going to Coney Island!" Maurice yelled into the phone. He gave me a wink from the kitchen. Then he went quiet for a while, listening to the caller. He laughed for a bit. "Oh, man!" he said. "That sounds good."

Half an hour later, Maurice hung up the phone. He buckled his belt, bit into his bagel, threw the rest of it on the counter, and slipped on his cowboy boots. "I'll be back soon," he said, pausing at the edge of the living room, his look straight out of a sitcom, the lowest common denominator kind. Guilty party retreats out of the room, having been given the direction "look sheepish" or "look like you feel really bad, but what can you do? You're a forty-eight-year-old man. The girl on the couch is only a girl, and Coney Island is a long subway ride from your apartment. Who's got the time for Ferris wheels?"

"Bye," I said. "I have my key."

"Careful in the city," was all he said. A moment later I heard his boots run down the stairs.

I got off the couch and moved a milk crate of LPs from the window. I made room for myself and sat with my legs extended down the length of the sill. I pressed my head into the glass. Rain fell in slow, heavy drops and below, the people went on doing their endless New York things, only now with umbrellas in their hands.

I saw Maurice pop out of the building, beneath me, his hair pressed back, looking unlike the people around him. He hopped into a cab. It sped off, down 9th, and became just another one of the twelve million moving pieces I was seeing, the swarm of the town that everyone dreams of.

I couldn't believe I had nowhere to go again. I had no money to spare on museums and was too shy to walk into the clothing stores. Going to a library struck me as a depressing defeat, and I couldn't stomach sitting in a coffee shop and pretending I was an NYU student or casually reclining on a park bench like I fully belonged in the city already. The only available option was strolling the streets, but what happened the previous weekend had soured me on the idea. I decided I'd stay in and read a book.

I walked up to the part of the bookshelf where Maurice kept his own books. He had four or five copies of each title. There were four poetry collections, a very short novel, and a memoir called *Still Falling*. "Which one should I read?" I asked Lexa, and it might've been the case that her upside-down head was pointed just slightly toward Maurice's memoir.

I carried the book back to the window and sat down, curling up against the wall and resting my head on the glass. I opened the book. It was dedicated to someone named Maude. "To Maude," it said, "You rock." The next page contained an epigraph with lyrics from "I'm Set Free" by the Velvet Underground. I turned to page one, chapter one. "I was born on a rainy Thursday," it started. I read aloud, for Lexa. "Do you like me reading aloud?" I said, but

Lexa said nothing. I skimmed the next few pages, which talked about Maurice's older sister, Lizzie, who shared his interest in hiding in the woods near their house. I guessed Lizzie was the person having all those problems that made Maurice's mother call. I skimmed past pages about a paternal uncle he particularly liked, who turned him on to music. His father's profession. His first guitar. His first best friend. I grew bored. I didn't want to read about strangers' children and their suburban, middle-class lives. I skipped ahead and picked a random page. I read silently.

Sixteen was when I finally took my place in the world. I was unashamed, brazen, aware it was not a choice. I felt like a place had been reserved for me at a beautiful table and I was merely sitting down into it. Sex. Fucking. The time had come. It was magic, it came from within me, it was spiritual and all that smoke. But it was also physical. I had the spirit and the god in me...

I skipped farther ahead.

We fucked in her basement, the low-ceilinged kind endemic in my suburb, with pipes twisting above us like snakes in a Greek myth. Horace. I remember a box of Christmas decorations rattling next to my foot. It was labelled with her mother's neat, housewifely handwriting. In the back corner, the boiler growled, like it was her keeper, telling me to get off of her already. I refused—not done yet, sir. Give me another fifteen seconds. When we were done, I imagined the family taking out all the angels and doves from that Xmas box in a matter of weeks. Because my family was Jewish, this was particularly hilarious. Meredith was pretty much done with me by that point, but she said something the meaning of which I only understood years later, when the Sateelites toured the west coast, right after our show at Mabuhay Gardens. We'd pulled off the road, on our way to Washington, at some idyllic park full of trees the size of the Empire State Building. I picked up a pine cone that lay at my feet. "Pinus lambertiana," Tim, our then-drummer said. "What?" I said. Tim repeated the Latin I hadn't understood. He was a smart one. Tim would read Goethe, Ovid, Schopenhauer, while the rest of us read girls, drugs, booze. "Pinus lambertiana," he said again. "That's 'Sugar pine cone' in layman's terms. They're massive."

I looked at the absurdly large, unabashedly phallic object lying in the cup of my hand and suddenly this eight-year-old memory of Meredith made sense. As she'd pulled her pantyhose up she said, "You won't have any trouble satisfying girls in your life, with that Pinus lambertiana." At the time, this sounded like "penis" and an Italian pasta dish. As it turns out, I was half right. I thanked her when she said it, stupid and ignorant, unlearned in dendrology, not like Tim our drummer, not like Meredith, who probably went on to become a forest ranger, though now, in the Oregon woods, I saw that thanking her was in order. She was right. After Meredith, it had only gotten better. I put the pine cone on the dash of our touring van and dedicated a song to her in Seattle.

I shut *Still Falling* and glanced over at Lexa. Her stoic jeans-model expression gave me the fortitude to try again. I opened the book and turned to another page, wanting to cleanse my palate of what I'd just read, but all I found was more prowess, conquered women, being an ass. I hated thinking of Maurice and his memoir voice, so unlike the voice he used with me. In the classroom, too, he had an altered persona. I understood there was a two-sidedness required of him and all somewhat-famous figures, and that I should take it as a compliment that I was getting the real Maurice, while the world, readers of *Still Falling*, students, listeners of the Sateelites, and journalists got the other side and that's all they'd ever get—the dry pit of the fruit I was getting to savour. I wanted to know what side Lexa had gotten, whether Maurice maybe had three, four, fifty of these sides that he doled out to friends even, each slightly skewed and temperamental, like phases of a moon. But of course, she could never tell me. Lexa was a page from a magazine.

IN THE LATE afternoon, I woke from a nap on the couch. I could barely see a thing in the apartment. The day remained gloomy and practically nightlike. The rain knocked on the windowpane now and then, whenever the wind changed direction. When I reached for the switch on the Saturn lamp, the bulb sparked, startling me. I let out a quiet scream, maybe enough for neighbours to hear. I remained in the dark for a while, sitting on the couch. Then I put on my shoes, which were not good for rain, and decided I'd circle the blocks near Maurice's place until I found the nearest pay phone.

I walked for about five minutes and once I found a lonely, graffitied phone box, I stuffed all the quarters I had into the machine and dialled the coach house. I heard ringing and a pickup. The moment I heard Alex say "Hello," I hung up. The coin dispenser didn't return any of my money. It might've been four or five dollars' worth I'd spent, just for a second of one-way conversation with someone whose voice I hadn't wanted to hear. The rain, by this time, had soaked through all the layers of my outfit. I walked back to Maurice's and changed into dry clothes in his bathtub.

THREE DAYS EARLIER, the day before I left for New York, Christopher had called me at my mother's. The way he'd left the last time I saw him, after bringing me my clothes, I didn't think he'd want to initiate contact. At first he wouldn't say anything, which made it awkward. I asked, in a stupid, insincere tone whether the Big Shadow had come. "Not yet," he said, sounding disappointed. He then asked about my poetry class. "Is that why you were carrying around Maurice Blunt's book all day? Are you studying his poems?" And though he sounded perfectly normal, in fact, his default flat self, hearing Maurice's name come out of him, at this juncture, when I stood to lose so much, was unsettling.

Maybe I betrayed something by how defensive I got. I said, "You think they'd put some has-been's vanity project on a syllabus?" I told him I'd signed up for a serious class, with poets like Blake, Herbert, and Dickinson, taught by a famous English lit professor. Thinking about it then, it made no sense why I'd told my cousin where I was really going for the weekend; the link between New York and Maurice was so obvious there was no way he wouldn't wonder. One inquiry at the English Department office about the summer poetry class and who was teaching it would've been all it took for him to connect the dots that mapped my recent behaviour. But Christopher didn't press me about the class anymore, other than an offhanded "I didn't think you could take classes before September." He then changed the topic entirely. "Could you do something for me?" he asked.

Christopher said he hadn't seen his mother and baby brother in over six months. I knew that, of course; it was something my mother brought up daily. He and Alex had the sense that if Christopher saw them, they'd start interfering with his Big Shadow preparation. My aunt was nothing like my mother, but Christopher had a weakness around her, which Alex attributed to a Freudian lacking. At one point all three of us had worried that if he hung around her too much, we'd never see him again. Of course, now I encouraged him to visit her, but he cut me off right away. "I'm not going there," he said, "I just want you to call or visit her and see how she's doing, generally. And then, you know, once I leave, kind of keep an eye on her."

I promised him I would, and then I heard Alex's voice enter the room, and Christopher pull the receiver away from his face. "Judy's calling," he said, though he'd been the one who called me. He then asked me, using a new voice, if there was anything else I wanted. I started to speak, only for his sake, but before I could finish a sentence, he hung up the phone.

MAURICE'S BUZZER WOKE me up past eleven in the evening. I was on the couch, wrapped in a blanket. The buttons on the intercom were unmarked and I'd never asked how to use it. I didn't want to speak to any of Maurice's friends anyway, so I stayed where I was. Two minutes later, Maurice came in. "I buzzed you from downstairs. I'm double-parked. Ready to go?" he said.

His eyes were bigger than normal, and his shirt was dishevelled. If it hadn't been for him telling me eight thousand times about how he'd quit drugs decades ago and was averse to them and anyone who still did them, I would've assumed he was high. When I didn't react, Maurice tossed his keys on the counter and leaned down to massage his wet cowboy boots. He kept his eyes on me the whole time, giving me an extended sheepish look. His slick-back had dislodged and two fat strands, congealed by mousse and rainwater, fell over his eyes. They added to his pleading look. I knew this was his way of saying sorry. Sorry for leaving me alone all day after promising me fun in the city. Sorry for saying he'd be back in a minute. A sorry for once felt nice. I asked him where we'd be going exactly.

"Coney Island!" he hollered. "What? Did you forget?"

I cocked my head.

"What's that look for?" he said, breaking into a smile. "Nighttime Coney Island is the best Coney Island. We can get hot dogs, go on rides, play in the waves, eat candy floss."

"I don't believe you," I said, making my voice deep and droning. "You're a liar." I was doing Dylan. The previous night we'd listened to the plugged-in part of *Live at Royal Albert Hall*.

Maurice gave me a long look, his mouth twitching, holding in a laugh. He called me "Judy the Judas," referring to the Dylan performance, then shook his head, like I was too much. He bent down to massage his boots some more. "All right, fine," he said, his tone also a joke, like he'd been caught in a lie and was confessing. "The truth is I need to park the van in Brooklyn. Come with me? Keep me company, please? I need more Jude-doing-Bobby-Dee. It's the greatest thing I've ever heard."

WE DROVE ACROSS the Brooklyn Bridge, my first time. And after locking a grey van that apparently belonged to Maurice behind a padlocked fence on a dead-quiet street somewhere in New York City, we rode the subway home in a nearly empty car, an endless trip during which I rested my head on Maurice's shoulder, keeping my eyes open because each time I closed them, all I saw were trees, forests and forests shedding phallic California pine cones.

"You were right. Nighttime Coney Island was a blast," I said somewhere in the middle of our rumbling, faceless ride. "The beachcombing was my favourite."

Maurice started laughing. This time he couldn't contain it. "Beachcombing," he said. His laughter ricocheted off the plastic seats around us and off the tuna-can walls. He seemed genuinely amused. Maybe surprised-amused. Happy at being taken out of some stagnant understanding of what people were capable of saying, of how people were. And I didn't get it. All I'd done was throw his lazy Coney Island joke back at him. But it worked. We hadn't gone to Coney Island. We never would. Was that funny?

I pressed my face into his side harder. His body bounced up and down as he laughed and laughed. I guess it was funny, my best one yet. "Beachcombing," he repeated after catching his breath. "Oh my God. Yes! You just *get* it!"

I WAS SITTING on the couch, reading back issues of *Rolling Stone* underneath Lexa the next morning when Maurice asked if I knew how to transfer footage from the little cassette in the camera onto a proper, big VHS tape.

"Of course," I said. "Do you have a blank tape?"

Maurice grabbed the chair from his computer desk and slid it across the apartment, bringing it to the front door. He looked up and put his hands on his hips. A short storage shelf ran partly along the wall and very close to the ceiling, just above the entrance and the bathroom door. It was packed with boxes, a small suitcase with wheels, two hard guitar cases, and an accordion file.

"Hold this," Maurice said, referring to the chair. It was an old wooden chair, bent and lopsided. I held the back of it.

Maurice let out a huff as he stepped onto the chair. His face was almost level with the shelf. He lifted his chin and surveyed what he had to work with. He zeroed in on a cardboard box marked "November" in marker. "This," he said. "I think there's tapes in here."

Maurice lifted both arms high over his head and as he did that, his T-shirt rose about a foot and his gut popped out, so that now there was a taut, snow-white ball with a blotchy pink rash between us. Maurice immediately dropped his arms and the T-shirt returned to its normal position. The November box he'd let go of came crashing down, a corner of it snagging his head. "Oww," he howled, grabbing his ear. "Fucking box! Fuck!" I jumped out of the way. The box landed at my feet, making a loud thud. Christmas lights and unused envelopes spilled out of its collapsed end.

I got on my knees and started stuffing the lights back in the box. Maurice stepped off the chair while massaging the side of his head. "I don't think it's that box," he said quietly. His hair was in his face. His cheeks were flushed. He wouldn't look me in the eyes.

I didn't know what to do. I'd not seen much of naked older-men bodies. Films and TV rarely showed them, and Maurice had always kept a shirt on. But it was only a gut after all. I cleaned up the box and put it back on the shelf.

"I don't think I have any blank tapes," Maurice said. He still wouldn't look at me. He pushed the chair back to the little desk and sat by his computer. He woke it and started typing slowly, using one hand. This is how my mother would look in front of a computer, if she had one, I thought. His hunched body faced the monitor with a mix of reverence and apprehension. I wondered if Maurice believed I'd never noticed he was fat.

AN HOUR LATER, we were eating toast on the couch. Maurice had turned on MTV and we made fun of the videos that came on. "Just kill this guy and put him out of his misery," he said about a musician standing on a desert dune, playing an unplugged electric guitar. "That girl is trying way too hard," I said about a woman gyrating inside a glass container. The November box was forgotten, it seemed. "God, we're so much better than everyone else," Maurice said. "They should be showing *us* on MTV."

I laughed and Maurice turned to look at me. He had the old, trained professional expression I'd first seen on the library stairs. "This isn't like what your insane friend does, right? You know I'm joking around. I mean, we *are* better than everyone else, but, you know, I'm not going to start talking about leaving for another planet. I just mean, we two have our heads screwed on tight, and that's rare, especially in this city."

"No, I know," I said quietly. "And my friends aren't really going to another planet. It's more complicated." I'd been waiting for

Maurice to ask me more about Alex and my cousin. Mainly, I wanted him to tell me that there was no way they'd stop me from moving to New York, even if they found out he was behind the class that I was taking, or about the things we got up to in his apartment on late weekend nights. That if they tried, he'd stop them first.

"Have they been bothering you lately?"

In my head, I parsed the word "bother." "Not really," I said. "But it's never clear what they're up to. I can never truly tell what's happening, but that's how Alex operates. He's never outward. He works in this odd background way. I can't explain it. I'm sure they're up to something. They might be trying to trick me."

A new music video had come on the TV, a pop song that we'd already made fun of the previous weekend.

"That makes sense. That's how these people are. They're schemers."

I liked that Maurice said "these people." It sounded like there were more Alexes out there, that he'd seen and dealt with them, and that there was a common solution to them, in the way you take one type of medication for a headache and another for a stroke. "He's a loser," he continued. He sounded pissed off and I liked that. "He was probably made fun of as a kid and then found that other friend of yours, figured out his weaknesses and latched on like a parasite. That's how it works. People feed off others. They need others to prop them up, to counteract their insecurities."

I nodded. I noticed Maurice left me out of the story. But I was there, too, of course. For a while, I was the other weak party, or maybe I'd just been lonely. Perhaps loneliness was the worst weakness of them all.

"You know, I really care about you. I really care about you being all right," Maurice said, holding my gaze. I looked back into his eyes and nodded. What I was thinking was that soon Maurice's class would end, and even sooner, I'd run out of airplane ticket money. I desperately wanted him to tell me how much it would cost to rent an apartment in his neighbourhood, whether I could live in his place until I found one, whether he had any leads on jobs or discounted sublets, whether once I was a bona fide citizen of this town I could still pop in on Sunday mornings and make fun of MTV over bagels or toast. If he wanted to save me, this was the way to do it—with some practical advice.

But Maurice didn't say a word. Instead, he brought his hand over my head and placed it on the same spot as before, just where my neck met my back. I braced myself. My elbows locked. He stuck his finger under my chin to lift it and gave me a wet kiss. My lips didn't move and my eyes remained open. They focused on a window across the street from his building, just the bit of window I could see over Maurice's hair. In the window, a grey human outline rubbed at the glass with a rag. The first person to appear in any of the windows facing us since I'd come to visit New York. Just a cleaning woman.

When Maurice was done, he removed his hand from the back of my head. Once free, I pulled away more forcefully than last time. It was only instinct. My face might've contorted. Maurice saw. "What's wrong with you? Never kissed a guy before?" he said. His voice was unkind and unfamiliar. He emphasized the word "guy" and underlined my immaturity, now suddenly a liability.

"I've kissed *a lot* of guys," I said. My face flushed. The apartment became bad-small. I would've given anything to be in the alley by the theatre, hanging on to Jeremy's shoulders, not there. Maurice just shook his head, leaned back into the couch, and turned up MTV with a jerky flick of his hand. Somehow, within half an hour, the page turned. We were laughing at music videos again, my inexperience and immaturity forgotten, excused, and underneath the rug now. And I was back to cool, carefree, and quick to forget. The necessary stuff of Mauriceland.

THERE WERE FIVE hours left before my evening flight home. I'd be back at my mother's by nine, in time to get ready for sleep in the bedroom where I'd slept since I was born. There'd be enough time before my mother's bedtime to have a conversation with her and make her believe I'd just come back from the countrystead. Just the uneventful undeveloped areas skirting our town, not New York. Not the centre of the world, the furrow into which everything that matters falls, the dustpan into which everything good gets swept.

"I have to run to the studio," Maurice said, hanging up the phone.

I nodded from the couch. I'd sat with my breakfast plate still next to me, watching MTV for the last hour as Maurice made phone calls. He said he'd leave me the number for the airport taxi. "I want you taking a cab. You're safer in a cab than riding subways alone," he said. He stopped moving about and gave me a long look like this was a life-or-death matter. I thought about the man with the writing on his forehead. And then I thought about money, and that I would rather take the train so as to have enough for more flights.

"I'll pay," Maurice added.

"Sure," I said, pretending I'd barely registered the offer.

I watched silently as he dug three twenties out of his wallet. "This should do it," he said. He then bent over the kitchen counter and drew scribbles on a piece of paper. "Could you also pick something up for me before you leave? I won't have time after the studio. I need to stay there late."

I liked the idea of an errand. It made me feel like I was part of the household, that by running errands I could pay my imaginary half of the rent. He asked me to pick up a blank VHS tape. I took the piece of paper from him and saw that he'd drawn a small map with directions to a place called Stove's Electric. Below was a taxi cab number. "Take this to the airport!!!!" Maurice had written.

"And transfer that video footage before you leave?"

I said I would and placed the paper with the map next to me on the couch cushion. Maurice ran out the door. I watched MTV for another half hour. Then I got ready to go. I put on my shoes and slipped the map in my pocket. Then I looked around the kitchen. I looked at the counter, and next to the toaster, and underneath the cereal box. Maurice had forgotten to leave me the money.

17

The next morning my mother woke me with a phone call. She asked if I remembered what day it was, and without waiting for me to say, she told me it was my aunt Tamara's birthday. "Everyone's hoping Christopher will come over for the dinner," she said. I said all right, that I would talk to him later, though of course the idea that his mother's birthday might be the thing that would make Christopher emerge from the countrystead, that would remove him from Alex even for one evening, got me so excited, I dialled the coach house the moment I hung up with my mother.

Christopher appeared to be expecting my call, or else Alex was nearby and he was set on affecting something like displeasure at hearing from me. His voice sounded wooden. "Yeah, obviously I know it's my mother's birthday. Check your mailbox. I left a card for her in there," he said. Then he reminded me about our deal, and asked that I make myself present at his mother's party in a way that made up for his absence. "Do it, or else," he said, sounding like a horror film script. "Do it or I won't screen for your mother's calls on any more weekends, ever."

When I left the apartment to go to class, I found the envelope he'd left in our mailbox, addressed in his avian handwriting, with its flap needlessly sealed. I walked a few doors down, in case he and Alex had parked somewhere and were watching. I hid behind a tree and opened the envelope. The act of reading Christopher's card hardly felt invasive. Any words a person could say to a mother, I already knew. I was probably born already knowing them, I think we all are. If anything, I felt I was owed a thank-you for thinking to screen the card. Sure enough, it was undeliverable. "Happy birthday, Mom," said the first line. "Whatever happens, know I'll always watch over you and Marco," said the second line, as if my cousin was planning to off himself.

HALF AN HOUR later, I walked into class with Maurice's apartment keys in my pocket. Over the weekend, he'd told me to keep them, that they were mine. But I still brought them with me, in case he asked for them back. I walked past the desks, moving them out of the way with my hip. I walked past Bettie Page, feeling she posed no threat to me now. Past the boys in rock 'n' roll clothes. I sat down next to the old man. He was wearing a T-shirt with the cover art of a New Order album on it. "Hi," he said. "Weekend good?"

"Yeah, pretty good," I told him.

I was past feeling giddy about the turn my life had taken. My new life was just my life now. I finally understood how celebrities felt, minus the having-money part.

"Did you do your homework?" the old man asked. He pointed to a book on his desk. He had liver spots on his knuckles. He could have been my mother's father.

"I don't do the readings," I said. "I'm not even a registered student at this school."

He gave me a long look. "Rock on," he said and smiled. The parts in between his teeth were solid grey as if packed with concrete. I assumed this was because the teeth were no longer his own. He didn't ask me any more questions. I really like this grandpa, I thought.

AFTER CLASS, MAURICE and I walked down the rose-lined campus path toward his faculty housing building.

"Jesus. Two more weeks of class," he said and shook his head.

"Two down, two more to go," I said and shook my head.

He put his arm around me and pressed me in by the shoulders. I wrapped my arm around his back and took hold of a bunch of his shirt fabric. We walked like that for a few seconds, the Dylan cover way, then let go. "So, I have some new ideas for shots," Maurice said. "Mark and Jamie were blown away by what you did. They came over after we were done at the studio last night. I showed them the tape."

It was a little odd that so many people were getting so riled up about fifteen minutes of footage, but I knew that part of transitioning from being a fan to just a normal friend of famous people was realizing they had less going on than you assumed. Maurice, for instance, enjoyed watching some terrible TV sitcoms, things that my mother liked. He spoke to his own mother on the phone a lot. He had ready-made foods like Campbell's soups and Hamburger Helper in his cupboards. He had shopping bags from Kmart, generic white sport socks with dirt on the bottoms, pills for relieving gas in his bathroom.

"So, Dana turned me on to something great. It's called Plexi-Star, have you heard of it?" he asked.

I shook my head no. I did not like Dana Miller.

"It's this thing…" Maurice didn't know how to explain it. He lifted his hand and made his fingers into triangles. "It's this thin, see-through plastic that you can use as a backdrop and it has a star pattern embossed in it and when you film and direct a light at it, it refracts this light or something." He made his fingers twirl. "And these stars just *fly* at you. It's pretty cool," he said.

I said nothing.

"I was thinking we should get some of that and shoot with it. I would stand in front of it, an indoor shot. The stars would burst out from behind me. I could maybe spread my legs, like I'm flying through space or something weird like that."

"Right," I said.

"You could do Mark and Jamie, too. It could be great footage for the tour promo."

I realized Jamie was Jamie from the Sateelites, their last drummer, as I'd learned from *How What Happened Happened*. This was the first I was hearing of a tour. "You guys are playing shows?" I said, casually.

Maurice stopped in the middle of the path. We faced each other. He looked around to see if anyone was within hearing distance. A bee flew past and he swatted it. Then he lowered his voice and said: "I mean, you can't say a word of this to anyone, promise? Obviously, I trust you like no one else in the world. Things fell through initially, but now it looks like Mark's on board again. Only a handful of people know about the tour. We don't want it to get out of control if people find out. At this juncture, it's top secret." Maurice looked into the distance, beyond my shoulder, toward the library stairs where we'd met, where it all started.

I nodded knowingly. I checked behind me, for anyone who could be eavesdropping. "Let's talk about this someplace else," I said. I pushed him so that he'd start walking. We continued down the rose-lined path. I tried to picture Maurice on stage. I'd seen photos of him on the backs of the Sateelites CDs and records he had in his apartment. He used to have a lean body that corresponded to the guitar that he played. In some of the old pictures, Maurice lay across the kick drum, his back arched over it, the guitar and one leg pitched toward the audience.

"It would be great if we could pick some up this afternoon. I called around. Turns out there's a place in town that carries this stuff," he said. "Plexi-Star," he added, a little annoyed, when he saw that I didn't know what he was talking about. "The shit that makes stars pop. We'll shoot some scenes on campus."

Maybe he saw that I looked uncertain. I didn't think Maurice would want promo shots filmed anywhere but in New York, not until the weekend. "Today?" I said.

"Yeah, today," Maurice said. "I have a ton of work to do tomorrow. And Wednesday I fly back home. Mark and Jamie and I were just talking on the phone last night, late into the night, on three-way, about how amazing it would be if you could be the band photographer or videographer or something. You could come on the tour. This is another secret—we might be playing Moscow. You could ride on the tour bus. Everything. Mark and Jamie are into it."

My mind was now trying to catch up with everything Maurice was saying. I was still having trouble believing that Mark and

Jamie of the Sateelites were talking about me in a circle, like teenage boys discussing a girl from homeroom. But I now existed in their minds. It was a fact. And because of how minds work, I'd be in there forever, even if they thought they'd forgotten about me, I'd still be there, crouched in some murky nook.

"Yeah, Jude!" Maurice said. "Think about it. Though I think it sounds pretty amazing. I'd take care of you, of course. I'd make sure you're okay."

I smiled and looked down at the sidewalk. My face, I could feel, had turned a visible red. In *How What Happened Happened*, a significant number of the women mentioned became part of the '70s New York punk scene by taking photos at shows, or writing about shows, or promising to take photos or to write about shows. *How What Happened Happened* made it sound so simple yet so fortuitous at the same time. They'd just fall into it like distracted pedestrians fall into open manholes. *Wham!* and they're a part of the scene, they start their own bands and make money off their art. They abandon all fear of ever having to leave New York and return home to their parents, of becoming boring people like their parents and every other boring person in the town they're from.

I told him it did sound good. I said it carefully. It seemed too easy to be real. I was standing in the middle of a quiet campus in the summer of my eighteenth year and I had everything a person could want. I had a job offer. I would go to Moscow. I would film men in a reunited legendary punk rock band. And after I was done doing that, I would move out of my mother's town.

Maurice said that sounded awesome and gave me a quick hug. "So, can we film tonight?" he asked. I figured my aunt's birthday would be fine without me, and Christopher would never hear about it. This was my life, my calling, and my profession now. "We should film tonight," I said. "There's no time to waste!"

Maurice said he liked how official I sounded. "You're the boss, Jude!" he hollered, lifting one knee. Two female students passing by looked at us and scowled.

MAURICE HAD WRITTEN down the address of KJ & C Supplies, the place that sold Plexi-Star in town. He told me to take a cab, and dug a twenty-dollar bill out of his jean pocket. "That's for the Plexi-Star, too, though you should really start keeping an expense tab. You can deduct this stuff, right?" He laughed at his joke. I didn't know what "deducting" meant in the context.

I put the twenty in my wallet and took the bus to the south part of town. KJ & C Supplies was located in a semi-industrial area and required fifteen minutes of walking from where the bus had let me out. Once I found it, I pressed the buzzer of KJ & C, but no one came to the door. I knocked on the window, a small square of frosted wire glass that seemed it could have nothing on its other side. I gave the door a kick, but no one answered. Around me, the street was deserted. The wind was especially strong that day and garbage rattled and hopped down the length of the ditch by the sidewalk curb. I wondered if everyone who worked on this street had taken the summer off. The sound of the trash almost passed for human chatter.

"What are you doing?" a voice said.

I looked around me.

"Up here!" the voice said, sounding annoyed that I hadn't located it. "What are you doing kicking on the door?"

A window was propped open on the second floor of KJ & C and a man's head hung out. His expression was unkind. "I rang your buzzer," I said. "Thirty times."

He told me business was by appointment only and disappeared, but a minute later he opened the door and let me in. I explained, "I'm here for the star plastic." The place had a smell like when one accidentally sets a bit of their hair on fire.

"Are you the daughter of the guy that called this morning?" the man asked. His fingernails were marbled in purple and black. He scooped up a tube of translucent plastic from the floor and tied a piece of twine around its midsection, handling it with surprising care.

I said, "No, I work for him," with a pride that perhaps had no place to land at KJ & C. Still, if this gangrened old man only knew where his plastic tube would take me. That I'd be travelling to Moscow, Paris, Amsterdam...

"Sign the invoice," he said. "I specifically told your boss to give me a call before you came to pick this up. We're by appointment only if it's anything past two o'clock." I signed the invoice. Plexi-Star was apparently forty-five cents per square foot. The bill came out to over forty dollars. I had no choice, I handed over my bank card, for an account connected to my mother's. "I prefer cash," the old man said, but swiped my card through his machine anyway.

The roll was heavier than normal plastic, the weight of a large baby. I walked out the door, holding on to it like it was my dancing partner. A gust of wind blew, pushing us both, the Plexi-Star acting like a sail. I instinctively grabbed hold of a utility pole and dropped the tube. The Plexi-Star bounced once, in a clunky, elephantine way, and tipped over the curb. It travelled slowly into the middle of the street, but nothing happened to it. There were no cars coming. The wind propelled it and it rolled down the block. I followed with a motherly patience. When I reached the first intersection, I picked it up and leaned it against the bus pole. There was no sign of the bus, no cars even on the horizon. It was almost disappointing. There was no one to stop and ask me questions, when for once I had such a good story, the story of how my life had turned around.

THE STAIRCASE of the faculty housing building was drowning in Iggy Pop's "Gimme Danger." The music grew louder as I climbed the stairs to Maurice's floor. After a minute of knocking, I tried the handle. The door was unlocked. "Hey Jude!" Maurice yelled. He was sitting on the couch, the grandmotherly couch he'd complained of. He'd lifted his beer bottle as he said my name. "I love that you just walked in without knocking."

I told Maurice to go downstairs and bring up the Plexi-Star, that I'd left the tube outside, on the stoop, because my arms hurt too much from carrying it across the city. "First things first," he said, putting his finger up to shush me. "Do you like Lester Pennet?"

I said I didn't know any Lesters, and then I told him again that the star stuff was downstairs and could he please bring it up before someone stole it. "Well then you're gonna meet Lester Pennet because it's a sin to not know the best guitarist in the world." Maurice lifted his beer again and took a swig. He shook the bottle and set it down on the coffee table. The coffee table was grandmotherly too, with fluted legs and carved scenes of nymphs and peaches.

"What about the stars and filming?" I said.

Maurice shook his head. "Grab the camera! Lester's better

than plastic stars." He sprang from the couch and ran to the bathroom. In a few seconds he was back, the smell of fresh hair mousse trailing him. Outside, a cab was already waiting. Maurice jumped into the back seat and motioned for me to follow. He gave the cabbie the name of a club. Turning to me, he said, "Start recording *now*!" The car accelerated and the automatic locks on the back doors clicked. I watched the tube of Plexi-Star get left behind, leaning against the front steps of the faculty housing building, looking like left-out trash.

BY THE TIME we got to the club, Lester's set had started. This wasn't a problem. The set, beginning to end, sounded like a single song, discordant and full of jarring looped melodies, like he was purposefully trying to annoy us. The show was all-ages, and the place was divided into a part for patrons who were old enough to drink and a part for the rest of us. Maurice seemed willing to stay with me in the minors' area, at least at first. We found an empty table in the back. More and more people entered the club but few seemed interested in Lester's guitar work. Lester was one in a series of opening acts for the headlining folk-pop band.

At one point, as the looped music kept playing, Lester lifted his hand over his head and announced, "Wouldn't you fucking know it, my best friend is here tonight!" Maurice nudged me once and then another time. The second nudge was more forceful. I didn't get what was happening. Maurice leaned his head toward me and said something that I couldn't hear. The looped music played, the same four notes over and over. It sounded like a skipping carnival track. The people near the stage were looking around, disoriented but intrigued, clapping and cheering. Maurice nudged me again and said, louder, more annoyed, "Why aren't you getting this?" He pointed at my bag.

I realized he wanted me to shoot him. I pulled out the camera and pressed the power button, but the green light wouldn't come on. The battery must have died after we'd filmed too many scenes in the cab ride over. Still, I lifted the camcorder to my face. "Love you, Lester!" Maurice yelled at the stage. I panned to the stage. A couple of people called, "Woo! Blunt!" Maurice slunk back in his chair and looked ambivalent, like nothing that had just happened mattered. I made a show of pushing the Pause button. "That was great," I said. "You looked good."

WHEN LESTER WAS done, Maurice went to talk to him by the bar, where I couldn't go. I moved to another table, closer to the wall so that I could plug the camera into a socket. I took out my film notebook and revised old notes. I made new notes about inserting Plexi-Star into scenes and making stars pop and fly. I was in the middle of adding stars to a scene when a hand brushed my shoulder. "Jude?" a woman's voice said. "Your name is Jude, right?"

I instinctively hunched my shoulders. My hand covered my notebook. Bettie Page, purple across her eyelids, her lips, and a little on her cheeks, pulled out a chair and sat down next to me. I must've looked afraid because she added: "Sorry, I heard Maurice Blunt call you that after our class. That's how I know your name."

Bettie Page appeared to be working at the club. A leather fanny pack sat clipped around her waist with a rag tucked into its belt. She asked me if I was a first-year student, and I said I was, "in a way." I asked if she was one too, and she groaned and said, "I wish. I'm more like a sixth-year student," but then immediately circled back to my answer. "What do you mean by 'in a way'?"

I didn't like how inquisitive she was. "In a way," I told her, Poetry and Rock 'n' Roll was my first class, and I wasn't sure I'd take more courses. I'd been asked to attend, like a guest or someone whose job it is to take a sampling of something. I tried to explain, without really explaining, why it was I was friends with the teacher. I was nervous and likely said too much in a way that wasn't at all clear.

Bettie Page seemed only more intrigued. "So you're just auditing the class?" she said. I didn't know what "auditing" meant, and anyway, at this point Maurice hollered, "Jude, c'mere, quick! Lester's on a fucking roll. I need you to film this." He yelled my name a second time, but then immediately lost interest as three women holding beers approached him and Lester. Lester pushed his stool aside to make room for the ladies. The five of them huddled. It appeared maybe Lester knew the women. Bettie Page remained sitting next to me. Her eyes travelled from Maurice and the ladies to me and back to Maurice again. I didn't understand why she didn't have work to do and could waste time sitting at a table. "You're *filming* him?" she finally asked.

Her eyes now stopped on the charging camera and my notebook, the cover of which said Film Notes. I couldn't read her tone. She was careful to not betray what she was really thinking. I could tell she was unimpressed, but I couldn't say whether it was with the idea of filming someone itself or filming Maurice Blunt. "I'm lending him support. We work together," I said carefully. "I work for the Sateelites," I immediately added, which made the whole thing sound more professional. I relaxed as soon as I said it.

Bettie Page lifted her painted-in eyebrows. "The Sateelites are still together? I thought they'd all overdosed," she said.

I felt she and I were destined to come upon a series of walls. "I'm moving to New York soon," I said, with the same confidence, feeling my story on a smooth track. I told her I was a videographer for the band and that we were going on a world tour. Bettie Page simply nodded, she seemed satisfied, at least enough to stand up after that. She said she'd see me in class soon and added, "Good luck with all that."

I watched her wipe down a nearby table and pick up an empty glass. I didn't like what those parting words implied. Any good luck was already mine.

I CAME HOME close to midnight and found my mother on the couch, eating grapes and watching television. I apologized for missing my aunt's birthday dinner and said I'd had a lot of work for a group assignment in class. "It's okay, your aunt understands," she said. "You're in university now and that's nothing to take lightly. Grad schools will see these marks..." She kept talking as I walked to the kitchen and grabbed a bunch of grapes for myself. I dropped my bag with the camcorder next to the coffee table. I sat next to my mother. She was in her pajamas and her bare feet were curled under her. I lay down and pressed the top of my head into her thigh.

"I'm so proud of you, little girl. Of how seriously you're taking school. Signing up for classes before the term's even begun. You're going to get so far in life. Not like me." I looked at the floor and my bag, and I could see the hard, blocky shape of the camcorder.

I turned my face into the couch cushion and started crying. It was a silent cry, barely physical. My mother kept changing channels and talking. I didn't know how I could ever tell her that I had taken a job as a videographer for the reunion tour of a middle-aged man's band, and that I would be moving away. I couldn't even tell who I felt more sorry for, myself, for not being able to do it, or her, because it would kill her if I did. When my face dried, I turned it back to the TV. At that moment, I didn't want anything. I didn't want New York, or Maurice. I didn't want my mother either. I wanted to be completely alone, in a no-place, with no memory of the past either.

"*Bo*-ring, *bo*-ring," my mother said as she flipped channels.

"Wait, Mommy. Go back to the last one," I said. I lifted my head. I wasn't sure whether I'd seen what I thought I had just seen.

On a tacky, glossy-floored stage with a fake skyline backdrop, a model-pretty girl was shaking her shaggy blond hair and singing the outro of a song. She was giving it to a black-and-white guitar, wearing a sailor style little girl's dress from the sixties, red leggings, and toe-less silver booties. It looked a bit derivative of Kim Gordon, but still, I had to admit, she looked great.

My mother turned the volume up. "Is this Letterman?" she asked.

Well, actually, it was Jeremy's band. I could see him behind the singer, waving his drumsticks around.

"This girl has a lot of confidence," my mom said as the blond woman pretended to smash her guitar against an amp at the end of the song, but then laughed and brushed her hand in the air as if to say, "Just kidding, everyone!"

The host ran out to shake her hand. Jeremy stood up, but

remained behind his kit, the way he'd probably been told to do by the show's producer. He was dressed in a stupid-looking denim jacket with acid-washed parts on the front. His hair was longer and fell over his eyes. He fiddled awkwardly with the tip of a drumstick, waiting for the host to finally be done talking to the singer. But the singer was telling a long story. She gripped the host's wrist, waved her free hand, and threw her head back in laughter. Then the credits started rolling.

"She doesn't have the class, the grace of a Judy Garland, though," my mother went on.

"You can turn channels now, Mommy," I said. I couldn't stomach it any longer.

She resumed her flipping. "*Bo*-ring. *Bo*-ring," she said.

18

O f course I still wanted Maurice, and I wanted New York City. Seeing Jeremy on TV only reinforced that. Imagine watching someone have their Beatles-on-*Ed-Sullivan* moment when only three months earlier they were making out with you in a sordid alley, and it seemed that sordid alley was as far as either of you would ever get in life. So, the next morning I left my house at eight and walked to Maurice's apartment. It took a while for him to answer the door.

"C'mere," he said once he'd let me in. He shuffled back to the bedroom while rubbing his eyes, fell onto the mattress, and wrapped the bedsheet around him, covering his face. "Nap with me for a bit?" he mumbled. "Lester came by after you left last night. I've had two hours of sleep."

I remained at the bedside, my arms crossed, and the messenger bag with Dana's camcorder and my film ideas notebook strung across my chest.

"No, Maurice," I said. "Let's go. I want to film in morning light. Get out of bed." I gave his back a hard shove and he started laughing from under the sheet. When he went quiet, I walked over to the window and threw the curtain open. "Rise and shine!" I yelled and I hit him on the back again.

Maurice lifted the sheet, exposing his hair and a piece of forehead. I could tell he was smiling. He pushed the rest of the sheet away and swung his bare legs up and out of bed. He sat on the edge, wincing from the light. His black jeans lay crumpled at his feet. The Plexi-Star lay unfurled, spread next to the bed like a rug. I knelt down, moved Maurice's boot off of it, and rolled the Plexi-Star into a tube. Maurice was still sitting there, rubbing his eyes, swinging his feet a little. "I love how you said, 'Get out of bed' and yanked on the curtains. You're the boss," he said and yawned.

THERE'S A HIGHWAY underpass in my city, northeast of the downtown, not quite suburban, but in a quiet part. It'd always been my favourite place to drive through whenever Alex and Christopher would aimlessly cruise the town with me stuck in the back seat.

"You'll see why it's great," I told Maurice. "You'll see once we're there."

Our cab stopped at the periphery of the underpass. On a late weekday morning, traffic was light. Maurice jumped out and I remained in the back seat, rooting in my purse for cash.

"Jude! Let's do this. What'cha still doing in the cab?" Maurice yelled from the sidewalk. "Just give the man some money," he said, then turned the line into a song, an altered version of the Beatles' "Money." He started clapping his hands to the beat, puckering his lips and lifting his face to the sky. I handed the cabbie a twenty and told him to keep the change.

Once the cab left, Maurice and I walked to opposite sides of the street. I turned on Dana's camcorder. Maurice stuck both hands in his pockets, elbows pushed back, torso puffed, chin up, and looked into the lens.

"Good!" I yelled. "Now walk slowly from one end to the other."

Maurice did as I told him. He looked ahead the whole time. These were good shots.

"Now lean against the wall, off-centre, by that thunderbolt," I instructed.

The walls of the underpass were uniformly covered in graffiti: squiggles, slurs, genitalia. It was sparse, its elements well placed, nothing trespassing on anything else, almost like it was curated. Taking up the central panel were two words. Pristine and protected from the elements by the shadow of the arch, they were spray-painted in plain black, childishly simple block letters; they'd been there my whole life: BIG DEAL.

I wanted Maurice right at the end of "big deal," an exclamation point capping that sentiment. I've always loved how it could go both ways. An ironic denunciation or a pompous remark. It all depends on the delivery and, of course, written words can't talk.

WHEN WE GOT back to his campus apartment, Maurice went straight for the couch. "Uff," he said, collapsing on the cushion. "You worked me hard today. I need a beer."

I set the bag with the camcorder on the armchair next to him and stood in front of the couch with my arms crossed. "Good job," I said. "Now I need some footage of Mark and Jamie, and the three of you together, obviously." It was the first time I'd said those names aloud. It still felt like a transgression, but my talk with Bettie Page the night before had left me feeling like I needed to prove my professionalism, to embrace my new career so that no one could question it. I was a videographer, hired by the reunited Sateelites. I could speak their names.

"Yeah, when we get back to New York we will. For sure," Maurice said. His head was thrown all the way back and his eyes were half closed. He wanted to take a nap, I could tell.

"C'mere," he said and put his hands out with a sloppy thrust, like a child that doesn't exactly know what it wants, only that it wants. I edged toward him. He rested his hands on my hips and pulled me the rest of the way toward him, parking me between his knees. He shifted forward and lay his head on my stomach. Gently, his forehead rubbed back and forth across my shirt. I uncrossed my arms and placed my hands on his hair. It was the first time I'd seen it from this high of an angle. I pushed my fingers into it. It felt coarse and brittle. I moved some of it around. The congealed clumps broke apart like two sides of a pea pod. Rivulets of grey that were invisible from the outside coursed through the cross-sections. I thought of dissections from biology class and the veins inside a mouse or plant.

Maurice shook his head. He wanted me out of his hair. He craned his head back to get a good look at my stomach. He lifted my shirt, to just below my bra. He pressed his cheek to my skin and then immediately lifted it away and gave the skin around my navel two very slow kisses. This was what Christopher and I had done to his baby half-brother for a while. Before he turned into a monster who demanded all of my aunt's attention, we would take turns kissing him, right above his belly button. Maurice let my shirt fall back down. I took a step back.

"Thanks for today," he said, "it was the best morning of my life."

I smiled and said that we'd done solid work.

"You're such a disciplinarian," he said. "But it's nice. You keep me on track. I need that. Thanks for getting me out of bed this morning. You're the perfect assistant. More than an assistant, obviously. Co-person. The person who makes sure I get shit done."

My face flushed and I said, "You're welcome." It was the first time Maurice had acknowledged that I was a professional, and that without me, his band might never go on tour. I took another step back.

"You're welcome," he mocked me, smiling. He reached across a couch cushion to grab the remote for a little stereo that sat on the mantle. He pressed Play. A CD started playing. The first track of *Initials B.B.* came on. I said, cool. I was feeling unusually shy. Maybe it was the compliment I'd just gotten, and the alien quality of the campus apartment, no Lexa, and bad furniture with a sweet lacquer smell. Still, I turned in a half twist, going one way and the other, like a swinging saloon door.

"Sorry, this apartment's awful." He lifted his arms, up over his head, and yawned. "Soon we can hang out in my place again. Forget about this nursing home."

"Yeah, your grandma's place."

"Exactly. New York's our home."

It was like he'd read my mind. Hearing the word "home" was what I needed. Just that, one syllable, to show me I belonged there already. I danced toward a full-length mirror and stopped before it. I smiled at my reflection. Maurice turned up the music, a call for me to do something, to take advantage of the mirror, this prop, like a girl in an MTV video would. I leisurely stretched my arms outward and up. I made starfish arms. I was Debbie Harry. No, I was Lizzy Mercier slinking onstage after an introduction from Serge Gainsbourg, my French television debut.

I pushed my hair up and let it rain back down. Maurice was still on the couch, three feet away, observing. I thought he'd love it and that it would make him laugh. "You look beautiful," he said, and I smiled without taking my eyes off my reflection and did another half twist, to the left. "With your tiny, underdeveloped breasts," he added, and my eyes remained fixed on my eyes, and my body finished its move by twisting to the right, so that Maurice wouldn't know I knew what he was talking about, so that maybe he'd think I hadn't heard despite him having been loud and articulate.

I STUDIED THEM later that day in the bathroom, as the soapy smell of my mother's asparagus slipped in under the door. I took off my shirt and looked, then pushed them up and together, augmenting them. There wasn't much there, but it was enough to form the general shape of spheres. I sat on the bathroom floor for a while. My shirt and bra were draped over the edge of the tub. I heard the oven door slam and the clatter of cutlery. Then I heard something new, a knock on the front door. I pressed my ear to the bathroom door to listen. I heard the overexcitement of my mother, greeting a guest. I put my clothes back on and opened the bathroom door.

Our table was set for its usual two, but Christopher and Alex were already seated there as my mother pulled extra plates from the cupboard. The table was so small that the plates, once there were four, encroached on one another, each plate lifting the one next to it off the table. The cutlery had to sit in our laps. "Just like in the old days, eh, Chris?" my mother said. Christopher hated having his name truncated, or to be reminded of a time when he'd spent more time with my mother, but he forced a smile. A casserole dish sat in the centre of the table, filled with pap the colour of toad shit.

"This looks great," Alex said, scooping up some pap and dumping it on his plate. "Thank you for accommodating us so last-minute." My mother answered that it was just "a humble mishmash." Alex shook his head no and Christopher tore the heel off a baguette.

I knew that everything happening before me was a feast of falsehoods, a little presentation: Christopher's half-assed smiles and Alex's savoir faire, the way they stomached the food and voluntarily scooped out seconds. I knew they were there to show me what they were capable of, that they could unilaterally arrange for meetings with my mother, sit across a table from her, and talk. Only I wasn't sure what they had to spill. I tried to catch Christopher's eyes, to gauge what he'd told Alex: New York City weekend escapades? Sharing a bed with an old man? Screwing him for airfare? I gave my cousin a gentle kick underneath the table, but he didn't react. Each time someone opened their mouth, I expected it to slip out, easy as a little belch, the one topic that could bring everything down: my supposed weekends at the coach house, my weekends in New York, the improbability of a university class being open to someone who'd not even paid her tuition, or of a perfectly functional phone breaking all the time, the drawer that at one point had a stack of money in it going empty, the way I'd clutched Maurice Blunt's poetry book that day. It was incredible, actually, how much live, smoking ammunition Christopher, Alex, and my mother had, and how, come to think of it, I had absolutely nothing on my end.

After clearing away our plates, my mother served dessert. She'd stuck wooden tongue depressors into a six-pack of yogurt cups like a coworker had told her to, and put them in the freezer. Her popsicles came out squat and cylindrical, tasting of watery milk, and it took a long time to lick them down. The conversation died and the sound of our disgusting slurps filled the apartment. When we were finished, my mother asked, "What next?" and Alex said it was best they got back home. My mother pressed her hands to her cheeks. "I figured," she said. "I'm jealous. One day I'll save up to buy a house outside of the city. I'd love to have my own chickens." She started talking about a fantasy coop, and of being woken by nature's alarm clock each morning. Other than her serving chicken for every other meal, I'd never known she had an interest in them.

"You want to be a chicken farmer?" Christopher asked. It was one of the few things he'd offered all evening. She laughed, wrapped her arms around his waist, and laid her head on his shoulder in an overly familiar way. He let her hang off him for two seconds, then wriggled from under her, walked toward the door, and out onto the stairwell, not looking back. In the end, the conversation about the chicken coop was as out-there as it got. We'd discussed Alex's mother's upcoming wedding, her fiancé, the weather, Christopher's half-brother's impending registration in first grade, the Pennsylvania woman on CNN charged with murdering her child, and Taffy, the missing dog, whose poster, Alex said, he had seen for the first time that day, stapled to a pole next to where they'd parked the car.

I SPENT THE remaining hours of daylight on the sill, looking out our living-room window. I'd forgotten about my breasts, but then I remembered. The breasts made me forget for a moment about the dinner. And then they switched places, the breasts would disappear, and the dinner would return, only to be replaced by the other things on my mind: the strange way in which Alex and Christopher could insert themselves in our apartment without notice. And how eager my mother was for their presence. How easily the hand had slipped into the back of my shorts in the used clothing store in Manhattan. The way Maurice manoeuvred in New York, slicing through its streets, almost cold in his execution. His dick a pine cone he wanted the world to know about. Every thought I had was an individual rolling wave, incrementally erasing the previous one, but only by covering it, and sending it back to where it'd originated. Nothing could be gotten rid of, only momentarily obscured. All of it remained inside, in the basin, cooking in the sun, the fish and the whales laughing at me. Within two weeks I'd amassed something like an ocean's worth of concerns.

The sun finally started setting, and it turned out to be a showstopper. Neons, purples, pinks, peaches, all mixed together in the bowl of the sky. The clouds were marbled, mottled, fibrous. One I could actually swear was shaped like a waving hand. I saw people walking below stop and look up, which inspired others to also stop. "So pretty," I said to my mother, who sat only a foot behind me, her fingers on the clicker, staring at the television. I rested my forehead on the insect screen and pushed my body weight forward; if the screen gave out, I thought, I'd go tumbling to my death. Or maybe three storeys wouldn't add up to death, and only my ribs would suffer, or a hip or shoulder. Suddenly my mother was behind me, no longer watching TV, but pulling her hands around my waist, the way she'd done with Christopher. She rested her chin on the top of my head and asked if I'd finished tomorrow's homework. "Who are you reading in class now?" she asked. "Is it a poet you like?"

"Plath," I said, because I knew she knew her, to make her feel a part of things. "I like Plath because she understands tragedy," I added.

"Yes. She's my favourite for that as well," my mother said, before starting on the sunset, how if a spectacle like this couldn't bring Taffy back, nothing could, she was certain of it. I made a sound like I understood and agreed, and leaned back against my mother, though I had no idea how the two things connected: a dog and a beautiful sky.

19

I decided I'd go to one more Maurice class and then quit. I didn't want to leave without saying goodbye to the old man. But it seemed pointless to attend any further classes when I hardly listened to what Maurice said and instead drew pictures, or took film notes, or wrote my own poems. Throughout the lectures, Maurice and I would give each other knowing looks. We were equals. Poetry and Rock 'n' Roll no longer made sense for me. Just before I'd left his apartment for JFK on the weekend, I told Maurice I might make Wednesday my last day. He'd responded with, "I said it from the start: you're a poet. You should be teaching *me* this stuff."

I'd hoped for a quiet, easy class of Maurice reading his poetry, but it turned out to be the day he announced the final assignment on which most of the course's grade would be based. If people wanted, they could write an essay on any topic involving poetry and the scene of mid to late '70s New York. Or else they could do a "creative intervention," and, working in a group, adapt one of Maurice's poems into another medium, like a play, a short story, or even a song. The catch was that the story or play or song would have to be performed in front of the class for it to count. "I'm not precious about my poetry," Maurice said. "Destroy it, cut it up, mash it up, reshape it, trample it. Make me unrecognizable to myself, I would love that best."

Someone raised their hand and asked if they could set one of Maurice's poems to the music of the Sateelites, and Maurice screamed, "Nooo! The Sateelites is still me! Gain distance, get as fucking far from Maurice Blunt as you can and make this your thing. I'm the fucking Old Testament God. Run!"

The class laughed and then the frenzy of students moving their chairs to form groups with other students started. I appreciated how the old man turned to me without needing to ask if we wanted to form a pair, though within seconds, Bettie Page pulled her chair up to us as well, barely making eye contact. It seemed she and the old man knew each other from other classes. He called her Jennifer and she called him Ron. Our group of three was officially constituted on some kind of understanding or vote I wasn't privy to. "I love it how we're limited to Maurice Blunt's poetry," Jennifer said, curling her painted lip and starting a doodle on her notepad. Ron scoffed, shook his head, and said, "Can we just jerk him off, get our A+, and leave?" They both laughed, not really checking if I found it funny too. Still, I smiled; it seemed that was required of me as one-third of the creative intervention group. I'd had the feeling that Jennifer wasn't crazy about Maurice, but had no idea about the old man, that he could joke about jerking Maurice off.

We tried talking about which poem might be best to adapt. Ron and Jennifer went off on tangents, talking about other classes they had and professors they knew. At the end of class Jennifer tore out a page in her notepad and wrote her phone number and address on it. The unilateral decision was made that we'd meet at her apartment that evening to properly start our assignment. "Let's order some food, put on mood music, and practise the best three-way hand job," she said. Ron said he'd bring the bananas. I took the piece of paper with Jennifer's number and address but secretly, happily, had already decided I'd not show up, that those two would never hear from me again. I said goodbye to the old man when I got up to leave. "It's been really nice sitting next to you in Poetry and Rock 'n' Roll," I said. "I wish you all the best."

TEN MINUTES LATER I was walking through the campus by myself when I saw a familiar object trundling down the drivable path. Given the slow and uncertain way it inched along, I knew the Honda was being driven by Christopher, which meant he was alone. My first thought was to hide behind some people or a tree, but a greater, wiser impulse overpowered the first and I ran toward the car, calling my cousin's name and looking like someone innocently flagging down her ride. Soon after, the car disappeared around a corner and when I looked down the way it'd gone, I couldn't see it anymore. A number of roads forked in various directions, some of them marked For Campus Vehicles Only. I walked home, hurried and nervous. Maybe this didn't make sense, but the picture that seemed most likely to me right then was my cousin on the living-room couch, commiserating with my mother, telling her about New York and Maurice after having just confirmed I was indeed in his class. And her of course not understanding the true meaning of Maurice, and the spectrum of friendships that could exist, especially in a place like New York.

When I reached the top of our street, I broke into a jog. At home, I found no one.

IT MAY HAVE been something to do with accumulation, and the human limit for carrying concerns stacked on you like bricks in a barrow, but on that afternoon I felt I'd reached a new level of despair. The concern over whether Maurice did or did not want me seemed for the time ancient and juvenile. If anything, now that I was officially hired by his band, his constant calling was annoying me and added to the worry that my mother would one day pick up and he'd forget to tell her "wrong number." It was Christopher I wanted to hear from now, but the phone sat silent. Once my mother arrived home from work and returned a look that told me nothing had changed in her conception of the world and her daughter's place in it, I felt a slight unburdening. Christopher hadn't blabbed. He hadn't paid a visit to the library branch where she worked and hadn't called her there on her private desk number to share any recent discovery.

Spurred by my luck, I said, "I'm going to my friend Jennifer's house to work on a school assignment." The rush of speaking something true for once made me delirious. I felt blessed for the opportunity, almost like I owed Jennifer and Ron a thank-you for being in on my grand Maurice plan.

Before I left, I said it again, at least two more times, very emphatically. "*I am going to visit a classmate named Jennifer and we will be working on a school assignment.*"

JENNIFER LIVED IN an apartment above a bakery, on a busy street near the university. "How's the movie business?" she said as soon as I sat down. Her tone was over-friendly, nothing like it had been at the club two days earlier. I didn't trust her. I also wanted to make sure she wouldn't tell people about the Sateelites tour, which I hadn't gotten official permission to advertise. I was about to answer when someone knocked on the door. I figured it was Ron. "Hold that thought," she said, lifting her finger.

A man about Jennifer's age stuck his head in. He was wearing loose orange jeans and a T-shirt with the sleeves torn off, had a ruddy beard, and held a beer can in his hand. He looked like he didn't have a home. Jennifer spoke quietly to him while blocking the entryway with her body. I heard her say, "Not now." The man turned around and left. Jennifer pushed the door shut.

"That was Ricky," she said, waving her hand to say Ricky was nothing. "So, anyway, how's your movie?" She sat back down opposite me. I asked where Ron was and Jennifer sighed and said, "We'll be lucky if we hear from him. He's probably out on a date or riding his motorbike or something."

I couldn't tell if Jennifer was kidding by listing activities that were the last thing that a man Ron's age would do. But then again, I didn't really know Ron. Until that afternoon, I hadn't known his name.

"My movie's a long way from finished," I eventually answered. I didn't like that Jennifer had called my work a movie when it was, professionally speaking, only promo clips, but I liked that I'd misled her and created at least that bit of distance between her and the truth.

"So, if you're auditing the class, why are you doing the assignment?"

Jennifer seemed intent on asking questions in the way of a hardline journalist. I merely shrugged and said something about wanting to be part of things and looking for academic experience. After that, we sat in silence for a long moment. "I've been wanting to ask, how do you like working for the Sateelites?" she finally said. The sheepish note in her voice made the whole visit worthwhile. I felt vindicated for how little I'd trusted her. I'd known she'd want to pry, that she was lying in wait and sidestepping the biggest subject: what it's like to be friends with a poet and his famous band from New York.

"I'm not allowed to talk about it," I said simply. "I shouldn't have mentioned the tour. Don't tell anyone." She nodded and I sensed a shift in power, it was mine now because I'd told her what to do.

There was nothing stopping me from leaving. The visit felt useless, beyond providing a narrative of campus friendships for my mother. But that was done now. I stood up and said to Jennifer that it was best if she and Ron did the assignment themselves, and that I wouldn't be coming to class anymore. It possibly came out sounding aggrieved, the way it was so sudden. Jennifer pushed out her bottom lip, then said, "Oh okay. But before you go, I thought you might be interested in seeing something."

She stood up and motioned for me to follow, past a brocade curtain, into a bedroom. I thought I'd indulge her. Or I thought I could get a good story for Maurice out of the visit. Inside Jennifer's bedroom, the walls were covered in roses. Roses exploding, roses wilting, roses blooming, roses losing petals, bees landing on roses. She must've seen how awed I was by the roses. "How did you do this?" I said. For the first time, I felt easy in her presence, or perhaps just distracted enough to feel easy. "I'd love for my room to look like this."

Jennifer told me she had an artist friend who only did work featuring roses. She'd printed the panels for her walls. "But this is what I meant to show you, actually," she said, pulling a wheeled clothing rack into the centre of the room. "Check it out!" she said, making a game-show-model gesture with her hand. She pushed the rack another inch toward me.

There were about thirty items of clothing hanging on the rack, mainly black, but some dark green and purple. I touched the closest item, slow and unsure of what I was supposed to be doing. A tag that had been pinned to the hem of a blouse read "Big Bad Wolf." There was a heart around "Bad" and a second, larger heart around the whole phrase "Big Bad Wolf." Most of the clothing had some form of rose pattern on it. There was a connection between the walls and the clothing as I understood it.

"Your friend made these clothes," I said.

Jennifer shook her head. "I'm Big Bad Wolf," she said, pointing at herself. "My friend designed the fabrics."

I liked the clothes a lot more now. They had a bit of a vampire quality, but overall I was impressed by how professional they looked. They had zippers and snap buttons. The hems were straight and the stitches didn't show. I held up a mod-style A-line dress with an oversized rose pattern that was the exact replica of the wall panels. "Pat Austin roses," Jennifer said and gently pulled the hanger out of my hand. She pressed the dress against me. "Try it on!" she said. "This would be great for New York. You can borrow it."

I wasn't sure what kind of transaction we'd initiated, but in the moment, it seemed a simple enough act to try the dress on, then leave it on her bed and walk out of her apartment once I was done. I started pulling the dress over my T-shirt and Jennifer shrieked, though she started laughing too. "Lift!" she ordered, holding my hands up. She peeled off my T-shirt and pulled the dress over my bra. I unzipped my shorts and Jennifer pulled the dress down, tugging near the hips so that it sat right. She didn't seem interested in my underwear or what I looked like without my top layer of clothes.

"Are you a professional fashion designer?" I asked.

"I wish," she said. "I mainly sell these on eBay."

I was about to ask more about that—it seemed absurd that this level of quality wasn't enough to get Jennifer's clothes into real stores—but I heard a faint, everyday human sound just then. Behind me, I saw the man who'd come to the door earlier, Ricky, sitting cross-legged against the wall, looking comfortable like he'd been there for more than a few minutes. He cleared his throat. Jennifer didn't seem to mind him. She'd entered a state of reverie, standing back and staring at the dress very critically. At one point, with her eyes still on the dress, she said, unconvincingly, "I told you to come back later," to Ricky. He answered, "It is later," completely without irony.

Once Jennifer seemed satisfied with the dress, she started scooping my hair in her hands, over and over like she was sifting flour. She hadn't asked permission. It was as if the hair was merely a continuation of the dress, and I understood that for a fashion designer there might be no border between where the clothing ends and a model and her hair begins. In that moment, in Jennifer's rose bedroom, it was easy to appreciate the allure of a modelling career, of becoming an art object. It was the most myself I'd felt in weeks, maybe because here was the freedom to hide behind the screen of supposed aesthetic appeal. I knew that neither Jennifer nor Ricky was looking at me, really, yet I was being regarded with such focused care and love. Jennifer stammered something and asked if I'd mind holding on for one second. She ran out of the room and returned with a metal toolbox in her arms. Her unself-conscious, frazzled energy had something very genuine about it. It would be hard to imitate or mask anything while acting the way she was. Minutes earlier, I'd believed her to be wrapped in dis-guises, and now here I was, with a stupid smile on my face.

Jennifer set the box on the bed and undid its latch. The box opened in the style of an accordion, revealing multiple floors, a whole staircase of little compartments stacked with bottles and jars. "Let's see, all right. Manhattan. Holly Golightly. Debbie Harry. Edie Sedgwick," she chanted. "Let's do this," she said, uncapping a blue crayon and bringing it to my eye.

"Jennifer's really good at this," Ricky said, sounding half-conscious. He'd moved so that he could see better and kept his lips slightly parted as Jennifer painted lines across my face. "That looks good," he said when she was done. His glum tone wasn't an insult. He spoke every word in that way, I realized. Jennifer took my hand and led me to her bathroom. Ricky followed us. He'd procured a tabby cat that he now held against him like a sleeping infant. There were more roses in the bathroom. A rose-patterned shower curtain. A bowl of rose-shaped soaps and a framed photo of a rose on top of the toilet tank.

"What do you think?" Jennifer said.

I brought my face closer to the mirror.

If only I'd been someone other than me, I wouldn't have looked half bad. I had the purple lips that Jennifer'd had one of the times I'd seen her. A halo of black, something like residue from an explosion, around my eyes. Eyelashes like daisy petals. And cheeks crossed with pink like I was running a fever. "So good," I said.

"This is how you'll conquer Manhattan," Jennifer said.

"Thanks," I told her. "I really appreciate this." My cheek muscles felt weighed down by the blanket of powder. The mascara made my eyes unable to open all the way. But I felt truly prepared for something by someone who understood how much it meant to look good, even if that involved becoming someone different. I decided I liked her, once and for all. She was a generous person, giving like a mother, but without the wild, unbearable parts.

I left her place and walked home holding a little zippered makeup pouch and the rose dress, which she'd packed for me in a brown paper bag. The change in reaction was startling. A driver rolled his window down at a four-way stop and asked me where I was headed, how my night was, how old I was. Men walking on the main thoroughfare stared me up and down. I figured women like Lexa and Jennifer got this all the time. It was an odd power to have. A power I wasn't sure what I could do with.

I thought about the man with the forehead writing and how my current look would keep him at bay. This look was an armour and seemed to tell others I had direction.

In the bathroom of the Burger King across the street from the repertory cinema, I soaked paper towels with soap and water and rubbed them into my lips and eyes until my old face came back. A Burger King employee walked in just as I was finishing up. "Tough day?" she asked, looking at the balled paper. I said that wasn't really it. And she said, "Gotcha," understanding, I guess, that sometimes a problem is best explained by holding back the details.

I dried my face by crouching underneath the hand dryer.

I felt better being the former me.

For the rest of my walk home, no one stopped me or looked my way.

THE PHONE RANG around one in the morning, waking me. I snatched the receiver, pressed it against my covers, and listened for my mother. I heard nothing. She was either asleep or accustomed to these calls by now.

"Maurice?" I said.

"Hey, Jude!" It sounded like he was on the street. "Did I wake you?"

"No," I said in a whisper.

"Wait, I can't hear you. I can't hear you. Call you back, okay?"

I said okay, even though I knew he couldn't hear me.

"Or, call *me* back in an hour, call me in an hour so I don't wake your parents."

I hung up, turned on my bedside lamp, and opened *How What Happened Happened*. When the time came, I dialled Maurice's number, I had no choice. It was my first time calling him from our home phone. I figured if my mother asked about the bill and a New York area code, I'd say it was a mistake and let her hound the phone company about it.

When Maurice picked up, I could hear a muted New York behind him. I asked what he was up to. I could tell he'd had some beers. He told me that after flying back to the city, he'd spent the evening with Jamie, and they'd gone to a friend's gallery opening. Then they went back to the studio. They'd been writing new material and practising old songs for months. He started telling me about the songs. The new ones and the old, in too much detail.

"So, what did you do today?" Maurice asked when he was done.

I glanced at Jennifer's dress, hanging on my closet door, its contour illuminated by the moonlight, or maybe just the electric lights on the street. "Nothing," I said.

"Are you sleepy?" he asked.

"Sort of," I said.

"You're in bed?"

"Well, yeah. It's past two in the morning." There was something about his question that I did not like. I felt it creep into my bed, simply by his asking about my bed.

"Is it a small bed?"

"It's normal." I laughed a stilted laugh. I imagined the mounting long-distance dollars for each second Maurice asked me about my bed, and my mother's hands combing the bill.

"Is it the size of *my* bed? I mean, would we both fit on it the way we do on my bed?"

"About that size, yeah. It's a twin."

"You wear your jean cutoffs to bed at home as well or do you change into something different?"

I wanted him to change the subject.

"No," I answered.

There was a long silence.

"Do you like your bed?" he asked.

"Not really. It's from a Sears catalogue, and when it arrived, my mother asked the men who were only meant to deliver the box to also put it together, and said she'd let them stay over for dinner if they did. They said they couldn't, they had so many deliveries to make. I think they could tell she was crazy."

For a moment I believed he'd laugh, but Maurice only gave a long sigh, as if I'd completely exhausted him with the story. "I'm going to sleep," he said. He didn't sound unkind, but it was more direct than usual.

"Wait," I said, "I have ideas for promo clips I've been wanting to talk through." It was a lie, but still, he stayed on the line.

"Oh yeah, what?" he said.

I told Maurice we could incorporate the content of the cassette tape Alex had made for me, about the pool of oblivion, all that strange ethereal nonsense, and play it as the stars shoot out of the Plexi-Star.

Maurice didn't answer right away. I heard a sound like he was turning over papers. "We can try it," he eventually said.

"Okay," I said. "So, good night?" I spoke slowly, hoping he'd interject and say something happy. I felt like I'd messed things up for no good reason.

"Sleep well," he said in the same grim tone, and after that the line went dead.

20

On Thursday morning at seven thirty, the phone rang before my mother left for work. It was Christopher calling from the coach house and it might've been the happiest I'd ever felt to hear his voice. I hoped for relief from the bricks that sat upon me and I asked about the pool first. I thought of it as an easy conversation starter, and I expected him to tell me all about his latest attempts at clearing bushes, and whatever it was they'd now graduated to believe the water would do for them. But Christopher seemed put off by the idea that I'd want to know.

"You never call," he said. "Actually, you've been kicked out, and never once asked if you could be readmitted or if we forgive you. And now you want intel about the pool? Yeah, right!" he said.

When I didn't answer, he added, "Is your poetry class over and you're bored now or something?"

I had no way in after that. I tried asking what was the matter, as if all the things that I'd done wrong and he'd listed couldn't be it. I knew they weren't it. Maybe for Alex they were, but not for Christopher. Yet he said nothing.

A few days earlier, I'd thought of something to use on my cousin. It was a direct confrontation technique, a type of undistilled honesty meant to come at a person with the suddenness and shock of being physically jumped upon in one's sleep. I'd hoped to do this in person—it was one of the reasons why I'd run after his car—but I could see now the phone was the best opportunity I'd get.

"Christopher," I started, "are you not tired of Alex's imperiousness?" I'd learned the word "imperious" from Maurice. I'd only heard it the last weekend, when he used it to describe his late father. I'd said, "Did you just say 'imperial'?" and he said, "Close enough." Maurice didn't ask me for my own father-story, but I told him anyway. I said my mother had gone on dates with a series of men, the year she turned twenty-six. She eventually became pregnant and had no intention of telling anyone, or even doing the math to figure out which of the men had spawned me. That was the plan all along. Then I said I believed all fathers aspired to that, imperiousness, and all mothers aspired to martyrdom, making for a very balanced situation in the home. Maurice laughed, and said he looked forward to being a father, with the implication I think being that he would never be imperious.

I could easily imagine that part, but not the part of Maurice actually having a child. It was the syphoning it would require, which seemed a type of death, something Maurice was actively and furiously averse to, from what I could tell.

Christopher seemed to have a very ready answer to my question about imperiousness, so ready I suspected he asked himself the same thing every day. Or maybe he just imagined me asking it and now he had the satisfaction of finally getting to answer.

"Life is imperious, everything and everyone is, the only difference is that Alex is actually *smart*." I had nothing ready to respond to that bumper sticker of a statement. And if I drove around in a car with that pasted on the back, I'd for sure leave whole highways of people scratching their heads. Smart how? He had large numbers of his father's books and records on his shelves, and he could maybe define "imperious." But other than that, he was just someone with money who'd recently graduated high school.

"Alex understands things no one else does, not anyone's mothers or fathers, not anyone who's written a book, not even you," Christopher went on. As he rattled off his list, I braced myself for a mention of Maurice: not even Maurice Blunt, the person you believe is smartest. Maurice, who hovers over every conversation, especially over every lie you tell your friends and mother, who hovers over your bed, your mother's apartment, your telephone wires, the trees on your street.

But Christopher never did bring him up, and I wondered how long something so present, large, and full could continue to exist only in a state of hover. Eventually he'd have to come down, crashing onto everyone and everything I had.

The only good that came out of our conversation was that I remembered about Christopher's mother. I apologized for not having checked in on her like I said I would, to ask her how she was and wish her a happy birthday. I immediately understood that that was the thing Christopher was angry about. Of course. It all comes down to mothers. Maybe Maurice came down to a mother, too. Maybe for him, I somehow came down to a mother. My cousin paused for a while, then said he'd known I wouldn't hold up my end of the deal, that I was so self-centred. "I guarded the line for the whole weekend," he said, "and the phone's been ringing a lot around here. The pool repair people keep calling, and Alex's mother. And sometimes the guy she's going to marry calls, I think when she's too annoyed and has questions about the pool progress." He said my mother did call once over the weekend, to ask if he knew what time I'd be back Sunday. It seemed like a completely random question, and like she was really only checking that I was there.

Christopher said she then went on to talk about Taffy, how Taffy's owner had gone around knocking on doors that weekend, to ask if anyone had any new clues, the whole situation having grown to the level of an unsolved murder. I asked if my mother had had a clue, and my cousin said he didn't know, he hadn't thought to ask her.

"I told her you were outside planting a tree for the wedding, so you couldn't come to the phone."

"A tree!" I said. "A wedding tree? What kind?"

I could tell he'd shrugged; I knew him so well. But I could also tell he was smiling.

"She believed you?" I said. "You have to tell me what kind of tree in case she asks."

"She's very imaginative. But I didn't say what kind of tree. It's all the same. Just make a tree up." He started to shrink away again and then said, more threateningly, "You have to see my mother by this Friday, ask her how she's doing, what my brother's up to, and get back to me. Or else I won't watch the phone for you this weekend, or ever again, I swear."

I said okay, that later that day I would pay his mother, my aunt Tamara, the greatest visit she'd ever had. I would ask her questions in the way mothers, universally, like being asked questions. Questions showing you care about their mundane activities, all their sacrifices, their recipes, and the shit they wipe up.

When we hung up, my mother stuck her head into my bedroom to tell me she was leaving for work. I now kept the kitchen phone permanently in my room and she didn't seem to mind. "That was an awfully early call," she said.

Perhaps too defensively, I snapped at her, saying, "Well it was only Christopher calling. So it's really not a big deal."

IN THE LATE MORNING, I started packing for my weekend in New York. I was leaving the next day. After I'd purchased the third ticket, my countrystead funds were reduced to a fraction of the final fifty-dollar bill, enough for the subway fare, perhaps a cab ride, and an airport pretzel. I wondered if it would be bad form to ask Maurice when my paycheque for the videos would come. Since he hadn't mentioned it, or my living arrangements, I assumed I'd be crashing at his apartment for the first little while, before we boarded the plane and the tour bus, before we headed into the heart of Europe.

I put the copy of Alex's tape in my backpack. I knew once he heard it, Maurice would see that the Big Shadow ramblings fit our aesthetic, in an ironic way of course. I'd respond by saying the tape was his, that he could have it. He could do anything he wanted with it. That was how over my friends and the Big Shadow I was, how successfully I'd escaped them and disavowed everything from my past life.

I decided I'd wear Jennifer's rose dress on the flight. I wanted New York to see it when I stepped off the plane and Maurice to see it when I stepped into his apartment. I laid out the rest of my clothes for the weekend—shorts, two T-shirts, two pairs of underwear, one bra, black socks—in a pile on my bed.

MY PERIOD STARTED at lunchtime. I bit into a sandwich and felt my underwear grow warm. I went to the bathroom and pulled my shorts down to check. The blood had come five days early. I felt betrayed by my body. This was the weekend I needed to be in top form. As soon as I returned to the kitchen, the phone rang.

"Hey!" Jennifer said. Her tone now came across as completely natural, free of spite or disguises, like we were friends. "Just wanted to check in before you leave. You got the dress packed, and all the makeup?" I told her yes and thanked her for it again. I asked if she'd ever been to New York. I realized I hadn't asked anything about her life. "Once," she said. "My sister had plans to be a model, and my mother was very into that. The three of us took a Greyhound there and my mother took her to some agencies with which they'd booked a sort of initial 'let's see if you're skinny enough' appointment. It was pretty depressing. I remember sitting around the hotel room, in Times Square, watching TV for most of the stay. I was fifteen, maybe younger. Old enough to know my mother spent too much money on that trip."

I could sense Jennifer wanted to share more about vain, beautiful sisters and ambitious mothers, but she was silent and I didn't want to pry. I decided I'd share and tell her about my period.

"I'm so upset I'm going to have it in New York," I said.

Jennifer didn't respond right away.

"Hello?" I said.

"No, I'm here," she said. She sounded pensive and distant. "I'm just trying to understand how that's bad. How is it bad? Having a period."

"I don't know," I said. The way Jennifer's tone had grown serious made me embarrassed. The answer to why a period was bad also seemed so obvious. "Periods are annoying," I said, unsure of myself now. "Cramps, changing tampons and stuff."

"No, I know," she said, her tone brightening again. She must've realized she'd made things awkward. "I know all about how annoying they are." She laughed once. "I guess I just meant—" She paused and took a deep breath. "I guess I just meant," she repeated, and I heard her cat meow in the background. "I just meant: is Blunt going to make that an issue? That you have your period while you're with him in New York."

I finally understood what she was getting at. She must've sensed I understood too because she immediately resumed talking, to cut me off before I could spill any secrets. "It's none of my business, I know. I only wanted to stress that it would be an asshole move if he had an issue with a *girl's period*. Because periods happen. Deal with it, Blunt."

I told Jennifer it wasn't like that. I said that I understood she didn't know Maurice, she wasn't close to him like I was, so it was easy to assume things about him. I said it was impossible to know him just from watching him teach poetry to us twice per week. "It's this artist friendship," I explained. "We talk about our work, and then collaborate on work, like these scenes I've been filming. I could tell Maurice about my period and he'd say, 'Ugh that's such a drag. Women have to put up with so much shit' and he'd probably say something feminist after."

"Feminist? Like what?"

I shrugged. I didn't know. "Something smart," I said.

There was another pause, long enough that I knew the subject was put away for good. Jennifer then asked me what time my flight was, when my return flight was, if I would fly back with Maurice on Monday or return by myself, whether I was scared of flying and if so, what moment was the scariest. We talked a little about travel generally. She told me she flew twice a year to visit her grandmother in Tampa, a grandmother who'd taught her to sew and whom she loved as much or sometimes, she felt, even more than her own mother. Before saying bye, she asked if I hated her, for implying that I was having sex with an old man who wrote bad poetry. She asked if I was now going to cut up the rose dress and torch its pieces in a ceremony in which I declared her a total bitch. She laughed after she said it, to show she was kidding, that she knew the answer was no, of course, of course I wouldn't. But her laugh was stilted, ending suddenly, like it had hit a wall it hadn't seen coming.

AT DINNER THAT NIGHT, I could barely swallow. My flight would leave in fourteen hours.

"Off to Alex's for the weekend?" my mother asked.

I nodded over the Chinese takeout she treated us to once a month.

"I'm glad you're spending regular time with them again."

I stirred my chopstick in the cardboard container. The bok choy looked like a dead bird with its wings peacefully wrapped around its body. I pushed the container away and by the end of the dinner, my mother had eaten my portion.

I COULDN'T SLEEP. Maurice, Jennifer, Ricky, Alex, my cousin, my mother, Mark Houde, they all paraded down the routes and channels of my head until what must have been close to sunrise. In the morning, riding the bus to the airport, I was haunted by the thought that I'd left something behind. I felt my backpack for Dana's camcorder and the tapes, my film ideas notebook, Jennifer's makeup, tampons, the crucial stuff. Thirty minutes into the flight, I remembered I'd forgotten to pack the pile of clothes I'd arranged on my bed. I smoothed out Jennifer's rose dress and dusted off the peanut crumbs from its crotch. The stewardess walked by for the last time, collecting our trash. The pilot announced our descent.

THIS TIME I landed in LaGuardia. Starting with my second visit, Maurice and I had a rule. I'd take public transit or a cab to his apartment, but had to call him from the airport after landing. He wanted to know I was alive and fine and that I'd be at his apartment in between forty-five minutes to an hour. I dialled his cell number from a pay phone near the luggage carousel. He didn't pick up. I walked around the carousel a few times and called again. He picked up.

"Hey!" he hollered. "Did you call earlier?" He sounded frazzled and distracted, like I'd pulled him away from something that was still happening in front of him.

"I'm in New York," I said.

"Shit!" he said. "Hold on."

I heard a sound like gurgling. Maurice had obviously pressed the phone against his shirt.

"Okay, Jude!" he said, returning. "I'm going to send Rory to get you. He's my manager. Don't worry, he's cool…what?" Maurice moved the phone away from his face and started laughing, wildly, along with two or three other people. I heard a woman's laughter too, quite piercing, young and comfortable. They were laughing like children. Like someone had fallen victim to a practical joke.

"Rory will get you," Maurice repeated, sobered. "You remember my van, right? He'll pull up in my van. A grey van! Yeah?"

I walked out of the airport and waited for the van. Forty-five minutes passed and I saw it. First just the van, hideous and square, then the glare on the windshield giving way to a rodent-like man behind the steering wheel. Rory had coarse blond hair and stubble growing out of a pointy chin. There were no formalities. I pulled open the door and climbed in, throwing my backpack between my legs. Rory slammed on the gas pedal. Soon we were on a highway with the city growing before us. We spent the whole ride in silence.

Somewhere in the middle of town, on an unusually wide street, Rory double parked the van and got out without saying anything. I followed him to the glass door of a five- or six-storey building I didn't recognize. I figured Maurice was inside the building, maybe in a studio, waiting for me to be brought inside. Rory was about to push open the glass door when he turned to me and said, "Wait, Maurice told you you're staying here tonight, yeah?"

I shook my head no. I no longer thought Maurice was in the building.

"Jesus Christ. Blunt!" Rory said and stepped away from the door. He looked over my head, at something very distant. "Okay," he said, still looking beyond me, then placed both hands on his cheeks and pushed up, hard, like he wanted to get rid of his face.

"So, Maurice has to finish some work," he started, "and his apartment is filled with equipment. He didn't know you were coming today. He got you a hotel room."

"Sure," I said. I looked at the glass door and nodded like this was normal, like I'd been led to glass doors and hotels in the middle of New York City before. "That's nice," I added.

"Yeah? All right. Okay. Let's do this," Rory said, relaxing. He pushed open the door and gestured for me to go first, now suddenly a gentleman. We walked up a short flight of carpeted stairs to a reception desk, round and tiny like a teacup. A girl my age was sitting inside the teacup. She wore an oversize maroon blazer, the sleeves so long only the ends of her fingernails showed. "Reservation for Blunt," Rory said and threw a credit card on the counter. I checked that the card was Maurice's card and it was really him who'd done this.

"I'll be fine from here on," I said to Rory, pointing my hand toward the exit. Rory hesitated. I could tell Maurice had told him to walk me up to my room and make sure I was safe. "I'm good," I repeated. "You can go and leave me now."

Rory pretended to hesitate again; I don't know for whose sake. Finally, he turned around and left. I watched him run back to the van.

I climbed more carpeted stairs, to the elevators. My room was small but perfectly normal. It had a bed and white curtains, a big window that faced onto the large street the hotel sat on. The street wasn't gridlock-busy, but seemed significant because of its width. There was a TV and a phone in my room. I peeked inside the bathroom. It too was clean. There was a tub. I didn't know what I was supposed to do. I didn't want to bother Maurice by calling him already. I sat on the window and watched the city for a little while. Then I filled the tub. I sat in the bath for an hour and read toursim magazines that came with the room. A bath always feels like a bath, no matter where in the world you are.

I turned on the television, but all it had was daytime TV. People arguing about exposed affairs, some overwrought soap operas. I filmed a little of the passing traffic from the window. I picked up a map that was lying next to the TV channel guide. It had a star for every place a visitor to New York should go. Central Park, Times Square, the Empire State building, the Chrysler building, stars for museums, Lincoln Center, Madison Square Garden. There were no stars for CBGB or Washington Square Park.

FIVE HOURS HAD passed since I landed. It was past three o'clock. I dialled Maurice's cell.

I could tell it was Rory who picked up. "Hold on," he muttered. He knew it was me, also. Maurice came on. "How's the room. It's okay?" he asked.

"It's fine," I said and regretted my tone right away. I sounded bitter. I sounded bitter yet I was in New York. I'd made the choice to come. I'd cashed in a fat golden ticket.

Maurice went quiet.

"Sorry, man," he finally said. "I totally thought you were coming tomorrow. I got the days mixed up. My place is a mess."

"It's okay," I said, trying to sound unharmed. I didn't understand why a mess suddenly mattered. It made no sense. I wondered if Maurice was hiding a woman in there, someone he was having sex with, a girlfriend I didn't know about, as if I'd care, as long as she didn't interfere with the tour. "Should I go walk around the city for a bit, or are you getting me soon?" I asked.

"Walk around!" He sounded relieved. "Go to a museum maybe. And then call me once you're done and I'll come pick you up in midtown. We'll have the evening to ourselves. Just us. *This* guy will be gone." I guessed Maurice had pointed at someone. But what good did that do? I wasn't there to see.

I heard ironic laughter, but it was so far away I couldn't tell if it was Rory.

"Bye," I said. I don't remember in what tone.

I LEFT THE HOTEL. I'd placed the map with the stars in my pocket. I figured as long as I stayed on the thicker-looking streets and close to the stars, I'd be okay. I walked north, up a street that grew busier and busier the more I walked. I figured I was getting closer to something good. I realized it was rush hour on a Friday. People were getting out of work, ready for a summer weekend. I walked with them. Eventually I saw a clearing, a change of scenery that could only mean one thing. I walked into Central Park. There were tourists ringing it and I pushed through the ring. They were people who looked like my mother, confused and frightened when life isn't all that scary. I didn't walk very far. After all, this was just a park—trees, bushes, Rollerblades, and dogs—and I'd left parks behind at home.

I thought to check how much it cost to go into the MoMA. I walked past the building two times, but couldn't tell where the entrance was. I walked on and pretended I hadn't intended to go in anyway. I bought a hot dog for dinner and ended up on Madison

Avenue. I called Maurice's cell from a pay phone, but he didn't pick up. I replaced the receiver and took my quarter back.

I turned south, toward the hotel. I was in my room by eight. I pulled the phone onto the bed and stared at it. "Tell me who to call," I said.

I dialled the first four digits of Jeremy's number and hung up. I hadn't meant to finish dialling that number anyway. For a second I considered calling Christopher, just to hear a familiar voice, to say something funny and check if he'd laugh. I dialled the coach house, but hung up after the first ring. I'd remembered the hotel would charge Maurice's credit card. I turned on the TV and watched the late-night talk shows that my mother for sure was watching. Eventually I fell asleep.

I WAS WOKEN by ringing and spent a few seconds making sense of the darkness. A curtain came into focus first, then the grainy cityscape behind it. I remembered where I was. I was upside down on a hotel bed, with my feet on a pillow, my body on a diagonal, head angled toward the window, the drapes open halfway, and the phone tucked into my stomach.

When I picked up, Maurice hollered "Jude!" I was expecting the girl from the reception desk. I thought if anyone were to call, it was the hotel that first called you and said, "Excuse me, you have a call from so-and-so, I am putting you through. Do you concur?"

I was still looking around, half risen and disoriented. The digital glow of the clock radio said it was 2:13 a.m.

"It's late," I said.

For some reason, Maurice found that hilarious. "I don't believe you. That's not the Judy I know. Anyway, I missed you so much today." None of it made much sense and everything was a non-sequitur.

But I couldn't help it, I smiled—big, pathetic, with teeth showing inside my standard-double room. "Oh yeah?" I said, then asked when I could finally see him.

I PACKED MY BACKPACK and took the cab Maurice had sent for me. It took less than five minutes to get to his building, including the formalities of paying my fare and saying goodbye to the driver. I'd known I'd been close to his building all along but still, the ride underscored the proximity, reviving the shame I'd been feeling for being a castaway in New York, the city he'd implied was my home.

I used my key to get inside. The staircase was as familiar as the stairs in my house. I could climb them with closed eyes. My soles knew the edges, the cracks, and the patterns drawn by the honeycomb tiles. The smell was homey: trash wafting from the first-floor garbage room and the leftover aromas of long-ago suppers. I knocked on Maurice's door, tired and ready to get into bed, under his comforter, which had its own special smell. I could hear Maurice's cowboy boots running and was buoyed by that clomping sound, happy that he was still willing to race across his apartment for me.

He swung open the door and I was about to fall back into my little tomb, the tomb of real New York, the only place that mattered in this town. He hollered my name, probably waking up the neighbours. I put my hand on the jamb and had to stop for a moment. My breathing paused. I thought I'd come to the wrong door even though it was Maurice who'd answered. Everything I saw behind him was off. His apartment looked like it'd been ran-sacked. A few of the things that were there before—the bookshelf and couch—were there still, but shifted to opposite walls. The computer desk and Saturn lamp were missing. There were new boxes of records, not on the windows but pushed against the wall. The rug had been removed.

He let me pass him. I walked in and turned in a circle. The couch now faced the window and was draped in a red velour throw. There was a tacky, bordello quality to the newly implanted decor: a lamp with a mint chiffon shade, a yellow mannequin with pink felt hearts on her nipples, a marble bust in the style of Greece or Rome. It was awful and kitschy, like the spaceship in *Barbarella*.

"Where's Lexa?" I said, seeing that the wall she'd lived on all this time was bare. The mannequin with the heart-nipples stood lean-ing against it now. Maurice put his hand on my shoulder. "She's somewhere around here. I don't know." He pointed his other hand toward a pile of papers and cans partly hidden by a new silver cur-tain. "Don't worry. Things will go back to normal. We just needed to move them around a bit this week."

I didn't want to ask why. Even at this point in our relationship, it felt like prying. I knew this was a world where one had to accept things and not care. It was the rule of Maurice's aesthetic sensibil-ity or something. His apartment was completely dismantled and if I asked why I would prove I wasn't meant to be there in the first place. But Maurice told me why anyway; he was too excited to hold it in. "This is all Dana Miller's doing. We finally got him to come shoot a video in here!" He smiled big and shook me by my shoulder. He was sure I'd share in the glee.

I pumped my fist ironically, but Maurice didn't get it. I was angry. Maurice kept going. "We didn't think he'd agree to do it—you met Dana, you saw what he's like—but he's on board!"

"Wow," I said.

"Yeah, it's so hard to get him to commit to a project that's not something huge, you know?"

"Right," I said. "I'm sure he's super busy."

"He's insane."

I gave up.

I walked over to the window, pushed open the tacky silver curtain, and looked out at my old view. The Friday night revellers were still out. Directly across from me, on the sidewalk, a girl my age twirled in a wobbly orbit as her girlfriend stood next to her, one foot on the curb, laughing. They seemed to be having a nice time. Maurice must have finally sensed something because he followed me to the window, stopped directly behind me, and put his hands on my elbows. "Dana's only shooting one music video, that's all. We wanted to use real film and get this whole Super 8 effect going. Just the new single."

I shrugged. I wanted Dana dead. If only Maurice had asked me, I would've used Super 8, too. He'd lied and made me believe a camcorder was good enough. I leaned back against Maurice's chest. It was like leaning against the letter *B*, he was so fat. In the window, I saw Jennifer's rose dress, reflected and imposed on New York's thousand buildings—a blooming palimpsest, stinky and wet, the only thing I had to wear and already it reeked of period.

"You like this dress?" I challenged him. I was aware that my voice sounded new, that this was not the kind of thing I'd ever said before, especially not to Maurice.

"It's beautiful," he said. With me still pressed into him, he arched his neck and looked over my shoulder to examine it. For a second, things seemed normal, like he was a good friend commenting on his good friend's new clothing.

"A designer friend made it for me." I made my voice sound like it was getting at something and not there yet. "Big Bad Wolf."

"Very talented," Maurice said, but by now his voice was a rustle. His face was somewhere in my neck, churning in small circles, the stubble gently combing my throat.

Maurice murmured, a relaxed, happy-feline sound. I looked ahead at the building opposite us. Its lights were out. I didn't understand why there was so little life there when we were in the centre of the world. Maurice's hands crept down and stuck to my hips. My arms were at my sides, wooden yet pliant. When we were kids, Christopher and I used to play D.E.A.D.—"Do Everything As if you're Dead"—on his mother's bed. One would lift the other's limb, an arm, a leg, hoist it by the wrist or the ankle, let go and watch it fall, laughing. Every part of my body was like that now, heavy as a dumbbell, loose as rope, and mutually agreed to no longer be mine.

Except for the eyes; those I kept for myself. I focused them like I was doing an eye test. I focused them on all the things Maurice's view had to give: buildings, buildings, New York. For the first time, I felt in control in this town; we were doing what I wanted to be doing even though it wasn't what I'd want to be doing at all. I figured I'd take it. It was all I could likely ever grab. Everything was a windfall and I was lucky to not be sleeping in my own bedroom or a hotel for tourists that night. I let go of my body and the barrel went over the falls.

"Mmm," Maurice said. His hands travelled in an S, starting from the hip, synchronized, up to my bra. I stood still. Their grip tightened as they drove past my breasts. The hands kept going. They stopped on my shoulders. Maurice's fingers locked into my collar bone and tried to spin me around, but I resisted, planting my feet more firmly on his floorboards. So he kept me as I was, with my back to his gut.

"Remember the note I left in your jacket after the first class?" I said.

"Oh, yes," Maurice meowed.

"Did you actually really read it?"

"Of course," he whispered. His hands clutched my shoulders.

"What did it say?"

"It said we should meet up sometime soon, so we could sit and talk and pretend we're on the set of *Rashomon*. I loved how you just said what you wanted then signed your name: so official. How you left it in my pocket and walked out of the room, no looking back." Maurice sounded nervous, like he was taking a test and could lose out on a lot by not passing it. So he went on, his hands still on my shoulders, massaging them, more formal now. "Yeah, that note was like nothing else. I put it in my wallet and showed Mark as soon as I got back. I said wait till you meet this girl. It blew his mind."

I didn't believe a word of it.

I believed a half to a third of it.

No, I believed ten percent of it, and despite myself that ten percent felt better than anything a more honest person could give me.

"It's probably four in the morning," I said, stiffening to an upright position and turning around so that he'd let go of me. I slipped back into myself. I'd tested something and found that it worked. But I could only do so much so soon.

"All right," he said. He walked backward and leaned against the bookshelf, which was partly dismantled to accommodate the new marble bust. He looked at me carefully, maybe afraid.

I kept talking: "The thing is, I woke up at six today to make it on the flight to New York. I forgot to bring a change of clothes. And I have my period. So, I need to get some sleep now." I looked squarely at him. Another challenge. But Maurice was unfazed. He was experienced; he'd been on this turf a long time.

"Three strikes, man," he said and grinned like nothing had changed between us. Cool as a cowboy, he turned and walked toward the bed. Or maybe he was an old grizzly bear retreating from a near-death battle.

21

"The heat today, the heat today," the cabbie mumbled as we stood stalled at a right-hand turn on our way to Mark's studio on Lexington. He yanked at his shirt collar and puffed his cheeks. It was Manhattan's go at it now—a heatwave as bad as the one that had hit my town just before Maurice danced his way into my life. The last time I'd had to live through a temperature this unbearable I was on my bedroom floor, owning nothing but the stupid hope of getting through the day without a phone call from my cousin and Alex. And here I was, three weeks later, sweating on a vinyl seat behind the plastic partition in a genuine yellow New York City cab. I had Maurice Blunt at my side and was on my way to see an even bigger New York cultural icon in the intimacy of his private studio. I didn't know what was up exactly, but as I understood it, the Sateelites had been using Mark's studio to practise their upcoming sets and to record a new single, for which Dana Miller had shot the video.

The cab still hadn't moved when I noticed that Maurice had locked his eyes on my face. He scanned the areas where I'd applied Jennifer's daytime Manhattan palette: a thick blue line on the top eyelid but nothing on the bottom one. Pink lipstick in a shade called "Flamingo Baby." And a smear of fever-coloured blush. "You made yourself up today," he said. The sappy way he smiled made me turn away. I didn't answer, as if he hadn't spoken. We finally made our right turn. The cab picked up speed. After a minute, I checked to see that Maurice wasn't looking at me anymore. With the back of my hand, I wiped my eyelids and my mouth, then stuck my hands under my thighs.

The cab stopped at a red light.

"Mark and Jamie are dying to meet you."

"Cool," I said flatly.

"You look pretty. I'm glad you started wearing makeup."

I pushed my hands farther under my thighs. I figured I hadn't rubbed enough of it off.

"I mean: it suits you," he said. "Keep wearing it. You look good. The pink lipstick."

My face flushed. I wanted to jump out of the car. I didn't know how Maurice had suddenly developed a talent for ruining everything that was subtle and good.

We pulled up to a building that looked like it could have multiple banks, the New York Stock Exchange, and Bloomingdale's inside. But when the elevator door opened, only a grey hallway greeted us, grey carpeting, grey walls, quiet, narrow, and lined with dozens of identical doors. It looked like the set of a David Lynch movie.

Maurice pushed open an unmarked grey door. I should have known that like everything else in the city, the space would be shockingly small. The studio's live room was the size of my bedroom and crammed with equipment all along the walls. Mark

Houde stood in the middle of it, his arms crossed, looking like the father of children who were more than my age. His face was round, much rounder than it had been in 1976. He had a salt-and-pepper brush cut and his glasses had square, arty black frames. His white T-shirt rested on wide, athletic shoulders. The T-shirt had a logo on it advertising the Long Island Ladies' Marathon. I shouldn't have been able to tell it was him.

Mark turned his head when he heard us shut the door. "Maurice, did you bring the cable?" he said. His voice was ordinary, on the quiet side, and polite.

Maurice pointed at me. "Judy's got the cable," he said.

I smiled and pointed at my messenger bag, where Maurice had told me to pack a cable that morning.

"Good," Mark said. He turned toward a line of guitars propped against a fridge-size amp.

"Mark, this is—" Maurice started.

"Oh, hi, Judy," Mark said, looking behind him for a quick moment. "Nice to meet you."

The shock of his address made my smile come out wrong. I tried tossing something casual at him, but the muscle above my lips seized up.

It didn't matter.

Mark had already turned back to the guitars. He picked up a red-and-white one and kneeled with it on the rug. The instruments and mics were arranged in a little mock stage setup. He started tuning the guitar, checking a pedal. He had more important business than my smile.

Maurice walked from the live room to the control room, and I followed him. The control room was half the size of the live room. "Make yourself comfortable," he said. He was unpacking things from my bag and throwing them on a couch. He pointed at its cushion. There was someone on the couch already. A woman with sharp features sat curled on its far end. Her pose was regal, and she had a lot of hair, pulled into a shiny bun askew on one side of her head.

"Hi, Judy," she said. She was probably my mother's age but knew how to take care of herself. She wore a gauzy scarf with criss-crossing silver threads wrapped around her neck and shoulders.

"This is Charlotte," Maurice said.

Charlotte tugged at her scarf to tighten it.

"Should we turn the AC off, Charlotte? You cold?" Maurice asked. "You know the city's melting."

Charlotte shook her head without looking at Maurice. She adjusted the scarf again. Her eyes were fixed on the back wall of the studio. "I'd rather boil alive than be artificially refrigerated," she said. "But there'd be a coup if I went near the AC switch."

"Charlotte's got a cold," Mark explained, still tuning his guitar. "Charlotte has an AC cold."

"It's better than an AC/DC cold. I got one of those once," said a skinny guy with a goatee as he shut the main door behind him. This was Jamie, the drummer, the other original Sateelite. Somehow he had managed to grow even skinnier than he'd been in 1976. No one bothered to introduce us.

BETWEEN THE FIRST and third hour of the Sateelites reunion practice, I sat on one end of the couch, opposite Charlotte, with my film ideas notebook in my lap. I composed elaborate pretend notes. My hand didn't stop moving. I wrote things that I already knew I wouldn't be able to read for years, because reading them would remind me of how I felt sitting on that couch.

I was an imposter, a fly that had accidentally gotten stuck in the room. Only I didn't have the freedom to slam into a windowpane and beg to be let out. I could tell that's how they saw me. No one asked my opinion about the music. No one mentioned videos, promo clips, or European cities where the tour would stop.

Eventually I started to draw, Maurice and the rest of them. I was too afraid to draw Charlotte in case she looked over and saw, but she was the best subject, with her angular profile, just staring into the back wall and sucking on a cherry lozenge.

"You're not bored?" she asked at one point, giving me a tired but warm look. I saw that she wasn't frightening, only ill.

I shook my head.

"Good," she said, and smiled.

The Sateelites played a few old songs I recognized, and a couple of new ones that sounded like they were trying to sound like the old ones. They mainly played the same four songs over and over, stopping at various points, opening the door between the live and control rooms and complaining about something that wasn't working. Maurice played guitar for the most part, switching to bass at points until a fourth person, Dale, showed up. I'd never heard of him, but apparently he played bass in the new Sateelites. He apologized for being late and said his daughter had twisted her ankle at dance practice.

"Blunt!" he yelled after setting down a neon green backpack that looked like something my mother would wear to the grocery store. "Coral said Uncle Maurice has to come see her dance. She's got a Parisian ballet instructor. When are you coming up?"

"What's her name?" Charlotte cut in.

"Who?"

"The dance instructor." Charlotte sighed and wiped her nose with a Kleenex.

"Laura something."

"Oh, never mind." Charlotte shook her head and wiped her nose again. "Maple danced with a Parisian woman named Claire something, but that was twelve years ago. Claire's probably dead. I don't know why I asked."

"I thought she was Russian," Maurice said.

The other men stopped what they were doing and looked at Charlotte.

"Claire? Not really," she said. "Claire was *born* in Russia, but raised in France. She was essentially French. She didn't even speak Russian."

"No, honey, she was not born in Russia," Mark said, shaking his head definitively.

"She was born in Morristown, New Jersey," Jamie offered and cracked up. He was clearly the buffoon in the group.

"*My* ballet teacher was from Morristown, New Jersey," Maurice said and he and Jamie nodded enthusiastically at one another.

"Fuck." Mark dropped to his knees and shook his head. "I was in tap lessons when I was seven. Can any of you believe that? The teacher was our neighbour. She was this sad, beautiful housewife that I wanted to save from her alcoholic husband. I was going to be a fucking tap dancer."

Everyone grew quiet. I saw Charlotte's expression change into a slow smile as she watched her husband drift to another time. They were all in there together, a soup of memories, intimate knowledge of one another's offspring, a web of friendships that I had nothing to do with. I kept drawing in my notebook: a crying poodle, a toothy pig, and a rhombus with a flower growing out of its middle. I'd never felt more invisible in my life.

AROUND TWO in the afternoon, Maurice stuck his head in the control room and asked if I'd mind getting them lunch. "Falafels!" Jamie shouted. Maurice dug in his jean pocket for money.

"Oh, no!" Charlotte cried. She rose from the couch and gestured toward Maurice. Her scarf fell to her elbows. "You don't send ladies out to fetch you lunch! No, no."

Maurice froze with his hand in his pocket. He smiled sheepishly and looked at the floor. Charlotte kept staring at him and shaking her head. They were like two cats on the brink of a scrap.

I looked to Maurice for instructions, but he kept his eyes on the carpet.

"I want to go," I said, laughing awkwardly. I desperately wanted out of that little space.

"See?" Maurice said. He resumed his movement and pulled two twenties out of his pocket. "Judy's the coolest, that's what you don't know, Charlotte."

Charlotte took a step back, lifted her scarf and surrendered. "Trust me, I know Judy's wonderful," she said, and sat back down on the couch. As I left, I felt her big brown eyes follow me to the door. "Bad Maurice!" I heard her say, just as I shut it behind me.

I BOUGHT FOUR orders of falafels from a food truck a block up from the studio and then circled the blocks until the Styrofoam no longer felt warm in my hands. The sidewalk was so hot by that hour that my shoe bottoms grew gummy. The rose dress stuck to my back and the tops of my thighs, bunching and rising with each step I took.

I walked into a coffee shop, went to its bathroom, ran cold water on my hands, and rinsed the sweat off my neck and forehead. I changed a tampon. I walked around the block two more times. As the elevator took me up to the studio, I stuck my finger in one of the falafel balls. Its insides were cold. I was glad.

When the elevator opened, I crashed into Charlotte. "Sorry, Judy," she said. Her scarf was balled under her arm. She took a step back to make room for me. It took me a moment to understand that Charlotte was trying to get into the elevator, that she was waiting for me to get out.

"Well, it was really nice meeting you," she said and smiled. She was close enough that I could smell her cough candy. I adjusted the falafel box and heard Styrofoam snap. The elevator started beeping.

"I think this wants to shut," Charlotte said, pointing at the door.

I didn't move. I didn't want to return to a Charlotte-less studio.

She gave me another smile. "I hope you have a nice stay in New York. Too bad I have to run." Her voice was patient and gentle over the alarm, which was growing louder and more menacing. "Maybe our paths will cross again?"

I nodded yes, maybe, and stepped aside for her. She walked into the elevator. Her eyes stayed on me as the door slid shut. She kept smiling, but her look was sad; sad and questioning, maybe disappointed. It searched me for my story, that much I could tell for sure. After three weeks in Mauriceland, I knew the look well.

22

We walked out of the building that housed Mark's studio. Somehow it had become evening. I made it, I thought. I survived. I would never allow myself to be trapped in that control room again.

"That was boring, huh?" Maurice said. He poked me with his elbow.

"Boring" was one way to put it. No one had spoken to me in the last two hours of the rehearsal. Just before we left, Mark had asked me to hand him "the capo." I didn't know what a capo was. It sounded like a fancy item of clothing, so I looked around for a blazer or a coat. Then Jamie stepped forward and grabbed a small piece of metal from next to my foot. "This is a capo," he said, holding the stupid thing up.

Maurice poked me again. "Do you hate me for dragging you to rehearsal?" he said. "We should teach you an instrument so you have something to do." He poked me a third time. "You could be in the band. Want to be our guiro player?"

I refused to play along. I could no longer tell whether I was tired or annoyed; the two had merged into one general feeling of wanting nothing to do with Maurice or the Sateelites. I knew he didn't really mean I could play in the band, and that that's why he'd named an absurd-sounding instrument. At this point, I couldn't see what exactly I was getting out of my visit. I'd wasted a lot of money flying to New York. I'd lied to my mother. And yet it was clear the Sateelites still didn't see me as an artist or an equal, possibly not even as their official band videographer.

"I got a lot of writing done," I said, giving my bag a slap. "I've been writing a book, so I got most of that done."

I didn't know why I said I was writing a book. Or, I knew why I said it, but I didn't know why I thought it was a good idea to say it.

"A *whole* book? That's commendable," Maurice said.

It took me a few seconds to remember what "commendable" meant. It was an unnecessarily long word. I suspected it could hold a lot of different meanings.

I looked at Maurice, to check if he was mocking me, but he was looking at the ground with a neutral expression.

We walked a whole block in silence.

"So, what did you think of the material?" he finally said. "Did you like the new songs?"

I knew this was my chance to make amends, but I only shrugged. I hadn't really paid much attention to the songs. They had sounded like one and the same song. They were not special. They had no hook.

"Don't know," I said.

Another block of silence followed, then Maurice started talking: "I think the songs are coming along well enough. It feels a little strange, there's something weird in returning to material you haven't played in such a long time. Mark has a vision for this stuff. We've been butting heads a little, but lately ... it's been good,

I mean, I'm glad he's into this project. We've known each other for so long that it's almost depressing. I mean, there were points in our lives when we tried to kill one another—really. He shoved me into an open window. Once I pulled a knife on him. Anyway, there's this risk, if I think about it for too long, of feeling down about reuniting. Like I'm returning to the past to redo something completed, and shut, and locked. That's hardly *creation*, you know?" Maurice gently pushed me leftward at a corner. We walked up a new street. He pushed me again when we reached the end of the block.

We were mainly silent after the second turn. The sidewalks were still and empty. They didn't feel like Manhattan. We were taking streets where tourists didn't venture. We passed an ordinary brown apartment building that looked like the buildings in the north part of my town, the kind one would see when driving to the countrystead.

At some point, Maurice made a joke, only I didn't realize he'd done so until it was over. He was waiting for my retort, looking eager. Keep your mouth shut, I thought, looking at his bunched face. I'd lost the power to pretend. I was making no attempt to hide how flat I found everything: Maurice, the streets and city, my feelings, the bohemian punk rock anecdotes about his relationship with Mark. I was completely over Mark, anyway.

We jaywalked across a multi-lane street.

"So do you like New York?" Maurice suddenly asked. He jumped in front of me and started walking backward as I walked forward. "I don't think I ever really asked."

"Huh?" I said. "Of course I do. I keep coming back and buying more and more plane tickets, don't I?" I watched Maurice's cowboy boots daintily hop in the wrong direction. I thought he'd stop after two or three hops, but he kept going, swift as a bunny. I counted the hops. We were at twelve. There was a protrusion in the asphalt. His heel snagged it and he wobbled, making a jokey scream. I couldn't help it, I smiled. He kept going. The curb was approaching. I said, "Maurice, the sidewalk's ending." I'd never seen a grown person hop down the street like that. Of course I loved New York. "Don't trip, Maurice," I said. "You're going to crack your skull. In three seconds, two, one…"

"Promise?"

"Promise what?" I said, covering my face.

"That you like this place," he said.

I was about to answer, but Maurice stopped and I crashed into his open arms. It was a clever trap and I didn't mind it. He wrapped himself around me, then picked me off the ground. We spun.

"I promise," I said as he set me down. I stumbled a little. I held on to his paunch. For the moment, I liked how fat it was. There was safety in that bigness. We both started laughing. Our laughter grew. In the end, I was crouched on the sidewalk, something was that funny. I might be going crazy, I thought. Two minutes ago, I wanted to push Maurice into traffic. All it took was him hopping down the sidewalk and here I am, not hating him anymore.

I was lucky to have him, I knew. None of what was happening was ordinary. No one else was getting to have this.

"Good! I'm glad you like it here," he said. "We're totally conquering New York. Soon we'll take over Moscow. We'll take over the world. *You'll* take over the world, actually. I'll just float in your wake. I'll just play these old, rehashed songs that no one wants to hear and float behind you as you make incredible films."

"Your songs aren't rehashed," I quickly said. "They're not rehashed, Maurice. Not even a bit." I realized that all along, he'd been waiting for a compliment. I appreciated this weakness.

"Yeah?" he said. That earnestness struck me, it was like when he'd asked about his music video and what I thought of it. I didn't know why my opinion mattered. But the way he said it, I believed it did.

We walked on. When things started looking like Maurice's neighbourhood, he put his arm around me, the Dylan way. I nestled in despite the heat. The smell of old beer oozed out of his armpit.

"I just want to take care of you, to make sure you're always okay," he said as he pushed open the door of his building. "You're just one of the special ones that's got a good head on her shoulders, you know?"

"Yeah, I think I do," I said. He found my answer funny, and as we climbed his stairs and I saw the old honeycomb tiles, I thought back to the story about him pulling a knife on Mark and being pushed into an open window, all of their highs and lows, that this was what I'd wanted so badly for myself, to be in the presence of someone who'd done all that, in New York City. Someone who'd done that yet found *me* special and good.

We reached the third-floor landing in silence. His arm was still around me. I snuggled closer, my hands clamping his shirt, clawing it a little as we took more steps. The wave of what I'd felt in our first days together was back. The euphoria of being with Maurice Blunt, being saved, and listening to his convictions about me conquering the world, like some Joan of Arc, which I knew deep down I wasn't.

I wondered if we'd always exist in an ebb and flow, with our frustration and appreciation see-sawing. "Thank you," I said. "Thank you for everything," I said as he pushed open his apartment door. I'd never said it, I realized. For three weeks, I hadn't said thank you once. He'd given me a home, made me breakfast in the mornings, played music videos for me and danced. I was ashamed at what I'd done. I'd spent three weeks being sheltered by a man who had plenty of other things to keep him busy. Maurice Blunt of the Sateelites, a genuine artist.

"I really appreciate it," I said. I hadn't meant to have grown so bored of it so fast. As soon as Maurice threw his keys on the counter, I ran back to him. I climbed under his arm and pressed myself into his gut. Even though he didn't seem upset, and he didn't seem to care too much that I kept saying "thank you," I was worried it was too late to make everything all right. I felt guilt. "Thank you for being so nice to me," I said again.

"Always," Maurice answered.

It was my favourite thing he said during our friendship.

My face was still buried in his black Western shirt, the old one with the roses on it. I planted a small kiss near its pocket. Maurice pressed me in harder. "Can we just listen to records and read poems all night?" I said.

He let go of me and pretended to fall back like I'd just shot him. "Yee-ah!" he yelled. "That's exactly what I wanted you to say!" He lifted his arms. He was on a high, too. He understood that I'd asked for forgiveness. He'd said "yes," in his way. He turned on the lamp, what used to be the Saturn lamp and was now a lamp with a green chiffon shade, and grabbed a beer out of the fridge. He threw a Coke can my way and ran to the record boxes by the window. He started slapping through his collection. "Oh my God," he said, lifting an LP. "Of course! Why haven't we played this yet?" Maurice pretended to be mad. "Judy is a punk!" he yelled, then ran to the turntable and threw on the Ramones' debut, side A, track three.

He started singing along with the song, loud, with an affected gruff. He closed his eyes, scrunched his lips, and shook his head around, dislodging his slick-back. "Judy is a punk!" He stomped one cowboy boot on the floor. At times he kicked it up, along with the crash cymbal. *Thump, thump, thumpa.* "Judy is a punk," he sang—words that, if you listen to it, aren't actually in the song. "Judy is a punk! Judy is a punk!"

When the song ended, I shouted, "More Judy is a punk, please!" like a rowdy fan in the stands. Maurice adjusted the needle. The song started again.

"Judy is a punk! Judy is a punk!"

He waved his arms in circles, whipped his head from side to side, his legs jauntily kicking, *thump, thumpa*, his breaths heavy. Clumps of hair bounced and came undone. "Judy is a punk! Judy is a punk!"

I watched from a lying position on the couch, my head on the throw pillow, vacillating between my grateful, pathetic glee and my now-honed composure. I was painfully aware of how much this scene, if I were to paint it for someone or even play it back in my head at a future time, would scream of pastiche, some awful plastic conjuring of what it's like to bum around New York with a music legend, a punk poet. But this moment, Maurice in mid-kick, singing my name to me, wasn't a movie, not even a documentary. It was happening before me, and in its genuine and unironic version it had the weight and appeal and magic that made it obvious why some hacky filmmaker would want to steal it, why another person would pretend it had happened to them or that they knew anything about spending one minute with Maurice Blunt.

"Judy is a punk!" Maurice grunted and heaved. "Judy is a punk! Judy is a punk!"

"Another round!" I yelled, saluting him with my Coke can.

Making a smooth transition from a leg swing to a lunge, he landed at the edge of the couch, sitting on his knees, his elbows planted on the seat cushion in a cherubic pose, and his face inches from mine. He grinned. Drops of sweat trickled down his nose. "How the hell did you get a song written about you in 1976?" he asked, and with no warning he jutted his face forward and stuck his lips into mine.

At first I did nothing; the way we'd crashed had startled me into a stopped state. But after a few seconds, I parted my mouth a bit, I don't know why. Maybe it was because his hand wasn't on the back of my head this time, holding me in place, as if he trusted that I'd grown less prudish since the previous week. Maybe it was because the music was still blasting and our night and our philosophy had been about no labels, no conventions, and no worrying about what the world thought of us. It was 1:08 a.m., I saw on the VCR panel behind Maurice's hair. It was time for me to stop being a child.

I shifted my lips, just a small gesture, a sip from a tiny spoon. Something, I thought, but not much. Nothing too horrible to live down.

Maurice pulled away after a few seconds. He smiled, his eyes on the wall above my head. "Judy is a punk," he said, again. "I *know* that song's written about you. I'm going to talk to Johnny Ramone and get to the bottom of this."

His humour, that he was unchanged, was comforting. Like there was a chance I was unchanged too and I'd been a kid to think two sets of lips touching would turn the universe inside out. I kissed my mother, after all. I kissed my aunt and my cousin's half-brother. At times, I'd given my cousin a kiss, a quick one on the cheek, if he'd made me especially happy.

Maurice jumped to his feet. I thought he was headed toward his phone, to pretend to call Johnny Ramone, but he jogged to the bookshelf and pulled out a title. He was on to something new. "Let's go to Pete Lootigan's tonight. Pete's gonna love you! He's having a thing," he said while flipping pages.

According to *How What Happened Happened*, Pete Lootigan was a poet. He was also in a band called the Thin Edges that lasted for one year in 1975. "Here, let me read you this one," Maurice said, spreading the pages and stepping into the centre of the living room. "Spit and tackle," he began.

The poem was about standing on a roof in the East Village, about thinking you've lost something and then thinking it's been found, but then in the end not being so sure about anything. After reading the final line, Maurice shut the book and threw it on the couch. "Up, Jude. Up!" he said, motioning with both hands for me to rise. "Grab the camcorder, quick," he said. "Let's go. Let's re-enact this thing of beauty."

I asked if we were going to Pete Lootigan's party. "Nah!" Maurice said. He was already out the door. Pete's party was forgotten. We ran up three flights of stairs, onto the roof, with Dana's Panasonic strapped to my neck. "This is your city now," Maurice yelled, out of breath, on the rooftop, pointing in a bunch of directions. "Take it all in, it's all yours now. You're a living poem. We don't need to be reading poetry, we are poetry. Take it in, Jude."

I turned in a circle to breathe in every side of it, the poem, the unending mash of buildings, a flickering bridge in the distance, a helicopter with its single red eye sliding across the sky. Everything that was holding me in its tight grip, a dead-tight grip that I didn't mind.

"Hey, get some skyline shots," Maurice said. "And make sure I'm not backlit."

I said okay, but in that moment I felt too happy to bother with promo clips. I wanted to savour the night, even the trite words Maurice was throwing at me. I felt I'd crossed a threshold and taken a step closer toward New York. I'd been in the city all along, yes, but those who were a true part of it could tell I was only a spectator. Now I'd stepped over a stanchion and its velvet border. I'd let Maurice kiss me without breaking out of it in disgust. I was something beyond an impostor, a non-New Yorker and non-adult.

I removed Dana's camcorder from my neck and set it on the floor. I checked if Maurice cared that I wasn't filming him, but he was busy looking off into the distance and talking to himself. There's plenty of time to film him still, I thought. This backdrop, the night, it's not going anywhere.

We paced the roof for a while. Every few minutes Maurice would lift his chin and check out the sky, pivoting his body in one spot, his cowboy boots making quick scratching sounds. Maybe he did think I was filming him, who knows.

I walked to the edge of the roof and looked down at 9th Street. There was no railing or wall on the roof—its floor simply fell away like the edge of a table. I took another step. I stood as close to that precipice as I could and sensed that I was doing something mildly dangerous, but it all seemed in line with what I'd done in coming to see an old famous artist-man in New York, in the spirit of us, and that evening, and the summer as a whole. Why did I think it'd be so hard to make this move, I wondered, looking at the street, the parked cars, and the few tops of heads swanning down the sidewalk beneath me. Coming to the city? Spreading my mouth a little and pressing it to the mouth of a person who cared that I'd always be okay, who saw to it that I'd make a movie?

Every wrinkle will smooth itself out—I figured that's what someone smarter than me would've offered as advice right then. I was on the right path. Maurice had come and found me. Soon I'd be here for real, and one day I'd be able to tell my cousin—and even Alex, if he gained enough distance from himself—that I'd taken up the Big Shadow on its offer. I'd let it take me away, as a transmuted, better version of myself. Except that none of it was what they'd predicted. They'd been looking in the wrong place! Maurice had nothing to do with clouds, he'd always been firmly planted, here on the ground, beside me.

I glanced back at him. He was standing in the centre of the roof with his face pointed at the sky. I looked at his hair and the shape of his body, the way the mass of his cheeks rolled down toward his ears. I wondered if I'd have to have sex with him one day, if that was simply how adults behaved, and if so, whether sex always meant something important or if could be only two bodies kissing in the faintest of ways, too faint to commit to memory even.

I peeked over the edge again. The tips of my shoes were flush with the drop. I shut my eyes and tilted my head back, letting the breeze brush the hair off my face. My body swayed with the air current. Below, I heard night revellers, a laughing woman and a laughing group of men. I smiled and spread my arms to the sides. I flailed them in a whimsical, birdlike way.

I heard a scream, so full it blew the sky off the city. I dropped my arms and looked back in time to see Maurice leaping toward me. His hair flew back, the fat on his face too. He let out a second, smaller scream and landed a few feet away from me. "Jesus fuck, Judy!" he yelled. "What are you trying to do? Stay back!"

I took a slow backward step and sat down on the tarpaper, nice and far from the edge to show him I wasn't going to fall. I supposed from where he'd been standing, he'd seen danger, a body on a knife's edge. "I'm all right, Maurice," I assured him. "I'm okay, obviously." The tone he'd used, like a tested and furious parent, made me want to cry.

He let out a long breath. "Sorry," he said, not sounding that sorry. "You just scared me, you just scared me," he said. He looked blanched and seemed angry. He'd placed one hand over his heart the way my mother loved to do.

"Nothing happened," I said. "Nothing happened, Maurice." I lay down. The tarpaper felt warm against my arms, as if it were a bed, waiting for me in this very moment when I needed to tuck myself away. Still, I laughed. "I didn't fall off the roof." I rolled onto my stomach and sides. "I'm totally good."

I thought Maurice would join me, or make a joke, or smile, but he stayed as he was, looking startled and stupid, still holding on to his chest. "You almost gave me a heart attack," my mother loved to say if I didn't pick up the phone on the first ring, if it took me a minute to answer her from behind my bedroom door after she'd come home after work.

I grinned up at him and made a jumping jack motion with my arms. "Right?" I said. "Look at how okay I am."

But Maurice wasn't in the mood. "Let's go back in," he said simply. "Your parents would've murdered me if you'd fallen. They would've killed me. Maybe think of that."

He turned toward the stairs, his boots rapping the tarpaper as he left me. *Rap, tap, tap.* I saw him brush back his hair with both hands, all that had come undone as he'd leaped to save my life. Sure, the cars were still honking and the bridges twinkled, but Maurice Blunt and I were done.

LATE NEXT MORNING, I sorted through the piles on Maurice's floor. I put the beer cans in a plastic bag and took them down to the garbage room. "Thank you," Maurice mouthed when I came back upstairs. He was on the phone, sitting on the couch with the blanket wrapped around him. He'd slept on the couch that night and given me his bed. "Yeah, no, I get it," he said into the receiver and gave me an encouraging nod. I continued digging through the trash and unearthed a bottle of Canadian Club, Maurice's socks, newspapers, magazines, and coffee cups, all victims of Dana Miller's video shoot. I could not find Lexa.

TWO HOURS LATER, Maurice and I stood next to each other in the centre of the living room, turning in circles, my backpack already on and an airport cab waiting. "She's somewhere," Maurice said, looking around. "It's just such a mess. I don't know."

I'd left the cassette tape with Alex's ramblings on the couch, and in the course of the night it had fallen on the floor. I could see it now on the hardwood, next to an old *New Yorker*. When Maurice turned his back to me, I picked up the tape and placed it on his bookshelf, next to the stereo and the postcard of the naked woman riding a horse in a cowboy hat.

A few minutes later, we started to say goodbye, but his phone rang in the middle of it and he raced to pick it up. I let myself out, and he waved, using the hand that wasn't holding the receiver. As I walked down the stairs, I could still hear his voice one floor below, but one landing beneath that, Maurice was no more.

23

The plane was having trouble landing. We whirled over my city, dipping in and out of a layer of purple clouds—*mammatus* clouds, which take their name from "mammary gland" and look like a field of udders. It was the start of summer storm season. The tree-bending winds would come almost daily and would stick around until late August. One such storm had just ended. I saw my block a bunch of times. I saw the flat, uninspired region where I'd gone to pick up the tube of plastic for Maurice's video shoot. Then came a severe tilt and we headed for the subdivisions of the suburbs. We're going to die, I thought. This machine will never right itself.

We touched down twenty minutes late. "Bad weather," the pilot crackled over the speaker. "Not much of a relief from New York," an old man lurching down the air stairs behind me said. I helped carry his hand luggage and he held my shoulder for support. The tarmac was slick and black from the soaking. The evaporating wet billowed around us. It was only six and as far as I knew, my mother wasn't expecting me at any particular hour. I called my cousin from a pay phone to ask if she'd called while I was gone.

The coach house line made a sound like it'd been unplugged. No one picked up at the main house.

I pushed past the people crawling toward the baggage carousel and was soon out of the terminal. I weaved between the idling cars in the passenger pickup area and headed for the bus stop. As I searched my wallet for a bus ticket, a hand grabbed me by the arm. Its owner said, "Your plane was late!" and I turned around, for a moment not recognizing the woman whose hand was now cupping my elbow. "Thank God I didn't miss you," she said. "I remembered when you said you'd be landing." It was Jennifer, I realized, only without any makeup on. Her face looked like a rubber stamp that hadn't been inked. I hugged her, out of some sense of relief, and she hugged me as well, more forcefully than I expected.

"You came to get me from the airport?" I said. She took my hand and pulled me away from the bus stop. We walked in this way to the idling cars. I saw Ricky's bored eyes in an open driver's-side window. He was wearing the same shirt as last time, a shirt with torn-off sleeves.

"Judy," he said.

I got in the back seat. Ricky put the car in drive and we left the airport. "You're wearing the dress," Jennifer said once we were on the highway. She turned around in the passenger seat and looked me up and down. "I hadn't even registered it. You look so nice." She was holding Ricky's hand, I saw, and I realized they were a real couple, that he wasn't just a neighbour or an oddly close male friend.

"I wore it for three days straight," I said proudly. "I forgot to bring my other clothes. It's a real nice thing to be stuck in."

I thought Jennifer would react with a smile, but she only looked more grave. "So, I need to tell you something," she said and immediately looked at Ricky, then back to me. "Your mother called me. She'd called your cousin, she said. He told her you weren't with him. That opened a whole Pandora's box."

Jennifer said more, but I could no longer hear her. My hands went for my seat belt, the part crossing my chest, to lift it, as if that would help, and of course it didn't. I'd expected this, and yet, in my truest deep parts, I'd held out hope that my cousin and I had an unshakeable deal, born of an unshakeable bond. I only remembered then that I'd forgotten to visit his mother the day before I left. The second after I'd hung up the phone with him, after so much promising, the thought had completely left me. What he'd said about my self-centredness was true and now I was paying the price.

"Did my mother send you here?" I asked.

Jennifer said no, but she sounded unsure. "I mean, when she called me after calling your cousin, I said you and I had plans to hang out today. So, it'll be good if she sees me dropping you off at home. That's what I'm hoping for."

In the rear-view mirror, I saw Ricky's eyes dart from lane to lane. I thought that if only he were a talker, he'd give me a more direct answer than Jennifer. Still, I relaxed a little. I released the seat belt and could now deal with particulars. "Oh, I know!" I said. "It's the clothes. She saw the pile of clothes I forgot to pack, grew suspicious and called Christopher, then called you to find me. She must've gone through my desk drawer." In my drawer, I had the piece of paper Jennifer had given me, with her name, phone number, and address. "So she thinks I've been spending the weekends with you? That I've been lying about staying with my cousin?" I scoffed. I hated my mother. I didn't blame her. Most of all, I was relieved she was all right.

"My mom's all right?" I asked.

Jennifer looked conflicted. "She was really worked up. She seems to know more. She guessed you were out with a guy, that a secret rendezvous could only be a guy, so I tried to sound casual about it. I had to say something. I said, yeah, okay, you sometimes hang out with a male classmate. She said, 'In that case, it's an eighteen-or-over boy.' She mentioned statutory rape. She sounded like a lawyer. I didn't realize she'd get so into it, that she'd go from 'classmate' to 'rape.' I'm so sorry."

There was no easy way to explain my mother. "She needs her own crime show," I said and smiled, to show Jennifer it would all ultimately be okay, that I was used to this. But Jennifer sighed again. She looked to Ricky and Ricky gave me a fleeting glance in the rearview. Jennifer turned her whole body to face me. She crumpled her featureless face. "I think she might figure out it's Maurice. That's the problem," she said. "Your mom called me a second time," she explained, "after calling the cops. She'd asked them about charging older men with statutory rape and finding them through phone records. The cops said if it's serious, they will look phone records up, they'll start an investigation. She said you've been taking a lot of calls, at all hours of the night. She said she'd been hearing a double ring, the long-distance way. 'So where does this guy live? In *another city*?' she said to me, all crazy, and when I said I didn't know, she hung up. I called back, but no one picked up."

I must have gone white in the face because Jennifer leaned forward, falling into the space between the front and back seats, and clutched me with both hands. I thought of the thread connecting my mother's phone to Maurice's apartment, so fine I hadn't noticed it. A wick on fire, gaining speed, catching up to a sleeping bomb. It could be that Maurice was slumped in a police station by now. Crimes against minors weren't treated lightly, I knew. I could picture his neighbours looking out of their doors and windows as he was led out of the building, wearing his Western shirt, jeans, and his cowboy boots, and not looking like other men his age. To the neighbours, this would be suspicious. They'd say "they knew." Even being New Yorkers, who are used to everything, they knew. The music, our dancing, it had all been too loud.

The waves that'd been so neat and apart, with their even, isolated rhythm, forgot that rhythm and crashed into one another. Every problem I'd had now massed into a basin too small to contain the tempest. "His landline, his cellphone. Stupid Maurice just kept calling and calling and calling. And I called him once too! It's all going to lead to his address," I said. In high school sex ed class, we'd learned about the tests that women undergo after rape. I thought of the Q-tips that would go inside me, swabbing for signs of Maurice.

Jennifer said it might take a long time to get phone records and link anything to Maurice Blunt. "Phone companies don't work on weekends," Ricky offered. But there was so much more than the phone calls. If only those two knew how far my mother could go. My sleepless nights, which she could feel and hear through the thin walls that separated us. The camcorder tapes that sat in the bag I'd left thrown around the house. My notebook, the plans for everything I would film once I was officially free. My mother could have gotten to it all.

"Do you think," Jennifer started, careful to dole out her newest theory as gently as she could, "your cousin told her more?"

Of course he had. I didn't know what mistaken notion of sibling-like devotion had made me believe that Christopher wouldn't talk. If only my mother asked him more than once, if only he waited until she'd climbed to the peak of her wrath—at that point he'd hand her the best clue, to really start her fire: look no further than Manhattan. Maybe he knew more. He probably knew more. "Look for the rhythm guitarist of the reunited Sateelites. He's *old* and shares a twin bed with your daughter."

I didn't answer Jennifer, only thanked her for picking me up.

"We'll sort this out," she said. "If it comes to it, we'll spin a tight story about where you've been spending your weekends. We'll get Ricky to corroborate." From the driver's seat, Ricky gave a hum of approval. I asked Jennifer why she was bothering to help me out, and with that, the tears came; I felt a wrenching pity for myself. Jennifer was even better to me than Maurice. I was surrounded by love.

"Because you're a cool and interesting girl, that's why," Jennifer said. She poked one of my tears with her fingertip and swiped it to the side. I cried harder. This gesture was more tender than anything I'd ever felt not coming from my mother. "Also, I've had enough of the Maurice Blunts of this world. But I'll save my rant for a different day." She reached her hand out to me again and pushed her finger into the next tear that'd started racing across my face.

WHEN I WALKED into the apartment, I saw that my mother had brought out the industrial fan again, and she'd also moved her bedroom fan into the living room. The two stood side by side with their blades still and arrested. The apartment stank of a stagnant, sweaty existence. For once, though, it was quiet. No neighbour sounds snuck through our floorboards, nothing from the row house next door, the street, or the passersby. It felt like our home had had the plug pulled on it, like I'd stepped into the aftermath of a disaster. "Mommy?" I called. "Are you in here?"

In my bedroom, the pile of New York clothes sat as I'd left it, with no evidence of a ransacking. Like the best in the game, my mother knew to cover her tracks. I checked my desk drawer. Sure enough, Jennifer's note lay at the top, a little more crumpled than I'd left it.

A workout VHS tape, Linda Spencer-Boyle's 6 Ways to Kick a Man's Butt, was lying on the floor of my mother's bedroom, next to a rolled-out exercise mat and a bunched terrycloth towel. The cover showed Linda Spencer-Boyle, beautiful and poised in a batwing sweatshirt and leggings. My mother's small TV-VCR combo was on standby, displaying a blue screen, awaiting the go-ahead. Her collection of exercise tapes stood lined underneath the TV. Cindy Crawford's entire suite, Abs of Steel, and a lot of kickboxing, all discards from the library.

Back in the hallway, I noticed that the bathroom door was shut, but a wisp of light shone from its bottom crack. It looked like more than light from the window. I tapped the door. "Mom, are you in there?" I said.

No answer came.

"Are you there?" I said again, tapping. I thought I could smell the moisture of a full tub, the way it roused the plaster walls to release a synthetic odour. At that moment, standing on the wrong side of the bathroom door, it struck me what my mother was truly capable of. I ran downstairs, where Jennifer and Ricky stood on the stoop of the triplex. Ricky was reading the Taffy poster that was taped to the door of our house. I asked them to follow me. "I need you in here, please," I said.

Ricky was the one who opened the bathroom door. Jennifer was behind him with her hands on his hips. My hands were on Jennifer's hips, capping our reluctant conga line. I pressed my face into her back. I could tell she was craning her head and taking a good look inside. "There's no one here," she said. I opened my eyes. My mother wasn't floating at the bottom of our bathtub.

"I don't know where she could be, then," I said. "She never leaves the house in the evenings."

Ricky offered that she could be at the police station. For a moment, I'd forgotten about the worst of it: the hysterics and rape charges, and the Q-tip going inside me.

"She probably went for a walk," Jennifer said, but didn't sound like she believed it.

"I don't know," I said again, and with that we left the bathroom and travelled farther into the apartment in that same conga formation.

THE THREE OF us had been sitting on the edge of my mother's bed for ten minutes when Ricky leaned down to pick up the workout VHS tape from the floor. He read us the description on the back:

6 ways to kick a man's butt:

1.   Don't look afraid

2.   Don't look back

3.   Show him who's boss

4. Keep your head up
5. Ball up your fist
6. Go for the jewels!

"These directions are bad," Ricky said. He shook his head and put the tape back on the floor. "They need to be more specific."

"It's just a tape for women to take out from the library," I explained. "My mother's afraid of everything."

"I'm sorry," Ricky said. "I guess these directions are okay, then."

We entered a peaceful intermission. My mother had drawn her blinds to stave off the heat, and the room had a pleasing dimness and cool. As we sat there, I began to feel inexplicably relaxed. It seemed we were just waiting; there was nothing else to do but to wait for her to burst through the door with Maurice's genitals in a sack.

"Wait, why don't we call your cousin?" Jennifer said at one point. "Why didn't we think of that?"

Of course I'd thought of it, but I felt too afraid; this limbo we found ourselves in, knowing absolutely nothing, had a real appeal to it. There was room still for the best version of the end of the Mauriceandjudyland story. And if it turned out to be the worst version, well, I wanted it to come to me on its own. The tide could creep up to me and do whatever damage it wanted. A slow death. There was no need to rush the end. Eventually my mother would have to come home.

"What's the point?" I said. But Jennifer was already pulling my hand, trying to lift me from the bed. Ricky stood up as well. We walked down the hall, maintaining our old order. I picked up the hallway extension and dialled the coach house. In the moment, I wanted very badly to hear my cousin's voice, the voice he'd used for months now: emaciated, disappointed in me, on the lookout for clouds—all this telling me nothing much had changed. "Nothing," I said. I held out the receiver. Jennifer and Ricky drew their faces toward it. "It's just a long beep."

Jennifer stuck out her bottom lip. "What could it mean?" she asked.

Maybe the Big Shadow had finally come and those two were gone for good. Maybe they'd merely unplugged their phone, the way I'd done to them, on so many occasions, when they wanted to talk to me.

Ricky cleared his throat. I thought he was about to offer a new game plan, something revelatory no one would ever expect of him, but he only asked for a sandwich. I pointed to the pantry. Jennifer opened the fridge and asked what kind of bread he wanted. Once Ricky finished eating, we went to sit on the living-room couch. Ricky and Jennifer sat on either side of me, and we waited like that, in silence.

AT SOME POINT Jennifer turned on the TV. She flipped through the channels, paused on CNN, and turned the TV off. "Did you think Maurice's arrest would have made it onto the news?" I asked.

"No," she said, sounding defensive. "I was just bored. I don't know."

"When you think about it, it's pretty crazy that you've been getting on planes and going to New York every weekend," Ricky said. "Who would ever think of that? I bet your mom wouldn't. I bet it's only the shock she's dealing with. The shock of finding out she doesn't even know her daughter." He smiled for the first time since I'd met him. It was also the most he'd ever said at once. He seemed impressed, like maybe one day he'd like to do what I did. To shock his mother with the knowledge that her child was a sea of secrets.

The phone rang just then. Jennifer said, "Pick it up!" and made as if she was off to pick it up herself. I grabbed her shirt and pulled her toward me. "No!" I screamed. She got to her feet and tried to lift me off the couch by my elbows. We performed a momentary wrestle. I said, "It's the cops!" And she said, "That's crazy. It's obviously your mother." What I was most afraid of was that it was Maurice, calling to ask how I could've let things get this bad. "I wouldn't pick it up," Ricky said, and in that moment, the ringing stopped.

THERE WAS A LOW bookshelf in the living room. All my mother's books were there. Ricky was sitting cross-legged in front of the shelf. He read the titles one by one to us. "Your mother has some pretty gory stuff," he said when he was done. "A lot of true crime, tons of stuff on death and murder." Jennifer and I were still on the couch. She'd tucked me into her lap and was trying to plait a French braid into my hair. She'd also put lipstick on me and mascara on herself. Two hours had passed since we'd arrived at my house.

"She's got a four-volume set of *America's Most Infamous Murderers*."

"By Casey K. Dick," he added when no one answered. "Is that Philip K. Dick's brother?"

"We can't go on like this," Jennifer said, as if the reference to Philip K. Dick had finally pushed her over the edge. She let go of my hair and stood up from the couch.

"Go on like what?" Ricky said. And at the same time, I said, "Let's just keep braiding my hair."

"We have to do *something*," Jennifer said. She put out a hand to each of us.

Ricky placed my mother's book back on the shelf. We got up and followed Jennifer out of the apartment.

24

Looking back on it, there was a peculiar smell as soon as we took the highway exit. But the country always has its smells and we forgive them and we ignore them. "I thought it was horses," Ricky said later. "Horses, cows, and pigs." Jennifer told him that what we'd smelled was nothing like what farm animals smell like. "It was more so the stench of human decimation," she said. Ricky then explained that he'd never been north of the city. He'd never in his life smelled country.

WE PULLED INTO the gravel driveway a little after ten. The sun had finished setting, but not too long before. The lights in the main house were on. They'd only ever been on during Thanksgivings or Christmas parties when Alex's mother still hung around. As soon as I saw the lights, I knew that my mother was inside, and the countrystead had been designated the Maurice Blunt Manhunt Headquarters. We parked behind Alex and Christopher's Honda and a gold SUV I'd never seen before. Did the police drive gold SUVs? Did their extra-special units drive them? The three of us got out of the car. I kicked the gravel as we walked toward the house. I wasn't afraid. I believe I was just exhausted. As I walked, the past three weeks reconfigured themselves as not adventure but some kind of trial, a cruelly long marathon unlike the normal order of life. What's worse, I'd gotten nothing out of it. No medal, no cheers, no job prospects or a mapped-out future. I felt cheated; my prize was consoling a mother who thought I'd been raped in New York.

"It really, really stinks here," Ricky said. He pinched his nose and coughed in an exaggerated way. I looked to the left, toward the coach house. I squinted and I stopped. Then I grabbed Jennifer's wrist and pulled her to a stop.

"What's wrong?" she said. "What do you see?"

What I saw was darkness that was more than just absence of light. I let go of her and started walking toward what was nothing, because that was the thing: what used to be there was now mostly gone. Jennifer and Ricky followed me, crunching close behind on the gravel. When my eyes adjusted so that I could appreciate the thousand shades of dark on the countrystead that evening, the outline appeared—something like the bones of a once-body, a prehistoric remnant rising out of the ground and undoing its poor burial. I was witnessing the skeleton of the coach house, my house in a way, too. Its edges were charred. The stench now made sense: all that burned vinyl.

"They burned down the coach house," I said and as soon as I said it, I realized I might be looking at Christopher's remains, too.

Jennifer said something but I couldn't hear it right. I answered by saying, "My cousin," then motioned for her to not follow. I heard Jennifer's acquiescence and some comforting words, her poorly masked confusion. I ran to the main house. My only thought was the last thing I'd said to Christopher. I strained to remember it, but couldn't. All I knew was that it had likely been steeped in anger, or even worse, the irony that made him so frustrated with me of late. When was his last phone call? I couldn't even say. Thursday? Maybe the day before. In a sense, I'd done this to him, I knew.

The side door of the main house was unlocked. I went in and ran through the dark kitchen, briefly grabbing on to the edge of its island to prevent myself from slipping. Just as I passed the fridge, a pair of hands took me by my waist, catching me from behind and pulling me into the unlit hallway. My shoulder crashed into a picture frame, then wall, and then a second picture frame. In the dark, I heard my aunt's scolding whisper, her breath heavy with a sour stench. "Bad girl! Gallivanting with college boys. For twenty minutes she thought you were dead. Do you know how hard I had to work to get her over it?" But her tone had already lifted at the last words. "You *know* how she gets. You've got to be *smarter*." Our backward clutch evolved into a proper embrace. We stood hugging for a couple of minutes. I let her calm and coherence communicate to me that her son was okay. And for a moment at least, I could be okay too.

I said, "What happened?" but my aunt didn't answer. She started dragging me through the entryway to the living room, making a grand entrance and revelling in the glory of being the one who'd found me. "Here's the lady of the hour!" she announced, releasing me with a light push and sending me staggering toward the centre of the room. It took me a few seconds to adjust to the light. All I could see was white, multiplied by waterfalls of dangly kitsch crystals. Alex's mother had powered on her two chandeliers. The place was much too bright, not that anything mattered now. Christopher was okay and my aunt had mentioned no old men, no New York, and nothing about what had happened on the library stairs in the rainstorm. I'd rather they'd thought I was dead in a burning building than discovered dancing in Maurice Blunt's apartment. He seemed farther away than ever, than even before I met him, safely tucked in some drawer of his city, putting on a record and getting ready to kick his legs.

THAT NIGHT, Alex's mother's living room was arranged like a boxing ring. Her couch had been dismantled to create four mini couches, placed in a square with the coffee table in the middle. The table's centrepiece was a glass sculpture of a bouncing horse meant to look like a drawing from the caves of Lascaux. My mother and aunt were squeezed together on one mini couch and my aunt was in the process of settling back in and draping her arm around my mom's shoulders. My mother's legs were curled underneath her butt. As soon as she saw me, she threw her head back in dramatic ecstasy. Wedged between her thighs was an empty wineglass.

Alex's mother had a couch to herself. She lifted her wineglass in salute. Its rim was completely red from her lipstick. Christopher sat on the third couch, bent forward at the waist with his head hanging. All I saw was his hair, but still, he looked unharmed. The fourth mini couch was occupied by Christopher's half-brother Marco, sprawled end to end, T-shirt hiked, and immersed in his hand-held game console.

"I'm sorry, everyone," I said. "I lost track of the time, I guess."

Alex's mother downed the last of her wine and set the glass next to the horse. "I've said it all evening and I'll say it again," she said, speaking unnaturally loudly. "Judy is a beautiful woman. She's going to start seeing handsome men." She then lowered her voice and cupped her hand to her face, showily pretending to convey a private message. "I said to your mother, 'Think back to seventeen. To what you were doing on hot summer nights.'" Before I could respond, Alex's mother wound herself up and let out a hoot. I believed for a second it was all part of being drunk. Then I saw that everyone, except for Christopher and Marco, had paused their movement and fixed their eyes on something behind me.

"Good evening," I heard Ricky say.

"Well, hello, young man," my aunt said. "Welcome and come on in."

Alex's mother placed one hand over her mouth and lifted her empty wineglass with the other hand. My aunt gave me a knowing smile and squeezed my mother's knee. Ricky said hello again and "How is everyone doing?" He walked farther into the room and on the way, tripped over a portion of the Japanese folding screen that stood behind the couch where Marco lay. The screen wobbled and Ricky grabbed it by its sides to steady it. Marco didn't notice. "Don't worry about that," Alex's mother said. She zigzagged her hand through the air. "I just had a heritage-designated coach house burn to the ground, and my guess is the insurance won't cover it since my son seems to have played a role in transforming it into a pile of ash." She looked at Christopher. "Right, Christopher?" She clapped her hands, but Christopher kept his face lowered. He appeared to be fast sleep.

"Poor boy," my aunt said. "Let's just be thankful the kids weren't hurt."

My mother's head was on Aunt Tamara's shoulder now and she looked dreamily at Christopher. "Yes, at least the kids are all right," she said.

I didn't want to ask where Alex was, but I guessed it was nowhere bad, a hospital, maybe, being treated for smoke inhalation, or more likely, upstairs, just ten feet above me, relaxing in one of the mother bedrooms and hearing everything that was being said. Either way, like Maurice, he'd stay in his world and his world would always protect him.

My mother perked up. "So, what's your name, young man?" she said to Ricky. She untucked her legs. "You've caused me a lot of grief these last twelve hours," she said. "You've woken me up countless times, at all hours of the night, these past few weeks. Calling my daughter, like some Romeo." She smiled as she said this and patted the bit of cushion at her side.

Ricky lit up, seeming pleased to be invited into the ring. The context of the invitation didn't matter. "I'm Richard," he said, swinging his long, skinny legs over the corner of the coffee table. "Nice to meet you." He made his voice deeper and gruntish, and it took me a few seconds to understand why he'd done it.

"Uh-oh," my mother said, using a flirty voice. "Richard was my father's name. That can't be good." She gave my aunt a coy smile. "Well, I finally get to meet you, Richard. See, I'm not so scary. You should come over for dinner sometime."

Ricky said thank you and sorry for all the calls. Then I tried to catch his eyes to say thank you, but he didn't look my way. He kept going, answering my mother's questions about who he was, where he'd come from, what he did day-to-day, where he believed he was headed in life, but how one could never truly know, right?

It seemed everyone had forgotten I was in the room and that I'd brought them together that night, to the lonely countrystead so removed from the ordinary course of their everyday. "Ain't that exactly how life works?" my mother quipped, and she and Ricky shared a laugh. I wasn't quite sure what was funny. I was no longer part of the conversation.

25

The day after the coach house fire was Maurice's second-to-last class. I slept past it without meaning to, not that I planned on going anyway. I turned on the fans in the living room. My mother had left me a premade breakfast in the fridge. She called in the late morning, bringing everything up again, primarily to say how lucky it was I hadn't been anywhere near the flames. "Richard seems like a nice boy," she said, though she'd already said it many times the night before. Since I'd woken up that day, I'd planned my response to this statement. I was going to call him "just a summer fling" and ease the way for telling her he would never come over for dinner, that that was the last we'd seen of him. But in the moment she seemed so glad, I couldn't do it. I told her Ricky had a sensitivity to him that I appreciated. I said he liked her very much too, and she said that was so nice of him to say but that she had trouble believing it was true. "No, it was true," I said to my mother. "With him there's a way of knowing, and when he said it, I knew."

I ate the breakfast she'd left me. And then I spent the rest of the day waiting by the phone. Only one person called, Christopher, just before dinnertime. I could hear his little brother wailing in the background. "I'm calling from my mother's. I have to live here for a while now, I guess." His voice was accusatory, though when I asked if he thought that his living situation was my fault, he said, "I don't know. I mean, by eradicating the coach house, we demonstrated to the Big Shadow how willing we are to let go of this material thing, our earth-home." And now Alex's mother had officially reinhabited the main house and stuck her nose in their business. A crew had arrived to properly renovate the swimming pool. There was nowhere to be them anymore.

I asked, "So, it didn't work? Why didn't the Big Shadow come?"

"It bypassed us, we think," he said. "We saw it, in the distance. I threw up that morning. It was so clear it was *something*, you know? And then it went elsewhere, looking for someone else. It'll take about a decade for it to come back. Alex says it comes in cycles. By then, hopefully it'll want us. I mean, a decade is a very long time. What am I going to do for the next ten years?"

Christopher went on, about escape and how I'd disappointed him. About how he and Alex had sat in the empty swimming pool with its shaved tunnels, watching their coach house turn to ash. But not once did he say he could've told on me. And he could have. He could have put an end to New York and Maurice long ago, with just one phone call to my mother. And when she'd finally gotten in touch with him—not after discovering the clothes on my bed, but after the countrystead's neighbours called Alex's mother, and mothers called mothers to communicate the frightful news of the fire—he could've told her then. All he'd said was that I was not with him that day, that I was safe and all right, with other friends who I'd been seeing a lot of, somewhere within the borders of our town, and to not worry. He could have said so much more.

"I'm sorry," I said. "I wish I could've helped you leave. I just don't think that shadow would've wanted me either. I felt nothing for it. I should've just said so instead of acting aloof and running away."

Christopher made a little sound, an "oh" mixed with a sigh. I think he was touched by my apology. I'd been a pretty nasty sister-cousin in the last months, but at least I had another decade to save him. He said, "We'll leave eventually, I guess," sounding unsure. "How was New York?" he asked, and I told him it was good, that I think he'd enjoy it and in the next ten years there would be opportunities for us to go together. He said, "I don't know." And I said that's okay. That maybe he'd know at some future point, that I now felt no rush about anything.

ON THE DAY of Maurice's last class, I stayed in my bedroom with the windows open. I held a book on my lap. The cicadas had arrived, a little early this year. At one point they soothed me into a long nap. In the evening, my mother returned. Her bare feet pounded along to the hip-hop of her workout VHS. She had latent stress she needed to rid herself of, she said. For a moment she'd believed her daughter had been swallowed by fire. For another moment she'd believed her daughter was dating a predator who fished young girls out of summer poetry classes—she'd read about such men in magazines. Later in the evening came my mother's dinner and questions about my new boyfriend. After dinner came Alex Trebek.

I summoned the courage to call Maurice on the weekend. I figured I should explain why I wasn't there, in New York, not that

I pictured him waiting. Rory the manager picked up Maurice's cell. "Can I talk to Maurice?" I said politely. I tried to make my voice not mine. But Rory knew exactly who was calling, I could tell by the pause that followed.

"Yeah, well, Maurice is in the middle of something," he said.

In the distance, I heard a guitar being tuned and the drone of idling amps. Rory wasn't lying, exactly.

"Who's calling?" I heard Maurice yell just before the line went quiet.

MAURICE DID CALL BACK, a few days later. He left a message. I'd told him to never leave a message. I was lucky to get to the machine before my mother that day. "Jude! I missed you last weekend," he said. "You've got to come down sometime." The lack of specificity was as obvious as a punch. "New York misses you," he added, and then he asked me to send him the videotapes I still had, registered mail, please, ASAP.

New York had all it could ever need and I knew it didn't miss me. I missed it, though. I missed Maurice, too. I put the ninety-minute tape containing all the footage I'd shot into a bubble envelope and mailed it in the morning. I put a note inside asking Maurice to send me back the cassette I'd left for him, the one with Alex's Big Shadow nonsense.

I thought I might have use for that tape. Just in case something ever came up. I pictured a documentary being made about him after the next idea he had, the thing that would finally get him the whole world's attention, not just his mother's. In the documentary, I'd play the audio tape and sit back and listen, the camera rolling, me smiling contemptuously, but also a little dreamily, maybe nostalgically, my hand propping up my chin, the lens on my face, very still.

Below, it would say: Judy, childhood friend of Alex, 1988–1998, the date range like a life span.

"Tell us how you met," the interviewer would say. "How did it begin?"

"It started with an overworked, pathologically anxious mother," I'd say, "and another lonely mother's remarriage, and a third mother's empty home, just outside of town."

26

A week ago, I received a call from Jennifer. She said she'd seen a poster, or rather Ricky had spotted it, for a Sateelites show in our town. They'd be playing at a midsize venue and were on their way to other cities, moving westward, then south and east, and eventually going abroad, to do four shows in England.

I haven't heard from Maurice since he left the message on my answering machine two months ago, saying he missed me and asking for his tape. He never did send me my Alex cassette, though I assume he got his videotape long ago. I sent it with the expensive kind of post, using the last of the countrystead money. I wonder if one day the footage will appear on a tour documentary or a history of rock 'n' roll show on VH1. I wonder if my name would be listed in the credits.

I could call Maurice. I could even visit; his keys sit in my desk drawer, in an old envelope I've resealed with tape. One day a long time from now I might call. When everything's forgotten, we could have a reunion, just like the Sateelites. Except I bet the same pall would hang over us, too. It's hard to relive a dead moment, and probably, on some level, wrong. Is the term "exhumation"? I think it's something worse.

IT'S THE DAY of the show and Jennifer calls. She says tickets are still available and the three of us should go; it'll be cathartic but also hilarious. "We can watch him, on that six-foot stage, thinking he's on top of the world, or whatever it is that sustains him."

I laugh and say I'll consider it. "If I call you back by sunset with a 'yes,' start getting our outfits ready." I'm gesturing to her favourite thing—the thing that sustains *her*, actually—the art of making yourself up, of revelling in disguises.

I've come to believe in that art myself, to a degree. I've started applying makeup before I go to class, and I've cut my hair in a new way, so that anyone who knew me in the summer might think I'm someone else today. In the mornings, if I'm up before my mother leaves for work, I take her by both hands, stop her from whatever she's stalking, pull her down onto the couch, and take out my little crayon. "I'll emphasize your beautiful eyes," I say. "Just relax, unclench your face a bit." As I work, I feel the tension leave her, brushing past me like a draught. It makes me shudder, the way I think I can feel it.

AS SUNSET NEARS, the phone stays silent. Jennifer knows to wait. She might even sense that I'm waiting for something, a "sign," or, in more earthly language, an invitation. It's the least that I deserve.

I've spent most of the day by the window. The hallway telephone has been relocated to the living room, onto the mantle next to the sill. It's so close that in the event of a ring, I wouldn't need to take my eyes off the view. I'd just draw my arm to the right and lift with a practised movement.

The weather today has everyone talking. I can hear it through the screen: "I wish it could stay like this forever," "I hope winter never comes!" Banks of clouds roll past. It seems the sky has no end. The sun is bewildering, and everyone is wearing T-shirts. On the lawns of my street, I can see shapes, the shadows cast by clouds, more tricks of light than my imagination can account for. And here comes another one, in the minutes before my mother usually rounds the corner. It floats by more self-assuredly than the rest. It might be real, not a shadow, or perhaps my mind has stopped setting the two apart.

The shape is a lot like a cloud, but with mass, pattering through the grass, stopping to sniff a protrusion. She steps around the paving stones; she's familiar with the landscape. Her tongue falls out from in between her fangs. She pants, then settles on the stoop and lifts her eyes at the building behind her, expecting a familiar face.

She is not a woman, but I think she looks like a woman in a painting. She has the relaxed air of arrival, and a radiance from having taken her time. I envy her for that, and my impulse is to lift my arm, to make a move for the telephone and set the world aright. The poster that was everywhere sits on our coffee table, acting as a coaster, and I only need to look behind me to see where I have to call. I will do that, but not just yet, I think. I drop my arm. I'd like to take in this view for one short moment longer.

ACKNOWLEDGEMENTS

THANK YOU TO Adam for your 24/7 support. Emma Patterson, for your superhuman levels of patience and care. Hazel Millar and Jay MillAr, for your enthusiasm and trust. Meg Storey, for your insight and bottomless store of solutions. Everyone at team Book*hug Press, for helping make this.

Thank you to dear friends who read, advised, and supported with kind words: Eric Magnuson, Jared Bland, Mark DiFruscio, Cathryn Rose, and Laurel Sprengelmeyer. Anna Culbertson, for guiding me through the alternative religions collection of SDSU's SCUA. Teacher Katie Farris, for wrestling with early drafts. Teachers Ilya Kaminsky and Sandra Alcosser, for encouragement. Kay del Rosario and Andrea Nene, for all the music and fun.

PHOTO: ANGELA LEWIS

ABOUT THE AUTHOR

MARTA BALCEWICZ's fiction has appeared in publications including *Catapult*, *Tin House* Online, and *Vol. 1 Brooklyn*. She spent her early childhood in Pomerania and Madrid. She lives in Toronto. *Big Shadow* is her first novel.

Colophon

Manufactured as the first edition of
Big Shadow
In the spring of 2023 by Book*hug Press

Edited for the press by Meg Storey
Copy edited by Shannon Whibbs
Proofread by Charlene Chow
Type + design by Ingrid Paulson
Cloud image: © Robin_Hoood/iStockPhoto

Printed in Canada

bookhugpress.ca